For those who have faced
many trials in pursuit of beauty.

"THE PROMISE OF BEAUTY BIRTHS
A NEVER-ENDING GAME; ONLY THE
OBSESSED WILL SURVIVE."

—Orléansian proverb

The Goddess of Beauty left behind her very own caisse for the first queen of Orléans. It contained four precious instruments she used to beautify the early humans.

First, a golden comb with the sharpest and widest teeth to ensure each hair had its place and to instill a sense of composure and equilibrium.

Second, her pomegranate leaves from which to brew her powerful nectar.

Third, a jeweled chalice from which to drink the sacred liquid and fill themselves with strength and a steadfast manner.

Fourth, a mirror made of glass to show them the truth of all things.

But when the God of the Sky cursed the humans and Beauty made the Belles, she imbued the caisse with a set of challenges. When awakened, an egg of death would hatch and loose the objects, each one setting forth a trial to determine which woman had the right qualities to rule Orléans with her divine blessing.

Beauty made a bargain with an enemy, the Goddess of Death, to keep the caisse safe in her caves until the kingdom needed it to select a new ruling house.

Every participant who failed the Trials would be Death's for the taking.

from The History of Orléans

 ONE

People are drawn to death. They flirt with it like the bayou moths that draw too close to our red sill-lanterns, coveting the heat, only to burn themselves alive in the candlelight.

Orléans is that moth now; the rooftops of Trianon flicker like ignited wicks, and three guards lift a dead courtier on a stretcher out of the Chrysanthemum Teahouse. Windy-season rain soaks her lace veil. I watch as one of her arms flops out, grayish in color and haggard, a broken branch at her side.

You're supposed to feel something when a person dies, when the light in their eyes is snuffed like a candle. A twinge in your stomach. A pinch in your heart. A fallen tear skating down your cheek. But after watching my sister Valerie die and since burying Amber and Arabella, nothing inside me moves. Maybe it's better that way.

Noelle, another Belle at this teahouse, rushes to my side. "Did she really fall from the balcony?"

My eyes remain fixed on the dead woman and the crowd of agitated onlookers. "She attacked Kata during a beauty session. Ended up falling from the tenth floor."

"But why?"

"Wanted more treatments than her ration token allowed. Thought she could bully it out of Kata. When she didn't get what she wanted, she cast herself off."

Noelle presses a hand to her waist-sash. "They usually just throw tantrums. Spit and curse. The attendants force them to calm down. I can't believe she'd do this."

"I can," I reply.

Anguished faces press against the teahouse windows from outside. The citizens do this across the kingdom every week when the teahouses open for ration appointments. Their fists knock; their hands wipe away streaks of rain to have a better look at the Belles. The handles of their parasols clobber the glass until cracks spread like lightning bolts, eager to storm in.

I should be afraid. Their energy hums with anger like bees in a kicked hive. They want a return to the old way— Belles in the teahouses and unlimited beauty work for those who have the right amount of spintria. But the banged-up windows will be immediately replaced, the rowdy visitors fined or jailed.

An imperial attendant shouts to the servants: "They're at

it again! Sill-lanterns out. Windows and doors double-locked. All Belles to the main salon!"

Iron shutters stamp out the morning light, while day-lanterns blaze like trapped stars.

Guards flood both sides of the staircase. Those outside use clubs to beat back the bodies. People plummet to the ground. I hear bones crack and the screeches of pain. Shackles and cuffs are slapped to ankles and wrists. Others scatter in all directions. The prison wagons line up, carting off the newly detained to provide more company for Sophia in her prison, the Everlasting Rose.

A hand finds my shoulder, and I jump. "Don't touch me!" I holler, then immediately regret it. Noelle's face is crumpled with upset. Her third eye sheds a tear. "I'm sorry," I say. "I was stuck in my own thoughts." I take her hand. "Let's go."

After three years, I've come to love the hidden Belles of the teahouses, those kept secret by the Du Barrys, forced to work as second-class citizens. They are anything but. Now they've become as much my sisters as those I was raised with.

Noelle and I walk together into the main salon. There, twenty Belles hover around a weeping Kata. I pull her to her feet. Tears drop down both her noses. "No scratches?" I ask. She nods and hugs me. "We'll try to make sure that doesn't happen again."

"But how?" She sniffles. The deep red of her skin never fades.

Violaine is pacing in front of a roaring windy-season fire.

"It's getting worse, Edel. They're more and more aggressive. My morning client slapped me." She lifts her veil to show me the handprint splayed across her translucent flesh.

"And the circuit-phones have been a mess," Ava adds. "Even with my extra ears, I had to take them off the hook. We're still working through the appointment ledger, and the waitlist isn't moving. And when we turn them down, they get angry."

"You have to push the queen and her ministers, Edel," Larue says. "Things have to change. That Belle's Bureau is supposed to set laws that help us—not make things worse."

"The palace attendants came yesterday and said we have to carry tracking pins on our cloaks," another adds. "For our 'safety,' they claimed. These Belle Laws have just turned into more restrictions."

"When I went to the Market Quartier this morning, vendors refused to take leas from me. Said my money wasn't welcome," Daruma says.

"I know. I know." I pull a parchment pad from my work apron, and a nearby servant hands me a quill. The thick pad spills over with my proposal for Queen Charlotte. I add their latest to the list of grievances and listen to their harrowing stories for the next few hours.

When Charlotte was first coronated, Belle amendments were passed, granting us freedom from the teahouses. Belles were registered and given rooms and a wage for honoring the beauty work ration tokens. We were given the promise that we'd be taken care of and protected.

That hasn't happened. Instead, I'm caught in a storm, pulled in a thousand directions.

The sky windows fill with gray light, scattering rays through the room. Servants slip from behind silk screens and push back papered wall panels. They wheel in afternoon carts with modest sandwiches and pots of tea. I remember how they used to brim over with raspberry cream puffs, sugar-dusted madeleines, beignets, honey croissants, and snowmelon slices. The kitchen made food as pretty as the world expected people to be. Now even that's changed.

"They think their beauty scopes will be back any day," Kata grumbles.

Ena races through the door, struggling to hold a bunch of hate post-balloons with her extra hands. She clutches their angry red tail ribbons. "How are these getting into the mail-room?" she asks. "The servants?"

"What is it this time?" I ask.

"Death threats. Beatings. Burning down teahouses," she rattles off. "The usual."

"Maybe we shouldn't get mail at all," someone says. "The only post-balloons we need are from Edel."

"I'll ask for more guards and mail surveillance," I say, scribbling another note down. "The Glass Isles teahouse just put out a fire last week. We need to take these threats seriously."

"I think it's the Jolie Society. They're loyal to Sophia, and they all wear pins like the emblem on these nasty post-balloons." Ena shakes the balloons, and the emblem flares; a white fleur-de-lis encircled with a red snake. "They want everything back the way it was."

The room erupts with upset.

"Everyone hates us. Feels like it's the whole world."

"They can't do that to us again. I won't work like that."

"I refuse," one shouts.

"Me too," another replies.

I walk over to Ena and the hissing, hateful post-balloons. I stab them with the quill. They sputter to the floor, and Ena throws their hateful letters into the fire.

"I won't let that happen," I tell them.

After that, the room settles. Still, as we eat sandwiches and sip our tea, an anxious thread tugs among us all—I gaze at them, taking an account. As I look at everyone who is here, I notice who isn't.

"Where's Delphine?" I ask.

"She left," Ena replies. Everyone shifts uncomfortably. "When the collectors from the Imperial Bank came to pick up our rent and taxes, she said she was fed up. Called it no better than the spice plantation and their overworked Gris."

I swallow an angry scream. Another Belle leaving the teahouses to live on the streets or peddle her wares in the underground markets across the kingdom. There have been others—three or four whose disappearance I've heard word of, and then no more. My heart knocks around in my chest. "Where'd she go?" I ask.

Silence is my answer.

"I love her just as much as you all do. Even though I didn't work alongside you in the same way."

No one will look me in the eyes.

"I'm not going to send the guards after her," I say. "But she could be in danger."

"We shouldn't have to pay money to the queen for doing beauty work," Violaine finally says. "We used to be tortured. That should be enough. We shouldn't have to pay another lea for the rest of our lives."

"I'm trying to make sure—"

"You have to tell them we're unhappy. You have to tell them no," Violaine says. "You can't blame Delphine or the others for deserting—from what I hear, they're being offered shelter and good currency. The teahouses aren't synonymous with safety anymore."

Other voices pipe up then, everyone chiming in to share their discontent, their fear, their anger. It's too much.

"I can't think," I reply, and dart up the stairs away from all their voices.

On the tenth floor of the Chrysanthemum Teahouse, I've transformed our Belle-product storage room into my experiment lair. Small blimps float overhead, carrying clusters of day-lanterns, dusting my worktables with light. Leeches cluster on the edges of porcelain bowls, while dried herbs sit in a mortar and pestle. Drawers expose their contents—bei powder bundles, wax blocks, skin paste pots, rouge-sticks, pincushions bursting with needles. The potbellied stove warms irons and tiny cauldrons and porcelain teapots.

I take a deep breath. I can't run away from my duties downstairs, but I can distract myself for a while. My experiments are laid out, ready for me to resume mixing—some days I have more faith in these elixirs to change the Belles' circumstances than I do in Queen Charlotte and her ministers.

I collect three skin paste pots, the deep colors now stronger when mixed with dye and herbs, and my newly developed contour cream. I use tweezers to pluck newly developed eye films from a shallow basin of water. I fill a small box with a variety to show Charlotte, including the liquid that began as my sister Camellia's elixir. I've been toying with it, using my arcana like a scientific instrument. With a little more tweaking, I think it could be something special—special enough that perhaps the people who flock to Belles for beauty work would embrace this instead.

"Tailor-made elixir," I whisper to the tiny glass bottles. "Maybe we open a shop in each city. Issue modification boxes. Each bottle specially crafted for the user."

Camille was focused on the blood—neutralizing the arcana. But why should we have to change? Instead, I want an elixir that will change the Gris. If they want to adjust themselves, that's their business—leave us out of it.

"Excuse me, Lady Edel," an imperial attendant calls out into the room.

I look up. "I'm not to be disturbed in here. You know that."

She enters anyway. A glittering gold-and-white post-balloon hovers above her left shoulder. "An urgent message," she says. "From the queen."

 TWO

"Would you like some tea, Lady Edel Beauregard?" my new imperial attendant, Adele, asks, drawing my attention from the carriage window. The world swims by. I glare into her eyes, where red is seeping out like blood trapped in blue-tinted glass. She'll need a treatment soon. One she won't be able to get without waiting on a lengthy list.

"You asked no less than an hour ago, and my answer still hasn't changed. Enough, all right? I'm not a teacup pet that needs looking after. I want to arrive alert," I snap.

"Only following Her Majesty's instructions," she mumbles before returning to her station on the other side of the carriage, carrying the tray. We would be the same pale shade of cream but a hint of gray lingers just under her skin.

If Camellia were here, she'd tell me to be nicer. Sweeter. But sugar and softness won't help extinguish the fires beyond the window.

I gaze out. The Chrysanthemum Teahouse is a blur behind us. Once a prism of lavenders and magentas and reds, now it's a dark mansion fenced in iron with shuttered windows and a guarded path.

This journey should feel like returning home, but it doesn't. Even after three years at court as a representative of all Belles. Even after all the time I've spent in Trianon, wandering what's left of its splendor, trying to force myself into its new rhythm. Even after sitting in on cabinet meetings with the Iron Ladies as they debated what to do with Sophia, how to reimagine the role of beauty work in the lives of the people of Orléans, what to do with us Belles as if we were merely colorful tokens on a game board.

Now nowhere feels right anymore.

Not Maison Rouge.

Not the Chrysanthemum Teahouse.

Not here.

The once-beautiful rose-shaped pavilions sit on their sides, their scent of snowmelon cider, peach champagne, and luna pastries replaced with the stench of ash and burnt wood. My sisters would cry, especially Valerie, to see those pretty pavilions crumbled like sugar houses.

At the thought of Valerie, my heart pinches. Her death is a deep bruise that will never go away, and my anger is fresh, even after three years.

We plod through the Garden Quartier, the emerald lanterns fluctuating in the darkness until the moon peeks from

behind the clouds. Posters on avenue boards and promenades show a portrait of Queen Charlotte with tomatoes con-
tinuously splattering over her face. A slogan races across the
top: THE LAND OF ROTTING BEAUTY.

Adele knits her hands in her lap and stares at me. Her
eyes gleam with questions.

I sigh. "What is it?"

"Is the new queen really going to release Sophia?" she
asks.

"Where'd you hear that nonsense?"

"The *National* and the *Orléansian Times* both reported it."

I scoff. "That's nonsense. You can't believe anything you
read now ... or hear."

"Both said after three years of imprisonment, the old
queen has to stand trial or be released. It's the law. They
interviewed the leader of the Jolie Society."

"Them! Silly idiots."

"They're building a case for Sophia's release and—"

I put my hand in the air and silence her. Anyone loyal to
Sophia is not worth listening to.

"The opera singer Geneviève Gareau is telling all her fans
and followers to support the Society. Their leader—"

"It's because she has the memory span of a gnat." I grit
my teeth. "They've forgotten what it was like when she was
queen."

"They want ..." She trails off.

I narrow my eyes at her. "What?" I ask, daring her. "Spit it out."

"For things to settle down. Maybe even go back to what they were..."

The look on my face silences her. "You can go back to what *you* were doing now," I say.

I turn to the window again. The audacity of her words. A headache begins to blossom as my jaw clenches. I clutch the box in my lap and try to push away all thoughts of Delphine and the other Belles who have chosen to leave. I know it was their choice and they were granted freedom. But I wish I'd been able to make them want to stay. And I wish I could know where they are now so I can be sure of their safety.

The carriage enters the Market Quartier. Wisps of ash swirl about like snow, and as the carriage navigates through the throng of bodies, I see the wealthy ordering their hired guards to chase away rioters from their limestone mansions, the night merchants rushing to close their shops and protect their wares. I catch glimpses of gray skin and red eyes. The city is unraveling, a spool of expensive thread tumbling from a sewing box.

Rioters have increasingly attacked the imperial carriages. Three have been flipped onto their bellies this week, sending courtiers to the infirmary. The rationed tokens cannot service all the needs and desires of the courtiers of Orléans. They tear up the city on days the teahouses are taking appointments.

And the rich are unhappy with only one change a month when they've had unlimited beauty work their entire lives.

The beauty magazines and scopes parade the fortunate members of Orléansian society who have found ways to break the rules. What is it like for those Belles who have left the teahouses? Beauty work in backward shops? How will they remain safe?

It feels as if a play is unfolding and at any moment all the actors will stop, take a bow, and wait for applause.

"Lady Edel," Adele says softly, and I glance at her. Her gaze is direct, as if she's gathered her courage. "I'm sorry. I want you to know that I'm no supporter of Sophia. I just thought you should know what the whispers are. You should be prepared."

As if on cue, a tomato hits my window like a bloody rock, its moldy guts exploding and streaking down the glass. Hands are lobbing rotten fruit at carriages like it will change the thrower's fate. Sling a maggot-filled snowmelon, and the grayness will disappear—teahouses back open, Belle-products as plentiful as post-balloons, beauty work for those with the most spintria.

I laugh. Adele gawks—surely she didn't expect me to cry. But I soften toward her. I don't want anyone afraid of me the way they were afraid of Sophia. I accept her apology with a nod and then move toward the back of the carriage.

"I'm going to walk," I inform her, and reach for the emergency panel of the carriage.

"Lady Edel!" she protests, jumping shakily to her feet as the carriage rolls on. "The emergency doors are only supposed to be used once the carriage has stopped."

"Not very useful if the emergency occurs while the carriage is moving."

"But this isn't an emergency!"

"Isn't it?" I say, rolling my eyes. "You can have my trunk sent to my apartments in the palace."

I tug at the slat, and the emergency panel snaps back, revealing the small hidden door that I'd installed three years ago when I took this position. The carriage is going slowly enough, I gauge. The sound of knocking floods the carriage.

I yank up the hood on my cloak to avoid being recognized. A few hands punch the side of the carriage. "Get through to the Imperial Carriage House quickly. Tell them no one is aboard. They'll let you pass and harass another," I order before grabbing my box and slipping out.

I stumble when I leap to the ground but catch myself. It was easier than I thought—I'll be doing that again, I think. The crowd moves on without me, following the carriage and thumping its sides. I give it a moment and then follow, keeping my hood low. A chilly breeze sends a ripple of gooseflesh over my skin. The scent of early flower blossoms pushes through the smoke; the God of the Ground sending his gifts, they say.

The carriage follows the road, but I branch off onto the walking streets, where the crowds are thinner, but closer—no wheels to avoid here, people jostling one another and shouting. Some race through the streets with their animated signs glittering with upset slogans and massive voice-trumpets. A newsie cuts into my path. I curse at her, but she doesn't hear. She's too busy waving her banner around. The headline is lightning illuminating the dark fabric—KINGDOM UNRAVELING AT SEAMS; QUEEN CHARLOTTE UNABLE TO KEEP ORDER.

"What kind of ruler is this?" someone in the crowd shouts. "Let's replace her, too. Just like her sister."

"It's time for a merchant house to reign," another challenges. "They know about real work."

"Sophia wasn't that bad," one replies. "She did more for us than her back-from-the-dead sister."

"At least people were afraid of her enough not to riot. Now we have *this* mess."

"Our queens used to be dignified, lovely, and, most of all, feared. I've seen nothing of that as of late."

"I bet this is all Queen Sophia's doing. I heard that some people are being paid to cause chaos. This is what she wants. And she's winning. Charlotte would do right to get it over with and let her out of prison!"

"The whole world will be gray before the new queen does anything. How are we supposed to live this way? Our traditions have been destroyed without regard for the ways things are, were, and ought to be."

I almost yell back at the woman and defend Charlotte, but two men flip over a pavilion. People scatter. I rush along the promenade past ravaged portraits of long-forgotten courtiers and reviled members of the royal family; vile words and gashes mar their faces. Bill posters scream contradictory messages—FREE SOPHIA! KILL SOPHIA!

Three boys push past me.

"Watch where you're going!" I yell. "I'm not a spirit. I'm right *here*, and you can see me."

They don't turn back.

With fists balled, I enter the Royal Square, spilling over with newsies and their navy story-balloons and black gossip post-balloons and flashing light-boxes. Many advertise their latest stories:

"The *Orléansian Times* has medical reports from the Palace Infirmary. Queen Charlotte not getting better. She may not make it through the next year of her reign."

"Interview with Minister of Justice in the *Imperial Inquirer*. Imprisoned Regent Queen Sophia will need to stand trial to be held for a life sentence."

"The *Trianon Tribune* interviews Barnabé Dene, head of political group the Jolie Society, who is petitioning the queen and her cabinet for the release of our one true queen, Sophia."

Other newsies attempt to haggle their way through the palace checkpoint flashing their press parchments. The guards bark about the entry list and the newsie restriction.

"Have your papers ready," an inspection guard hollers. "Official invitations only."

I take out my travel parchments, and the portrait of my

face stares up at me, the eyes winking every few seconds. Wax stamps mark the numerous trips I've made back and forth between Maison Rouge and here, or to meet with other Belles who have been given residence in the teahouses. I push my way to the front. "Move aside. I'm an honored guest."

"Are you expected by Her Majesty?" a palace attendant demands.

"I'm returning from the Chrysanthemum Teahouse on the queen's orders."

The official palace invitation glows beneath the night-lanterns with the queen's glittering seal; the word *Urgent* thudding in animated ink.

He nods and steps aside. As the checkpoint gate closes behind me, a palace blimp slithers overhead, dropping a silhouette screen of Queen Charlotte. An egg flies above the crowd, narrowly missing the blimp.

I hope she'll listen.

 # THREE

The palace is a fortress now. The promenades are punctuated with guards, populous as night-lanterns. The gardens are littered with camps, tents, and stalls for weaponry. An arsenal built to keep the people at bay. The once-twinkling windows are adorned with bars.

Not a place for queens and court.

When I first arrived here with my sisters years ago for the Beauté Carnaval, I couldn't take my eyes off its glittering arches and sparkling turrets. I remember the fountains and plazas and pavilions, boulevards lined with manicured trees and shrubs, shimmering pavement, marble terraces, white stone buildings trimmed in gold, gardens exploding with color, and a river snaking along full of glistening boats overflowing with laughing courtiers. The hair rose on my arms the first time I saw it, even though I wanted to hate it. We'd been swept into the world of a storybook and told we were heroines, ready to save this world from grayness. My heart had fluttered despite my protests. Beauty swept us along in its tide.

But now as a trio of attendants walk me and two other guests from the checkpoint, my stomach constricts. I look up at the building with its barred windows and bleak light, and it reminds me of a morning-lantern about to go out.

"Why aren't the palanquins still here?" one of the guests complains, fussing with her dress and flapping her fan. "Did all decorum go away? Is there not a drop left? This is quite the walk."

I laugh and feel her glare. She reminds me of the one friend I've made at court: Gaelle Marchand, from the House of Fortunes. She will be bored and smug, waiting for me in the Belle apartments, fussy about me being gone so long. Hopefully. My one solace in returning to deal with the chaos.

We approach another gate, its bars thorned and glistening with the promise of poison for those who dare climb it.

The door slides open. An attendant steps forward with a night-lantern. She snatches its ribbons, pulling it closer to us; its light is almost blinding. "State your names."

"Edel Beauregard," I say with a sigh. "Again."

"The Belle," she replies, then gasps with embarrassment. "Excuse me, I—"

"Yes, one of those. And I have a name—which I just stated."

"Welcome back, Mistress Edel, and my sincerest apologies."

"Not accepted."

I used to be able to rein in my rudeness—at least some of the time. But too much has happened now. I am out of patience. Her white face pinches, and she bows as if that will sweep away everything her words represent. She ushers me toward the massive staircase, where guards have replaced the statues on every step. We climb in silence, the roar of Trianon an echo.

A woman waits at the east palace entrance. She wears a small pillbox hat boasting the word *servant* in a cursive gold stitching. The thinnest of nets is draped over her face to hide the gray. "Her Majesty has been awaiting your arrival," she reports crisply, eyeing me.

"The carriage traffic was terrible. Angry crowds blocking the Imperial Mile. Getting through Trianon is getting more and more difficult," I explain.

"Nothing appeases them," she replies. "Nothing quiets them. Not the windy-season rain. Not the darkness of night. Not the sleepy hours in the early morning. All hours of the day, they're out there in the Royal Square and throughout Trianon." She leads me down a winding series of corridors. All the walls are blank, plaques and portraits and art stripped, while guards and attendants stand with watch-balloons primed to capture every movement.

"She's waiting in the Cabinet Room."

"Is there a meeting? There wasn't one scheduled until later this week."

"It's been moved up," she answers. "It's urgent."

As we enter, the Beauty Minister, Rose Bertain, rushes over and wraps me in a warm hug. She wears a jeweled eye patch, a casualty of time spent in Sophia's prison, and her skin holds a rich licorice color, one that will last long. "You're well, my little poppet?"

I nod and squeeze her hand. "What's going on?"

Charlotte's ministers and advisors sits around a circular table; jaws locked in grimaces, exasperated glances exchanged, and heated words echoing in the high ceilings. Several of the Iron Ladies enter next, pacing and grumbling. Lady Arane, their leader, nods at me, her eyes black as obsidian. A mask hangs from the waist-sash of her spiderwebbed dress.

"Come, come. I haven't been told, but with this group, you know there'll be much to discuss," she whispers, taking my hand and leading me deeper into the room.

Charlotte pivots to face me, and her eyes fill with light. "Edel, I'm so glad you're here."

"Your Majesty." I bow. Charlotte is always happy when I return, as if the mere sight of me will somehow clean up this mess.

She reaches for my hand and squeezes. Her fingers hold a tiny quiver. The poison left a permanent yellow to the whites of her eyes despite the beauty work I did for her last week. But the rich brown of her skin catches the beauty-lantern light and she looks beautiful.

"Our troublemaker has returned." The Fashion Minister flaps his fan in my direction as he stretches across a chaise in front of a fireplace. The sight of his brown face softens me.

"Good to see you, too," I reply. "I know how much you missed me."

"I can tell by the look of your hem that you need me," he says with a raspy laugh.

I sneer at him, then smile. All the time I spent distrusting him in the past feels so silly now. His warm smile is a comfort.

Charlotte takes her seat at the head of the table. "Edel, I've been staring at the hourglass ever since your last post-balloon, waiting for your arrival. I've made a decision that I must tell you all about."

"And I have a few things to show you, and an idea to put before the cabinet," I say, lifting my box. I'm eager to discuss the elixir with her—a more practiced hand than mine may be able to take what I've accomplished and make it truly useful.

"I'm afraid it will have to wait," she says before I can say more. "I must face the Orléansian press corps in less than an hourglass."

"For what?" the Minister of News asks.

"I will tell you in just a moment. Everyone, please find your chairs," she orders.

An unease settles in the room. I find my seat, and the

Iron Ladies sandwich me. I place my box on a table spilling over with old documents, among which I see a map of the kingdom detailing that week's casualties.

"As you all know, we've reached a new crisis peak. Several women from merchant houses in the Silk Isles have died. They broke into a courtier's home to steal Belle-products, and the personal house guards killed them. Very unfortunate."

The Beauty Minister gasps in shock. "How beastly!"

"Camellia is working as fast as she can to make and ship out more products," I interject. "She wrote to me just yesterday that Padma was setting out a thousand boxes on the pier for the imperial boats."

"It only feeds their addiction," Lady Arane interjects.

"And creates continued disparity," her disciple Lady Violetta adds, placing her iron mask onto the table. The left side of her head is shaved close to the scalp, leaving behind the pattern of a spider's web that matches Lady Arane's dress.

I again lift my traveling box, the elixir glittering inside. "If you would let me show you—"

Charlotte interrupts. "No amount of products will appease them right now. Nor additional ration tokens. The regulations aren't working as we'd hoped. A few of the other Belles from the secondary class—my apologies for using that unfortunate term—continue to use their gifts illegally. This feeds everyone's taste for the old ways."

"I am investigating and gathering more information about where those Belles might be," I say. "Every time you've sent me out to those reported locations of illegal teahouses, they've already closed and moved on. But none at the Chrysanthemum and the Silk Isles Teahouses are involved—I know for certain." I almost add that Delphine has abandoned her post, but it would only derail the conversation. I tuck it away for another time.

"We've caught one—Antoinette. She's been jailed, and we're preparing to question her," the Minister of Law adds. "Our covert guards will roost them out of their nasty little nests."

My head snaps in his direction. "Pardon me? They're not birds. They're young women," I snarl. "Why was I not alerted? Consulted on the terms of her punishment?" Anger rises in my voice. "Am I not the head of the Belle's Bureau? I should be the one to question them. Why was I not told? And were those people who were harboring her jailed as well?"

"You are being told right now, Edel," Charlotte replies, skipping my last question. "This is what these meetings are for."

"Not good enough," I press. "I want immediate post-balloons sent to me on all Belles-related matters. No matter where I am."

"We should reopen the teahouses fully. No more twice a week. No ration tokens," the Minister of Law interjects. "A quick and temporary peace until we test more solutions."

"Or create some sort of new teahouse system," the Minister of Finance adds. "Our economy is hemorrhaging.

The Imperial Bank will not survive without the flow of spintria. The tax on leas is not enough."

"We've been over this plan before," I snap, "and it's off
the table. Belles will not agree—"

"We know, we know," Charlotte replies, raising her hand
to silence me.

I continue anyway. "Allowing the Belles to live and work
at the teahouses—under their own free will—and earn their
own leas is the right start. But the taxes must end. Entirely."

The Minister of Finance balks, pressing a well-manicured
hand to her chest.

I ignore her and push onward.

"We need more protections in place. The teahouses aren't
completely safe for them anymore. But if you'd let me show
you what I've discovered"—I tap the sides of my box—"it
could help us draft new regulations. I've intensified the
effects of Belle-products and am on the verge of personalized products that bond with a unique individual's—"

"Take them," Charlotte says, waving a hand at an attendant. "Take them to my desk with the other things for review.
But now is not the time."

I seethe as the attendant plucks the box from my hands—
his nails are painted gold. I've never seen an attendant with
painted nails before. Charlotte changing more of Sophia's
rules, perhaps. The attendant disappears with the box.

"We should close all the teahouses and build one giant

one on the isle of Chalmette. Maybe in the outskirts of Nouvelle-Lerec will do. One central place. Guarded and monitored," the Minister of War offers.

"Oh, like a prison!" I respond, eyebrows arched. "Why not the Everlasting Rose?"

"You think Belles can just live *among* us—like regular citizens of Orléans?" he challenges, his brow furrowed.

"What are we, then, Minister? Teacup pets? Animals bred for slaughter? Dolls from a child's nursery?" With my box of elixir gone, I ball my fists. "We are not game tokens. Not anymore. You need us."

"And *you* need us," he shouts back. "You aren't safe without our imperial guards; the masses would not just be at your door—they'd be inside and wouldn't take no for an answer."

"The need is too great." As the Minister of News shakes her head, the headline segments on her hair-tower whip and snap like flags.

Frustration binds my stomach. The problem is a tangled ball of yarn. Untangle one string, another one forms a knot.

"We need to do this in phases," Lady Arane replies. "We've spent the last three years putting bandages over the wound, only to have this infection grow." She glares at each of us. "You should've never started the rationing so soon."

"I thought you were the Iron Ladies," I say. "Against *all* beauty work. You'd have us still imprisoned—and working under those terrible conditions?"

"Addicts must be weaned. Stripping it all away in one swoop breeds desperation. We must work with the addiction and then master it," Lady Violetta says, pounding a fist on the table.

"I will have to train thousands of more soldiers to quell all the uprisings and provide protection to Belles," the Minister of War adds. "Taxes will have to rise. Unrest will flare even more."

"Citizens will go bankrupt using their spintria underground," the Minister of Finance warns. "The royal infirmaries will fill with botched bodies. Even now, they're reporting an increase in bizarre occurrences—people who have used dye to change their skin and ended up poisoning themselves. A woman just died for trying to have a set of her ribs removed by a butcher. People are scalping their teacup pets for wigs!"

Charlotte groans. "No one wants to embrace a new age, a new way. The Jolie Society has amassed a gargantuan following, all of it soaked with the poison of my sister. They want her back on the throne." She shrugs. "They've even petitioned for an audience. Courtiers and celebrities have been storming the court, flooding me with new policies and demands. And we don't know who is funding them."

"Do not cave to the pressure," the Beauty Minister replies. "Sophia will face her punishment for what she's done, and that will show the world none of her nonsense will be tolerated any longer." A teacup leopard crawls out of her hair, down her shoulder, and onto the table.

"But perhaps we might have an audience with them just for show," the Minister of War offers.

"To show what, exactly?" I snap. "And to *whom*?" All these fools—none of them Belles, and all of them with opinions of how to cater to the needs of those who have lost power, and not to those of us who never actually had it. I'm at this table among them and still not being heard.

The Minister of War's pale face pinches with annoyance. "I suppose you have a better idea?" He gestures for me to share.

"I agree with Madam Bertain. Sophia needs to be dealt with. Put her on trial. Expose all her crimes to the world. Finally issue her a punishment," I say. "She used to relish in the carriage tours, waving at visitors and sending letters to scandal-loving newsies. Remember? The press and the people haven't seen her in three years. She has become a mystery ripe to be rediscovered."

"I stopped allowing her to send those letters because it enabled her to breathe air into those fantasies," Charlotte says. "Instead, I send *her* weekly letters and remind her of why she's there so she will no longer have delusions of grandeur. Food, water, a bed, and a bath are the only comforts I will allow her right now."

"Still, bring her to court. Let them see her in all her disgrace," I demand. "Send the world a message, Your Majesty." I pound the table, and the teacup leopard squeals, dashing back into the Minister of Beauty's hair. "Squash the rumors.

Show them a campaign of your strength. Give the newsies something to fill the papers with. Cut off her head and drape it across the hourglass in the Royal Square!"

The room gasps in horror.

"You speak about severing heads as if it's as easy as slicing a banana." Charlotte waves a hand in the air to silence everyone. "That is not the path I've chosen. She will be tried for her crimes this year, as is Orléansian law. I cannot indefinitely imprison a member of the royal family. But we must solve this problem in order for the prosecution to be seen as legitimate."

The ministers fidget and look away from one another.

"The solution I have decided to propose will put an end to Sophia's shadow—even mine. What Orléans truly needs is a fresh start." Charlotte stands. "And that is why I called you all here."

My heart flips in my chest; its beat angry with anticipation.

"I don't think *I* can fix this," Charlotte says slowly. "I've tried. We've tried. Tirelessly. My patience and energy have been depleted with this endless endeavor."

"You are the queen," I tell her.

"A queen that no one wants," she says, sounding as weary as she looks. "A queen that can't keep her cities from burning and people from dying. A queen that can't convince her people that beauty work has to change if we're going to survive." Tears glisten in her eyes. "I'm calling for the Beauty Trials."

 # FOUR

"You're doing what?" the Fashion Minister screeches, sitting straight up on his chaise.

"The tournament from fairy tales?" I laugh, the absurdity catching me off guard. The Beauty Trials are among the favorite stories told to children who have questions about the world; questions that can only be answered with such tales. The kind of stories that make gods and goddesses close enough to touch, rather than ancient entities whose magic remains like fossils. I snort. "Surely you're joking. Surely—"

Charlotte waves a hand in the air. "Give me a moment to explain. We've been at this for three years now. All the arguments. All the fires. All the mess in Trianon and our other beautiful cities. I must do whatever it takes to protect us all. Even if that means removing myself." She steps away from the table. "Being the ruler requires sacrifice. That's the main role of a queen. My mother taught me that."

Everyone immediately kisses two fingers and places them over their hearts to give respect for the dead Queen Celeste.

"This might bring even more instability," the Minister of War says.

"Or it could breed goodwill," the Minister of News replies.

"Our finances may never recover," the Minister of Finance adds.

I stare at Charlotte in disbelief. "We've spent so much time trying to make things better," I tell her, "and you're just giving up? Gambling with this make-believe?"

Charlotte turns to look at me. "When you first stayed behind, I told you I would most likely abdicate. I always wanted to enact the Beauty Trials. This shouldn't be such a surprise to you."

"I never thought you were serious," I admit. I reach through my memories for those conversations we had years ago.

"I am *very* much serious," Charlotte insists, her voice sharpening to an edge.

"Then you are *seriously* foolish," I cry.

"Watch your tone," the Minister of War says to me.

"Relax, Bernard," the Fashion Minister interrupts. "Edel's in shock like the rest of us." He uses his cane to stand, then takes an empty seat at the table. "Your Majesty, you must forgive all of us. We were not prepared for this tonight."

"You think this is easy for me?" Charlotte's eyes narrow and flood with grief. "My maman passed this divine right to me. I would not do this without deep thought. But I've been wrestling with it since I took those oaths and ascended to this throne. I can never be the queen Orléans truly needs. Not a queen like her."

"May the gods bless our beloved Queen Celeste," the Beauty Minister whispers. "May she be sitting at their table enjoying their feast, for she has earned eternal rest and glory."

Like a signal has been given, two side doors snap open and three attendants march in: one holding a velvet robe, another a cushion displaying the queen's crown, and a third with a voice-trumpet. One of the attendants drapes the robe over her, and another affixes the crown into her thin hair.

"The imperial librarians have excavated the Goddess of Beauty's caisse from the Goddess of Death's caves. I will inform the people of Orléans tonight." Charlotte turns to the Minister of News. "Tell the attendants I'm ready. Alert them to allow the newsies onto the palace lawns. I want the whole world watching."

"You're doing it right *now*? This instant?" My mind is a mess of anger and confusion and worry and frustration. All the angry things I want to say bubble up, threatening to explode. I bite my bottom lip to contain them as the arcana swell and hiss just under my skin. I don't even have time to write to my sisters. What will Camellia say? What if this big show fails? How will they treat the Belles after this? And if it happens to be true, what if the woman who wins the Trials puts us back in the teahouses?

"I just…"

"I understand." Charlotte flashes me a weak smile. "But I must at least try. Nothing we have done has worked thus far."

"What if it isn't real?" I ask. I wonder if she can sense that part of me hopes it isn't. "It hasn't been done. It could be myth, story. Many people say that Belle magic is the only magic left in the world."

"Then we're no better than we were. But we must see," Charlotte says. "This will reinforce goodwill within the kingdom. It will allow everyone to be part of the governing process—or at least feel that way."

"Your Majesty," I say, desperate. "Please. Can we discuss this more? Can you just see what I've brought?" I look around for where the attendant went with my box.

She doesn't reply, instead moving in front of the window that looks down on the palace lawns. A side door opens. King Francis appears, followed by Queen Celeste's other partner, Lady Pelletier. Everyone bows and greets them. They smile at Charlotte in support of her decision.

I can't stop this now. My heart backflips in my chest.

"All is ready," one of the attendants says to Charlotte.

The knot of betrayal in my stomach coils tighter. As the glass windows are opened, the windy-season air rushes in, sending shivers across my skin. A blimp hovers right outside like a bulbous moon, and a silkscreen drops from its under-belly. Sky candles push through the wrought-iron bars and bathe Charlotte in light. Her portrait is projected. The noise of newsies below is a melodious roar growing louder than the crackling of fire in Trianon.

Frail and thin, Charlotte looks like a child still, a young girl playing dress-up in her maman's closet. She nods at one of her attendants, and the woman holds up her voice-trumpet.

Charlotte gazes out at the masses. "My dearest subjects," she says. "I have read every post-balloon sent and noted every complaint you shared with me. All of it has made me think long and hard. I have come to a decision after careful thought and consideration." She takes a deep breath, and it feels like the world below takes one with her. "I am invoking our most sacred ritual, the Beauty Trials."

The newsies are silent, stunned into shock. Then a flock of quills scratch parchment and thousands of navy story-balloons lift into the air, followed by black gossip post-balloons. The skies fill as they turn in all directions headed for the outer isles.

Charlotte puts her hand in the air, signaling silence. She is obeyed.

"In three days' time, we shall let the Goddess of Beauty choose our next ruling house and queen as tradition demands. Our new queen will be beautiful inside as well as out, ready to usher in our new age and reconcile how we must move forward and embrace the change that has been placed at our feet. The Trials will be fair and just in the choosing—as Beauty intended. Though it means the end of my line and the reign of the House of Orléans, I hope my mother, our beloved and departed Queen Celeste, is watching with our gods and supports my desire."

The newsies respond with thunderous applause.

Her eyes drift to the left and find me. A sheepish smile tucks itself in the corner of her mouth. Her light brown skin is flushed, a rosy bloom dusting her high cheekbones. Sweat slicks her forehead, soaking the tight curls around her hairline. It's the happiest I've ever seen her. She seems almost relieved.

I look away, a sick anger swirling inside me. I'm a teapot boiling over, ready to spill. From here I can just make out the Everlasting Rose, where Sophia feels nearer than ever. This tournament reeks of her influence—she's an expert of seemingly leaving things to chance; meanwhile, she's four moves ahead, skipping along and laughing. Has Sophia been moving pieces, guiding Charlotte into this decision? I imagine the long line of whispers that leads from her mouth to the headlines. This feels like just one more salacious story.

The crowd on the palace lawns extends out to the Royal Square, growing by the minute. Some stand on the royal hourglass and cheer and dance. The rumble of terror and delight fills the night. A thousand voices chant with a charged happiness.

"It is time for our world to start anew. It's time to engage our gods," Charlotte proclaims.

I gaze out at the city beyond the Royal Square. Clouds of smoke curl around rooftop spires and escape to the sky above from whatever is burning below. All the women and girls ready to enter the Beauty Trials will burn, too. Their hair and flesh turned to ash. The kingdom will feast upon their bones as the newsies report every detail in their papers and newsreels. They'll lap it up like blood-infused milk.

 **FIVE**

The next morning, I board a carriage heading to the Royal Harbor. Before the driver even pulls off, I set a lilac post-balloon out of the small carriage window headed for the Rose Quartier and my friend Gaelle Marchand's home.

> *Gaelle,*
> *I'm thinking of you. I'll be with you soon. You've heard the news of the tournament, I'm sure. I look forward to your thoughts.*
> *Edel*

I'm too angry to face Charlotte yet. I'm too frustrated to even eat. Her decision sits like a flaming weight in my stomach, swelling and churning and burning my insides. I have to tell Gaelle all that's happened. I have to know what she thinks of this idiocy. I have to ask her what she'd do. Perhaps she can consult her cards. The first time we'd met, she said her prophetic cards could tell her everything about me. I challenged her, and she rose to the occasion, making her one of my most trusted friends. I need her counsel now. I will go to her as promised.

But I have one thing to do first.

Camellia would call this plan foolish, and she would be right. But I stayed up most of the night after Charlotte's announcement writing letters, sending post-balloons to my sisters, and pondering. And the only thing I couldn't stop thinking about was Sophia—seeing her face-to-face, confronting her for all she's done, finding out if she is continuing to set up her sister with violence and instability. If this move toward calling for the Beauty Trials was actually her doing. If she has spies inside Charlotte's cabinet.

If this is all an elaborate trap.

The tiny bulb of my post-balloon drifts through a near-empty city, headed toward Gaelle. Today, my carriage easily traverses the streets without the threat of being flipped over. The rioters are still in bed, appetite satiated by the news of the Trials. Trianon is calmer than it has been in weeks, months—years even. The only people running along the Imperial Mile are newsies claiming to have more information about Charlotte's Beauty Trials proclamation.

As the Everlasting Rose comes fully into view, I see the lines to board the wire-carriages to the island snaking around along the pier. Charlotte should've shut down these wire-carriage tours, but she thought if she allowed the world to see her sister inside the prison, it would send a message. I fear it sent the wrong one—a message that says Sophia may be quiet, but she's still there. Perfecting her poison. Weaving her web. Biding her time.

Newsie boats buzz around the Everlasting Rose like flies, each wanting to get the first portrait of Sophia since Charlotte placed her there, each hoping for a quote to print in their papers, a small bite of what she might think of all that's transpired since being locked away. Does she agree with her sister's decision? Would she have done the same thing?

I could answer their questions easily.

No.

Sophia will not think this make-believe tournament of trials is the right plan for Orléans. She still thinks her reign would have succeeded. She probably planted this poisonous seed in Charlotte's mind. Somehow.

I will find out for myself today.

Newsies race along the pier holding their papers. "The *Chrysanthemum Chronicle* has the official report first. Sophia's access to Belle-products and beauty work restricted by the queen," one newsie hollers. "She's plummeted into grayness. Never to see the light again."

"The Beauty Trial preparation underway. Excavation of ancient documents has begun. Imperial librarians seen going into the catacombs—one of the entrances to the Goddess of Death's Grottos. The *Trianon Tribune* has the exclusive portraits. Don't miss a single moment."

"Wonder what disgraced Queen Sophia thinks of all the Beauty Trials news? We've analyzed the signs. Read the *National* for the most accurate theories."

Vendors weave through the throng offering windy-season treats—tiny pots of tea for the journey, flower-shaped cookies soon to return to flower boxes, petit crème-cakes dusted with sugar snow to bid farewell to the cold, and little hot cakes to welcome the heat. I watch it all with a combination of nostalgia and disdain.

Nearby, a well-coiffed young man steps onto a small platform and hollers into a voice-trumpet: "The one true queen of Orléans to give her first interview to the *Daily Rebel Rose*. The Jolie Society has supported her from the very beginning. We are her loyal flock." He's reed thin—a strong gale could carry him away—and his hair is the color of fresh snow, almost the same shade as his skin. He plays with his crimson top hat, the brim of which is covered with curious copper butterflies, his fingernails gilded. "No more conjecture, no more speculation, no more biased lies. The truth unvarnished. Get it here."

My eyes burn into him. I've seen their posters and heard their shouted slogans at court—*With Sophia, our Defender and Vindicator*. How could anyone support the monster in the cage? How could anyone forgive her crimes?

"Line up for the first tour of the day," a porter calls out as he herds the line through a series of aisles.

I pluck a flower from the wall, hand a few leas to the

driver, and descend. I hold my breath until I pay for a ticket and board. There I join fifteen passengers, including the well-coiffed young man from the Jolie Society. I shift away from him. His proximity needles me, and I need to focus.

The inside of the wire-carriage is larger than it looks from outside: a plush velveteen jewelry box with teakwood benches and goldenrod cushions tucking us safely away from the wind and the water below. Riders ooh and aah as they glance around. Chandelier-lanterns tinkle as the wire-carriage slides forward across the pier and lifts into the air. Stormy light pushes through the sky window above our heads and scatters gray rays across the floor.

Servants whizz in and out, slipping from behind silk screens. They wheel in carts brimming over with beignets and honey croissants and sticky saffron cake. "Only three leas, gentlefolk of Orléans. Have a taste from the trolley carts as you take in the sights."

I haven't eaten yet. My mouth waters, but I don't want to risk lifting my veil to reveal my identity. Plus, a glamour would be a waste to use now, when I'll still need one to get inside the prison. If I even get that far.

Women chatter behind their veils and ornate fans, interrupting the cacophony of my thoughts.

"You think she's shriveled and gray now? She was changing her look hourly right up until she was imprisoned," one asks.

"Let's hope we get a glance," another adds. "A tiny peek. I just have to know."

"Not shriveled. She's still quite young, and her natural template will cling to youth. But definitely gray as those clouds overhead."

The women burst into chuckles.

A uniformed woman steps into the middle. "Welcome! I am your guide and fountain of knowledge for all things related to the Rose. Please direct all your questions to me. We'll be coming up to the south of the prison in just a few minutes." She holds out a tray of eye-scopes. "Please feel free to borrow a pair. It's an architectural gem, a marvel, a true Orléansian feat despite its purpose. Nothing comparable has been built since our glorious Coliseum."

Like everything in this place, the ugliness of what the prison means at its core is glossed over: a cake you can smell the rot of, with everyone only talking about the icing. I sit seething as the carriage rises, hating every passenger who gleefully reaches for the eye-scopes. But I'm here for a reason, and I take a pair, too.

I gaze out the wire-carriage windows. The Everlasting Rose glows like a pearl trapped on the ocean. Licorice-black spindles curl into rose-tipped railings along the face of the building. When I was captured, I woke up in one of those cages. The memory of the cold floor I slept on flickers across my skin.

But now I fixate on the landing dock hanging off its side. The entrance I know is just for deliveries and guards.

"The queen's cell lies just ahead." She points. "The third from the left across the top row."

Sophia's window.

The scent of seawater is nauseating.

As I lift the eye-scopes and look for movement, an arm brushes my shoulder. I glance up, and it's the young man with the white hair from the dock.

"Mind sharing the view? I'd like to get a glimpse of our one true queen," he says.

"She is *not* our queen." Still, I grit my teeth, scowl, and scoot over.

He removes his hat, gold nails shining, and his white hair seems stark against the wine-red color of the carriage. As I watch, he fusses with his glasses, then removes a few of the copper butterflies from his hat. He lines the curious creatures along the carriage window ledge. In an instant, they stretch their tiny wings and flicker away out into the wind. I watch—they're almost too tiny to make out in the open air. But I think they land on Sophia's windowsill.

No one else seems to notice.

"What are you doing?" I snap, nudging him sharply. "What was that I saw you do?"

He winks. "You might need a monocle, pretty, for you saw nothing." He replaces his hat, tips it at me, and saunters away. Everything in me wants to rush after him, grab him by the collar. I almost do. But then the guide's voice rises:

"You can see more of the grounds to the right," she instructs us. Onlookers rush to the other side of the carriage. Our path has begun to shift over the landing dock. I don't have time to deal with the man and his butterflies, or I'll miss my chance.

"Now or not at all," I whisper to myself.

Moving quickly, I remove the flower I plucked earlier from my dress pocket. I wedge myself near one of the carriage windows, ignoring other passengers' protests, and set the flower along the ledge. Silently, I summon the second arcana, Aura, pulling it from my blood like chords. The veins in my arms and legs swell with heat and my hands flush red beneath the white.

No one notices how the flower's stem thickens before crawling up the carriage's side like ivy along a trellis, nor do they see when it twists itself into curling knots along the cable wires.

The carriage jerks. Screams tear through the tiny space. The passengers tumble in all directions as we grind to a halt.

Perfect.

 # SIX

The wire-carriage sways left and right like a kite caught in a storm. The arcana dissipates, but its work is done: the thick vines tangle the cable line, preventing it from moving even an inch along its path. I flatten myself against the wall and clutch my stomach, pretending to be overcome with nausea and preparing to leap as soon as I find my opportunity.

"Everyone find their seats," the guide shouts. "Quickly, quickly!" She rushes to the circuit-phone perched on the carriage wall and speaks in a hushed tone to someone on the other end.

The white-haired young man is across from me, squinting intensely as if that will allow him to see through my veil. "You look nervous," he says to me.

"Aren't you?"

"You look familiar."

"I don't know you, and you don't know me," I say.

"That remains to be seen."

The guide hangs up the circuit-phone and rushes to the middle of the carriage. "Don't be alarmed. All wire-carriages will dock here momentarily while they clear the cables. A bird's nest, they think."

"Land? *In* the prison?" someone replies.

"This is highly irregular," one guest says.

"Are we able to get out and have a look around?" someone asks.

"Absolutely not," the guard barks.

The wire-carriage jolts as the attendants work quickly to switch it to a nearby cable line. We inch forward. Now the courtyard comes into view. Women gasp and clutch their purses to their chests. There is a grand tower at the very center, where a watchman overlooks the floors of cells and cages. Prison window-boxes hold magnolias and roses and jasmine like carts of petit-cakes. Even a cage must be adorned.

A woman appears at my side. "I've taken this tour so many times, and nothing like this has ever happened!" she squeals.

"Everyone remain seated," the guide instructs. "You are not to leave the carriage under any circumstances."

As I look around the courtyard, I shudder. Memories flicker through my head like a newsreel—how the tower haunted me the days I was trapped here, how I could never see the watcher reporting every detail of our torture, how they brought in the needles and the vats to drain my blood, the midnight melody of my sisters' screams. I shudder when the carriage comes to rest on the landing dock. Do I have the courage to enter this place once more?

Then a flicker of bronze darts past my eyes. One of the man's butterflies. A breath later, it ignites like a tiny firework.

An explosion sounds. Dust and smoke choke us. Everyone scrambles to push their way out.

"Don't jostle me," someone yells.

Women scream that they can't breathe.

"I will not have my fine dress reeking of smoke," another says.

Passengers in other carriages begin to pour out onto the landing dock.

"There's a fire in that carriage!" one hollers, pointing.

Guards and guides try fruitlessly to herd them all back in.

The tangle of chaos provides the perfect cover. I slide out into the crowd, then slip into the shadows of the nearest hall until enough of the passengers shift from view. I know this place well, because although I hate the tour guides' insistence on showcasing its architectural beauty, it's true—this place was never really built to be a prison. It was built as a showroom—Sophia too obsessed with beauty to even consider that security, perhaps, might be one thing more important than aesthetic. When I was freed, I'd walked its halls, determined to know it inside and out. I'd been shocked by how little effort it required.

Now I sprint past empty cells, the Rose an easy map in

my mind. But it's not the only thing I picture. The image of Sophia floods my mind. Her wild eyes. Her perfect mouth. Her lavish hair-towers. Will I be able to keep from throttling her when I find her? And will I find her in time, before the wire-carriage line is repaired and the chaos contained?

I don't have to search long. The tour guide had told us all the location of her cell—top row, third from the wall. But Sophia herself makes her easy to find. I freeze in the corridor as the sound of her laughter echoes like a screech. My feet follow its sound, unable to turn around even if I wanted to. I can still hear the shouts from the courtyard, but in this moment, finding Sophia is the only thing I care about.

Behind bars, Sophia perches in her chair. It looks more like a throne. Over its high back hangs a golden chain. Sapphires and rubies dangle from it like glittering fruit, ripe for picking. The jewelry around her neck catches the morning-lantern light, while her pale white skin is powdered, any hint of gray masked. Eye films maintain a bright blue color, while a decadent scarf swaddles her hair. Her blouse boasts a seed pearl pattern, and her petticoats bloom with crinoline. She looks like a massive, upside-down teacup.

Not a prisoner.

Her eyes comb over me. "You're looking lovely, Edel. So nice of you to come see me."

"You're well kept," I spit back, glancing at her bed, fluffed with feather pillows and gossamer comforters, her teacup monkey, Singe, playing in the disheveled folds. A low table holds a lavish spread of cheese, fruit, and bread. A vanity with an array of Belle-products explains her lack of gray.

In the cell Sophia locked me in, I slept on a mat. My food was full of mold and maggots.

As if she can read my mind, Sophia says, "I am a queen."

"You *were* a queen."

Sophia stands. I can see the chains that ring her wrists like iron bracelets.

"I suppose you've come for something; otherwise you wouldn't have gone through all the trouble."

"If you're a queen of anything, it's manipulation. I know what you are. Trying to undo all the things Charlotte has done. You're responsible for all the unrest in Trianon and Orléans. Poisoning newspapers—encouraging newsies to reject the laws and regulations we've been passing."

"Me?" she says, pressing a grayish hand to her chest. A smile dances across her mouth. "What could I possibly do from in here? My sister monitors everything I do. Her spies poke and prod me. They even check my bowel movements."

"I'd have done even worse to you."

Sophia clucks her tongue. "You're just a Belle. Nothing more than a puppet bred to service us. You will *always* be beneath us. Even below the Gris."

Her words burn my flesh while the noise from the courtyard grows louder: there are shouts for passengers to return to their carriages. I don't have much time.

I grimace at her. "You made sure Charlotte would never

be able to rule effectively—sending your supporters out to cause the riots and chaos. You knew it would be too much for her. You knew she would follow the rules, that she'd trigger these nonsensical Beauty Trials."

Sophia laughs with a sharp-pitched glee that echoes up into star cutouts in the domed ceiling. Even here, she can see the sky. When I was imprisoned, there was only darkness.

Sophia moves toward her tea table. "I would offer you some tea, but I'm not feeling particularly hospitable. You've been so mean after all." She digs a tiny metal spoon into a canister, dumps the contents into the steep net, turns her back to me while pouring herself a cup. The comforts of her prison send more rage through me.

"I have to make my own tea now. There's an art to it, you know? Oh, of course, you do. You had to serve us Belle-rose tea."

I want to wrap my fingers around her throat, but I force my mouth into a smile and show a gentle sliver of teeth. "You think if there's a new queen, she'll let you out of here. But you won't be able to control those trials," I say.

She whips back around, lifting the teacup to her mouth to cool it with her breath. I get a whiff of the liquid—a strong floral odor, almost enough to sting my nose. Sophia makes her eyes large and innocent as she blows.

"If it were up to me, you'd be dead," I say. "I would've left your head in the Royal Square until the northern vultures pecked your skull clean."

"Another would grow back," she says, and sips her drink with smug satisfaction. "You'll never be able to get rid of me. Even if you do successfully kill me."

I work hard to conceal the concern that her words plant in me. What does she mean by that? My sisters, my fellow Belles, will never be safe until the world is rid of her, I do know that.

"I'll make sure you never get out of here," I growl.

"You and I both know that isn't true." She winks. "When I am released, and I most certainly will be, I will make sure you and your sisters, even the degenerative ones, will be put back in their rightful places—the auction block and the teahouses. I will restore order. I will give my subjects what they truly want. The way things used to be. You are in service. That's what you were born for. That's why the Goddess of Beauty sent you here."

I lunge forward, gripping the bars. "You will never put me or my sisters in a cage again. You will never come near us again."

"No one cares about your freedom, Edel. No one wants you liberated. Don't you understand this by now? The only thing that matters is beauty. The only thing that matters is spintria. Your little insignificant life doesn't."

She smiles. I see her teeth for a moment. They are bright red. She looks like an animal who's bitten into a fresh kill.

I step back in horror.

"Yes, Edel . . . it's exactly what you think."

Dread thrums through me as if it has replaced the arcana. It can't be.

"The rich proteins in your blood, the blessed arcana gifts, help me maintain my beauty from within." She drains the cup, then sweeps her finger along the rim for the remaining bits and shows it to me before licking it off.

My head turns fuzzy, like I'm waking up from the worst possible nightmare. The missing Belles that everyone assumes are working back-alley teahouses—are they actually giving their blood? Or are they—part of them—ending up here?

"How . . . ?" I breathe.

"I am a queen, and you are nothing more than a pretty puppet with gifts you don't deserve."

I let my eyes burn into hers. From a distance, the eye films look like one solid color, but up close you can see all the details, how each iris is filled with different-shaped petals, fanning out in color bolts of white-blue and gray, like storms caught in the middle.

"No matter my current circumstances, you can *never* take that away—even in death. It is my birthright. It is my destiny. It was written by the gods. And my earthly supporters will never betray me. They are, we might say . . . at the center of all things."

She grins hugely; then the door in back of her cell opens— three guards and three servants march in, bearing a gilded tub filled with frothy bubbles releasing a heavenly scent. One servant ladles scoops of honey into the water. Another removes the iron cuffs around Sophia's ankles and examines the bruises. Their movements are routine and practiced. How can they treat her like this, while she is a prisoner?

They don't spot me. But as they begin to undress her, Sophia grins. "We have a visitor, my little darlings!" she says, clapping.

They all look up at me in shock. At the same time, footsteps echo throughout the hall. A crowd appears at the end of the walkway—newsies and guards. With them is the white-haired man with the crimson top hat and strange butterflies.

"Her cell is this way!" a newsie yells.

A phalanx of guards tromps down from the opposite side. "You are out of bounds," one barks. The newsies turn and run. I race behind them before I'm caught here again.

"Bye-bye, Edel," Sophia hollers, then whistles a tune that echoes off the domed ceiling, tangling in each and every empty cell, chasing us as we descend the stairs and exit the Everlasting Rose.

Her words echo inside me: *I am a queen, and you are nothing more than a pretty puppet.*

Her Belle-blood tea sickens me, chokes me with rage. I swallow the impulse to vomit. But it has given me an idea.

I will keep the Belles safe. I will make sure she never gets out of here. I will enter the Beauty Trials myself before I allow her tyranny to resume.

Maybe the new queen of Orléans should be a Belle.

Maybe it should be me.

 SEVEN

In the morning, while the palace apartments are still quiet with dawn, I slip behind a gauzy curtain in the Imperial Library, striding into the Belle archives, where Charlotte asked me to meet her. The sky of stained-glass windows is now covered in black drapes. Law ledgers and copies of the edicts Charlotte and her cabinet have passed since she ascended the throne fill the tables. I comb through them while I wait. A single reading-lantern floats beside me.

I used to come here when I first stayed behind to help Charlotte, fishing for historical documents that revealed how all the beauty laws came to be over time. I'd walk through the aisles, pulling out all the books on the laws related to Belles. It's what my maman would've done. She loved the library at Maison Rouge, dragging me there when I was small whether I wanted to go or not, telling me everything I needed to know was captured in ink—all the answers to all the questions. I use the opportunity of silence to scan all the edicts Charlotte's cabinet has prepared for the meeting.

Belles will be given free room and board at all teahouses, and a wage of 1,000 leas per beauty work appointment.

All teahouses will open twice a week.

All residents will be given a monthly beauty ration token to be honored at every teahouse and by every Belle.

Belles will be compensated by the Imperial Bank for each appointment honored.

Beauty work will be taxed at 150 leas per appointment to be collected by treasurers from the Imperial Bank monthly; all citizens, including Belles, are subject to the kingdom-wide fee.

I frown at these edicts—more middle-of-the-road nonsense. Trying to please everyone instead of doing what is right. But my eye catches on another one—this one in a stack with sketches of vultures and what looks like a caisse. I recognize Charlotte's neat handwriting:

If the queen calls upon the tournament in order to abdicate her throne, and the tournament fails to produce a new queen, then representatives from each isle will be called to choose the successor.

My frown becomes a snarl. Representatives from the isles? The isles whose richest and most influential desire more than anything for beauty work to return and Belles to be thrown in the teahouses again and forced back into the old ways? There's no way they can be depended on to make a decision even resembling ethical. My hands shake with the impulse to rip all the documents to shreds—it wouldn't matter anyway. I turn to the bookshelves in frustration, and my hand falls upon a tome of fairy tales.

I recognize its spine, and memories yank at my heart-strings. Pulling the book free from its neighbors, I run my fingers over its brocade cover with a gilded title—*The Tales of the Gods*. A copy just like it sat on the nightstand I shared with my maman—and probably every child in the kingdom. As I open the book, the memories tug me in like a ship caught in a terrible storm.

I close my eyes. Images hit me in flashes, and I'm back beside my maman in our old room at Maison Rouge. The red sill-lanterns flickering patterns across our bed, and a dining cart whistling with steam.

Maman sits perched in bed with a book. Her warm brown face holds a clever smile, and she clucks her tongue, ready to fuss at me about one of Du Barry's numerous complaints about my behavior: *Edel didn't write all my lines* or *Edel didn't complete the arcana lesson* or *Edel didn't follow instructions the first time.*

"Am I in trouble?" I ask, ready to apologize for whatever it might be, because the look of disappointment in Maman's amber eyes is the only thing that would make me sorry.

"You always think that," she replies.

"Because usually I am when you look at me like that."

"So flushed. Your temper shows in your skin." She pats the spot beside her. "Come lie with me. I'm cold and you're always warm."

She touches my cheek. Her hair smells of honey soap, and her hand makes my arms and legs relax. I sink into the familiar shapes left behind in the mattress. "Why are you reading that fairy tale again?"

"Why not?" She shows me the book. "I like fairy tales. This tells the story of the Beauty Trials."

"I want *real* stories," I sneer. "Not made-up ones."

"You were never one for make-believe," she replies with a chuckle. "Will you let me read before you dismiss it as untruth?"

I sigh and pull the blankets over me, tangling my limbs with hers. I nuzzle closer to her and peer at the pages.

Maman kisses my forehead. "After the Goddess of Beauty selected the first queen of Orléans—"

"Marjorie!" I say.

"You've been paying attention in your studies."

"Barely."

"Beauty was preparing to return to the sky. She needed to determine who would look after the first humans. She took her caisse and—"

"Like ours?"

"Just like ours, petit. But this one held only four objects. A comb. A chalice and pomegranate leaves. A mirror."

"But why?"

"Ever the eager one." She shifts the book between us. The illustration of Beauty's glistening caisse opens and shuts on the thick parchment pages.

"Beauty selected attributes she thought would be best for a queen. She placed a comb in the caisse to remind humans to be composed and balanced. What are the next two?" She points to the flickering image.

"A cup with rubies," I answer.

"A *chalice* of pomegranate nectar brewed from those leaves, of which the first humans could drink to fill themselves with strength."

I stare at the fourth object, a mirror that reflects tiny images of Maman and me.

"And lastly, a mirror that would always show the truth."

The red sill-lanterns cast patterns across our bed.

"You know this part of the story. After Beauty's husband, the God of the Sky, cursed their babies with skin the color of a storm, eyes as crimson as roses, and hair as stiff as reeds, Beauty made us. But she wanted to make sure that if Queen Marjorie and her descendants couldn't rule, another could. These objects represent a divine tournament where competitors face a quartet of obstacles."

"What were the challenges?"

"It doesn't say."

"How did Queen Marjorie win? What happens if you lose?"

Maman turns the page, and I gasp. A terrifyingly beautiful woman shrouded in black and red stares back at us. "If you die during the Trials, your soul with be given to the Goddess of Death, Beauty's enemy."

"But why?"

Maman chuckles. "It was the bargain that was struck. Queens must be tested, petit. Power requires examination."

The memory of Maman lingers like a ribbon of perfume, and I gulp down the swell of missing her, the desire to be back where none of this exists. I return the book of fairy tales to the shelf.

"Excuse me!" a librarian barks at me, her eyes severe and full of annoyance. "You are *not* supposed to be in here."

Before I can answer, Charlotte, her attendants, and guests sweep in behind her.

I bow.

"Your Majesty, good morning," the librarian mutters with a bow.

"I asked her to meet me here," Charlotte says, commanding and stern. "Please bring out all of the documents related to the Beauty Trials."

I give the librarian a smug smile. She nods and curtsies before scampering off.

A stream of librarians floods the alcove, their hair fashioned into large disks, and their arms full of books, parchment stacks, and boxes. They release a few reading-lanterns loose into the room. Their light bathes us in golden speckles.

The Iron Ladies, a few important-looking people I've never met before, and all Charlotte's attendants assemble around the table ready to see the documents.

One librarian steps forward. "Your Majesty, the instructions await your review." She motions to a large table covered in tissue-paper-thin parchment. "It has always been rumored that these parchments are made of the flesh of our beloved Goddess of Beauty, and thus indestructible," one librarian informs. "But there is no way to test it without potentially damaging them."

An attendant presents a pair of white gloves to each of us. I pull mine on slowly. Being invited into this process reminds me how angry I am with Charlotte, the feeling of betrayal that knots inside me. Still, as I approach the table and all that it bears, my chest buzzes with anticipation. I think of Maman and what she would've said: *Keep an open mind—and most importantly, an open heart.*

"I'm excited to show you what we excavated," Charlotte says, staring into my eyes, oblivious to all my hidden feelings. "We found the caisse near the island of Minnate. The documents that detail the proceedings of the Trials have been kept in the royal archives for as long as anyone can remember. Those documents said the caisse would be at the entrance of one of the Goddess of Death's caves. Did you know that there are four entrances? One for each direction the wind blows."

I cut my eyes at Lady Arane, leader of the Iron Ladies. She once trapped me in one of those grottos with Camellia when we sailed to dethrone Sophia. "I am familiar with them." Lady Arane averts her eyes.

Charlotte motions to a beautiful round woman whose hair frames her plump cheeks. "I'd like to introduce you to our newly appointed Minister of Games, Madam Bisset," Charlotte says. "She will be overseeing the Beauty Trials along with a Gamekeeper, as is tradition."

"A pleasure to meet you, Madam Bisset," I say politely. "Gamekeeper?" I ask Charlotte.

"A Gamekeeper shall emerge from the caves of the dead, summoned by the Goddess of Death's vulture," Charlotte says, quoting.

"You act as if we've always had these trials," I say. I almost laugh—it seems absurd that every one of these officials is taking seriously what very well might be a fairy tale from the very book I still hold in my hands. "As if this is an ordinary affair and not something out of a children's story."

"Ever the skeptic," Charlotte replies. She affixes a monocle to her left eye and leans over the table to study the parchment. "It's miraculous that these have lasted thousands of years," she remarks, and begins to read, her voice ringing out into the small space. She seems relieved, like the Trials will ease a burden from her shoulders. And it will, I realize. She wants this change for herself as much as she does for the kingdom. I can't decide which I am more: spiteful or sympathetic.

"Herein lies the divine instructions to invoke the Beauty Trials," she reads. "A series of challenges set forth by the

Goddess of Beauty to select the queens of Orléans in her image."

"And who wrote them?" I drawl, determined to make my suspicion known. "The Minister of Fairy Tales?"

An imperial librarian stares down her nose at me. Another one tries to shush me.

"The documents were recorded by the most ancient of ministers, transcribed directly from the Goddess of Beauty. Have you no respect for tradition?" a third replies, aghast.

"It hasn't exactly served me well," I reply, but Charlotte has begun to read and no one pays me any attention.

"Awakening the eternal caisse will animate four objects: a golden comb, a jeweled chalice, pomegranate tea leaves, and a mirror.

"Each object represents a challenge that will test a contestant's mettle to measure her right to be queen—for the Goddess of Beauty used these objects to make the first humans.

"The jeweled chalice holds pomegranate nectar to be brewed from the enclosed leaves. The nectar seeks to identify the proper spirit of women who should be blessed enough to compete for the hallowed responsibility of queen.

"The enchanted pomegranate leaves will choose eight competitors, and Beauty will mark each of these Anointed Eight with a Belle-rose on her left cheek.

"The Goddess of Beauty's comb ensures each hair has its place. It reminds one to carry oneself with a sense of equilibrium.

"The mirror of glass will show the truth of each competitor and reveal the inner self.

"To unlock the caisse, a Belle must willingly sacrifice blood and place one drop along its filigree. Once opened, stewards of the throne must brew the pomegranate tea and serve it to hopeful competitors. Within a day's cycle, the marks will appear."

Charlotte's eyebrows furrow slightly here, as do my own. It doesn't say how many competitors are allowed to enter the Trials. Is it unlimited? What if there are dozens? Hundreds?

"Beauty made a bargain with the Goddess of Death that, in exchange for the safekeeping and guarding of her divine caisse, those who failed the Trials would be hers for the taking. Each of the Anointed Eight is to write her last will and testament, because to enter the Trials means success or death."

Charlotte pauses only for a half breath, swallowing.

"The objects will set forth their trials in succession. Each challenge will be clearly identified and the Gamekeeper shall reveal its objectives. As each one is completed, the objects will retreat to the caisse, and upon completion of the challenges, the entire caisse will return to the Goddess of Death's caves. May you always find beauty. Let the Trials unearth it."

The room sits in stunned silence. Then the ministers begin to buzz.

"An excellent opportunity to unite the kingdom around a common purpose," the Minister of News chatters. "It'll restore faith and joviality and sell a heap of papers."

"Shall we design a special wardrobe for competitors?"

the Fashion Minister ponders aloud. "That would give them something to be excited about."

"Look at the depictions of the first trial," the Beauty Minister says, pointing at an illuminated manuscript. A labyrinth of underwater caves, stalactites and swirling shadowy ink depicting the depths of seas. Would the Trials be the exact same challenges—or new ones? My stomach tenses at the thought of all that water... if it turns out to have any truth to it.

A librarian clears her throat loudly.

"By your leave, Queen Charlotte, we will present the caisse," she said.

"Bring it out, then," Charlotte says, still lost in the parchment.

"Here, Your Majesty?" the librarian says uncertainly.

"We are secure," Charlotte says, looking up. "I would like to examine the contents with the benefit of these texts rather than cart the whole library to my quarters. Don't you think it best?"

"Very well."

The caisse is massive—at least three times the size of our beauty chests, nearly the length of my cell in the Everlasting Rose. It's so caked with age it looks like it is made of dried mud, or brick. Something tugs at me, begging me to move closer. My fingers tremble with the desire to find its edges and dig them out. Claw away the mud to see what's beneath. Put this whole fairy tale nonsense to rest. It's just an ancient caisse. This is all pomp and circumstance.

I take one step.

My chest rises. My arcana awaken. Veins swell in my hands. A noise floods my ears like the hum of the beehives near the greenhouse at Maison Rouge.

I take another step. The hum grows louder, and I wish my sisters were here.

Could it be real after all? My skepticism from a moment ago feels fragile.

Behind me, Charlotte speaks. "To open Beauty's caisse, a Belle's honored blood is to be used. This assures that the Belles, Beauty's divine gift to Orléans, are engaged in the determination of its queen."

She doesn't want to ask me, and in that moment, my spite melts temporarily into sympathy. Charlotte, still fighting the effects of poison, trying desperately to keep everyone happy. But I don't care about everyone—I care about my sisters, the Belles. I wonder if the Goddess of Beauty ever imagined one of her divine gifts would ever take the throne. Maybe not. But she likely didn't imagine a queen of Orléans sipping our blood from a teacup either. I hadn't wanted the Trials—I had hoped the elixir I've been experimenting with would be enough. But, staring at the caisse before me, the traveling box of my potions seems small and insignificant. Here in the library, a real change could begin.

"I will do it," I say softly. I don't take my eyes off the dirt-caked caisse.

"Are you sure?" Charlotte whispers. "Perhaps there is another way...."

"I doubt it," I answer. "If this is real, as you insist, then the means are the means."

In the end, she sends for a nurse, bearing a tray of needles and glass bottles.

"No ceremony?" I say, to hide the thumping of my heart. "No *once upon a time*?"

The nurse tuts at me, and I lift my arm, allowing her to draw a small vial of blood. The pinch is always so hot, and as I watch my blood trickle out, it occurs to me that if I could become queen, no Belle would ever have to give her blood again. I could make it so. I could keep them all safe forever.

"The documents say it's supposed to be put in the filigree of the caisse," the Beauty Minister reads. "How can the blood penetrate this debris?"

"Blood is powerful," Charlotte says. "Especially when it's shed."

She takes the vial of my blood from the nurse's hand and stands considering the caisse. Then, with grim resolution, she drizzles it over the top.

Layer by layer, the crusted exterior begins to wear away, and the filigree to reveal itself: a wall of golden snakes pulsing with aggravation and anticipation. The caisse shakes, listing left and right like something within is trying to escape.

I step back. My doubts about the Beauty Trials, already quieting, shrink to near silence inside me. Something under my skin twitches. The nearness of magic makes my very blood hum. This is something. Something real.

There is a terrifying grinding sound, and we all clap our

hands over our ears to shield them. With a final shriek, the lid of the caisse pops open. There's a long moment of silence, and then I step forward to look inside. Behind me, the various ministers merely crane their necks to peer in.

Inside are the comb, chalice, and a mirror—as well as what must be the dried pomegranate leaves. I had expected them all to be as ancient and ragged as the caisse itself, but there's not a speck of grime on any of the objects. Their precious metals glint softly in the light of the lanterns, as if winking at me. I feel their pull, calling me toward them.

Above them a single glass orb rises, connected to each of the objects by delicate chains. They pulse and glow as if they're angry fallen stars happy to be released.

"Lovely," the Beauty Minister says. "How lovely."

"But what is that?" the Fashion Minister murmurs. "Comb, chalice, mirror...egg?"

I have seen it, too—small and smooth and black. It seems to tremble. A sudden wave of nausea catches me by surprise, as if whatever trembles in the caisse trembles in my stomach.

"The documents said nothing of this," Charlotte whispers.

The egg shakes more violently, and I'm afraid I may vomit.

"Look...it's hatching," another librarian says, her voice rising.

The shell of the black egg cracks, and I clutch my middle. Out of the egg climbs a small, squeaking vulture, its feathers slick with mucus. Its eyes are dark marbles, rolling in its sockets. Those eyes find us, then make their way to the chains. It stretches its wet wings, then begins to nip at the chains. The bird is so tiny, but something about it roots me to the spot. It is terror personified. But no one else seems stricken by the horror of the creature.

"What if it ruins the objects?" Charlotte says with alarm. "This is unexpected. All the old stories say that vultures are the messenger for the Goddess of Death. I see no message."

One librarian attempts to stop the vulture, doing what I wouldn't dare do—reaching out to touch it. The flash of blood from her finger is immediate, and she cries out, shrinking back from the curved beak. Has anyone noticed the bird seems to be growing? Doubling, tripling, quadrupling. Right before our eyes, becoming stronger and bulkier and bigger.

The vulture finally snaps the chains. It has untethered the glass orb, which now lifts above us. Like the bird, it too seems to have grown—it's big enough for me to wrap my arms around now—and releases a hum. We all stare in silence, even the hunched vulture.

Then the orb shatters.

The sound is like a roar, and several of us shriek—myself included. The shards fall like a rainstorm, drops that can slice through your skin, taking blood and flesh as their price.

The vulture stretches its now massive wings. A chorus of cries erupts all around me with Charlotte cowering under the protective arm of an attendant. Three out of four objects spin wildly, then, as if released from a bow, set off in separate directions like post-balloons. They rise and rip through the ceiling, releasing another hail of glass. With a beating of massive wings, the bird of death follows.

My nausea recedes with it, but not my heartbeat. Only the bundle of pomegranate leaves remain.

Guards and attendants scramble to clear us out of the room—Queen Charlotte has already been whisked away to safety in the moment I took my eyes off her. But now I can't take my eyes off the ceiling, watching the shapes of the objects and the bird disappear, until someone hollers, "Look at the caisse!"

I whip around. The lid of the beauty box has slammed shut, and the filigree pattern shimmers and twists, reassembling into cursive letters.

My fingers yearn to touch them, and I reach out. An imperial librarian steps in my path. "Don't," she says desperately.

I push past her and place my hands on those words. They pulse and hum along with the arcana in my veins.

"What does it say?" the Fashion Minister asks, panting. Pinpoints of blood appear on his face from the falling glass.

I read aloud, and I'm shocked by how steady my voice sounds.

"The Beauty Trials have begun, my children. Let the nectar decide who is worthy to move forward."

 # EIGHT

In the Royal Square, women and girls clutch blood-ink pens in the air, ready to injure themselves or forfeit their lives to the Goddess of Death for the chance to become the next queen of Orléans. I watch from my room's balcony as they scatter about like this is some sort of festival or party game, and not a potential death sentence. And yet I'll be among them. Won't I? Am I really going to do this? If it means protecting my sisters, now and forever...yes.

I turn away from the window and resume pacing. I'm waiting for an answer from Camellia. I hurried to send a post-balloon to her yesterday, writing so fast my fingers could not keep up and smudging all the letters. I haven't heard back from her or Gaelle. It's hard to contain the frustration. What could Camellia be doing if not answering? I consider my letter, which I kept short:

Dear Camellia,

The Goddess of Beauty's caisse has been opened. It's real. Even writing this phrase feels strange and unnatural, but the fairy tales are true. I'm entering the Beauty Trials. I will do whatever it takes to make sure we are safe and never have to return to a teahouse again.

Edel

The guards clatter bells to silence the excited crowd. The newly appointed Minister of Games, Madam Bisset, perches on a high platform, shouting into a voice-trumpet:

"Please maintain order. All will be able to enter." She waves her dark brown arms in the air, her glittering bangles scattering the sunlight. "You will have today to submit all proper parchments. You will be ineligible if you don't follow the procedures. All must include a detailed last will and testament—all things must be accounted for. Send your post-balloons to the Imperial Mailroom to be sorted. They must arrive before the morning star. Listen up! Listen up!"

A light rap on the door yanks me from the balcony. I perk up, hoping it's Gaelle, knowing it must be her.

The door creaks open, and Adele enters. My heart sinks a little.

"I have the ink and parchment you requested, and mail for you has just arrived." A trio of crimson post-balloons float behind her, their tails dragging, the Belle-symbol blazing on its side.

The pulsing sight of the fleur-de-lis and its curling ribbon of blood disgusts me now. How we've been marked as Belles in a way that was supposed to make us feel special, but instead it became a brand, a mark of property. As if it's been burned into our flesh. If Sophia had had her way, more Belles would have been grown in her perverted tanks. The emblem carved into the foot or neck of each child.

"My sisters," I murmur.

"What was that, my lady?" Adele asks.

"Nothing. Were there no other post-balloons?" I ask.

"Just the three."

She studies me, looking concerned. There's something about Adele that is sisterly, and I regret being so harsh with her. When she's not acting nervous, she has a shrewd way about her—the kind of girl who would always tell you if you had something in your teeth rather than letting you embarrass yourself. I avoid her eyes as I reach for the post-balloons, biting my lip and wondering why it's taking Gaelle so long to respond to the note I sent before I saw Sophia—or better yet, why she has yet to come see me at all. "Thank you." She hesitates for a moment before she goes, nodding on her way out.

I tear open the back of the first post-balloon and fish out the parchment scroll.

I recognize the handwriting immediately.

Camille.

Her quill marks are hurried, stark with worry and anger.

Dear Edel,

You entering the Beauty Trials couldn't be true. You are my sister. You are a Belle. This is a death sentence. I cannot lose another sister. I will not lose another sister. This is foolishness. I need you.

Come home so we can discuss this. There's got to be another way. We are strongest when we work together.

Camille

I open the second post-balloon to find a letter from Padma.

Edel,

I can imagine the tiny flicker in your eyes when you decided to do this. And I know there's no way to talk you out of it—though Camellia will try to.

I don't know what to tell you other than to be safe—and that I trust you and love you.

Padma

I open the final one, even though I know what it will say, and who it's from.

Hana.

Dear Edel,

I can't believe Queen Charlotte is actually doing this. The things we've been told have proven to be a mix of falsities and truth, and I am so confused. I fear I'll never understand it all.

That beauty-box looks disgusting. How could that have come from the Goddess of Beauty? It looks like it's been wrestled up from the depths. Soiled by the God of the Sea himself.

The papers are reporting that there will be a ball for competitors, and then the imperial ship will set sail the next afternoon for the Gravier Palace, where they'll all live throughout the tournament. Are the rumors true? Are the challenges only three days apart? That's not much time to heal if something should go wrong. But you've probably already thought of that, crafty Edel.

Write to me. I need to know.

And I love you. And I know you will win. You always do.

Hana

PS Camille is threatening to come to court if you go through with your plan. Don't tell her I told you. But be prepared!

My sisters' words echo long after I'm finished reading.

I go to the desk in the palace Belle apartments. Every time I sit here, I imagine what Camille's life must've been like as the favorite. The rhythm of attendants and servants shifting in and out of rooms, the melody of food carts and the snap of post-balloons, the faint echo of circuit-phones and parties. Seeing Elisabeth Du Barry's smug face daily filling the Belle appointment ledger.

The scents of her old life remain—the honeyed candles and bei powder and the perfume of rouge-sticks and pigment paste pots and rose creams. Her signature colors still tint the walls, wrapping me in a gift box of fuchsias and magentas.

I never wanted that. But my life these past three years has been anything but a fairy tale. Camille's perfumes mingle with the smoke and ash of the burning capital city.

The thought of Padma's warm smile and Hana's excited eyes and Camille's anxious gaze fills me with resolve. I will do this to keep them safe. And I will make sure I know and see all that is happening.

I take out parchment and a quill, and begin to write.

I, Edel Beauregard, being of sound mind and body, not acting under duress or influence, and fully understanding the nature and extent of all my property, do hereby make, publish, and declare this document to be my last will and testament.

I bite my bottom lip, then stare back at my Belle-trunk. My mind makes an inventory of all the silly objects I've amassed in eighteen years—it's not much.

All of my property of every kind, which I may own or have the right to dispose of at the time of my death, I bequeath in equal shares to my sisters Camellia Beauregard, Hana Beauregard, and Padma Beauregard. Except for the caisse, which should be given to Gaelle Marchand of the House of Fortune. Should the preceding persons die before me, then I bequeath the said property to the Maison Rouge estate as a substitute beneficiary to be sold and proceeds used to take care of any remaining Belles.

I make two copies of the will and put it into a letter case. I take a post-balloon from the desk hook and write a note to my sisters.

Camille, Hana, and Padma,

Keep this safe. It's part of the rules. Unfortunately.

I hope I'm selected to compete. Belles should be given the opportunity just like anyone else. The caisse wouldn't have been able to be opened without our blood. And I gave mine. They owe that to me.

If they choose me, I don't plan on losing the Beauty Trials. We will never return to the old way. No teahouses. No favorites. No competition. Not if I can do anything about it.

I hope you understand that I must do this. That I can do this. You did so much for me—and our sisters. Let me do this for us.

Edel

PS Camille, stop worrying about me. You'll make the others worry, too.

I stare at the words and run my fingers over the parchment before folding it, stuffing it into a post-balloon, and sending it off the balcony. Then I march from my bedroom into the main salon. "I need to see the queen on urgent business," I tell the first attendant I see. "Please send word."

She curtsies and scurries from the room.

I pace back and forth, only the noise of my dress sweeping the floor to keep me company. I watch the large hourglass on the mantel, fixating on every falling grain. I think about the comb, the mirror, the chalice, the pomegranate leaves that would soon turn into nectar—the hideous bird hatching from its egg. What sort of challenges will we face? How will the challenges truly showcase the qualities of being a queen? Did the Goddess of Beauty wish for her subjects to die in the process? Maybe it's all a gamble—Sophia was queen, after all, because of nothing but the blood in her veins. Nothing to do with justice or wisdom, and if anyone bothered to ask me, I would say a queen needs to at least value both. What she does not have herself, she is wise enough to look for guidance on.

My attendant returns then, interrupting my stream of thought. "My lady, the queen is dining with the Minister of Games," she reports. "She said you are welcome to join them in her private tea salon."

We snake along the long corridors and over a bridge leading to the private residences of the queen. The candles that line the walls ripple and dance, painting the hallway with buttery light.

Charlotte and the Minister of Games sit across from each other while servants wheel dining carts back and forth to the table. A pack of teacup wolves gallop between plates and cutlery, chasing a tiny ball. Beauty-lanterns crest overhead, bathing the room in light.

"Lady Edel Beauregard," the attendant announces.

I bow. My hands quiver clutching my last will and testament.

"Join us for a late lunch, Edel, will you?" Charlotte motions and a seat is brought out for me. "It's been a big morning."

I can't possibly eat. I must do this now, before anyone else has a chance to interrupt me. I hold up the papers. "I'd like to submit my name for the Beauty Trials."

Charlotte sits straight up as if she's been struck by lightning. The Minister of Games drops her fork and the clatter makes the whole room flinch.

"You couldn't possibly," the Minister of Games replies, aghast.

"Why not?" I place the will before her.

"You're a Belle," Charlotte says.

"I haven't forgotten that detail."

"And neither will the other competitors," the Minister of Games snaps.

"The whole world knows who I am. What of it?" I reply.

"The whole world knows you have *gifts*," Charlotte says. She seems to be scrambling for words, for a reason. "The arcana. It's an unfair advantage over the others!"

"The arcana? I won't use it."

The Minister of Games crinkles her brow, the brown of her skin an accordion. "We can't only have your word on the matter, Edel. Who knows what the three challenges will be or how they will manifest? You may be forced to in order to survive. I will not allow it."

"Where in the rules did it say that Belles couldn't enter?" I demand. "Show me."

"It doesn't," the minister admits. "But—"

"Then I can enter," I almost shout.

"It's not that simple, Edel. And please calm down," Charlotte says. But her frown is flustered, as if she, too, is inching away from composure.

"I *am* calm," I reply, opening and closing my fists as the tide of anger shoots through me.

Charlotte touches the empty chair to her left. "Have some of the steamed salmon. It's delicious. We can discuss this further once we're all well fed. My maman—gods rest her soul"—she kisses her two fingers and presses them to her chest—"used to say decisions should be made with a full belly."

Adrenaline floods my body. "I don't want to sit and I definitely don't want to eat."

Charlotte sighs. "Well then, Edel, I'm afraid I can't accept your entry into the Beauty Trials. I thought we'd be able to discuss the difficult details of the situation, but if you don't want to have a thorough discussion, I'll get straight to it. You will delegitimize and undermine the competition."

"Am I not a citizen of Orléans?"

"You are," she replies.

"Am I not part of the women and girls of Orléans?" If I could open my mouth and breathe fire, I would—my anger tries to find its way out of every part of me. "Then I deserve to enter. To at least drink the pomegranate nectar—let Beauty decide. She may not allow me; she may strike me dead on the spot. But why should I be blocked from trying?"

The Minister of Games pushes back from the table and crosses her arms over her chest. "Such defiance. Such disrespect shown toward your queen."

Charlotte's eyes fill with irritation. She purses her lips and tries to look sincere. "Join us for the Competitors' Ball tomorrow night. You can still be part of the festivities even if you aren't allowed to compete."

My whole body clenches. "There would be no Beauty Trials without me—and my blood, Your Majesty."

"I need you by my side. I need you alive."

"And I need to compete," I say. "I insist on being part of what happens to us."

"I promise you that the new ruling house will take care of Belles. I will ensure it before the transference of power. We are your stewards." She means it as a comfort, but it sounds like the creaking door of a gilded cage snapping shut.

"Not any longer," I reply, steadfast. "Belles will take care of themselves."

 # NINE

The next morning, the bed curtains snap open.

I sit up, a headache punching its way into my temples. My dreams were plagued with images of that vulture and drowning in dark water.

"Lady Edel, I'm sorry to wake you, but the Beauty Minister has made an unexpected visit," Adele explains, helping me from bed. "She is waiting in the main salon."

I rub my eyes. "Tell her I'll be out momentarily." I race to the nearby water basin and splash my face. My hands tug my blond hair into a Belle-bun with practiced instinct, and I pull on a robe. I know why she's here. I'm sure my so-called defiance during my audience with the queen has gotten around to each of the ministers.

I find the Beauty Minister stretched across the long chaise, her rich dark skin a decadent smudge of chocolate against the cream. Her vivant dress mirrors a rainbow after a windy-season storm—stripes changing every few seconds. Her teacup leopard stalks around chasing the droopy tail ribbons of the post-balloon Gaelle sent back to me last night, telling me she'd gotten trapped with her cousins at a wedding in the Gold Isles.

"Good morning, Edel," she says before taking a long sip of tea.

I consider the pastries on the breakfast cart before choosing a powdered luna pastry and a carafe of snowmelon juice. "I suppose you have come to convince me not to argue with Charlotte," I say. "You won't be able to talk me out of it."

She lifts her teaspoon, squinting to admire the fuchsia color painted on her full lips. "After these few years, I've learned to save my breath with you," she says with a chuckle. "My, the gray really does push through when you're not constantly refreshing." She sets the spoon in the saucer; then her eyebrow lifts. "No, I'm not here to dissuade you."

"Oh," I reply with surprise.

She points to a black-and-crimson box sitting beside the door. "I've brought you a dress from the Fashion Minister for the Competitors' Ball."

I lure the teacup leopard into my lap with the promise of a strawberry from my luna pastry. The tiny cat tussles with the bright red fruit bigger than its paws.

"But answer me," she says, pursing her lips, "why do you want to do this?"

"I never wanted this life," I say, scowling. "Any of it.

But I don't want anyone telling Belles what we have to do anymore."

"That's not exactly an answer," she replies.

"Are you going to ask all the competitors the same question?"

"If you succeed and win, you'll be telling everyone what to do—including the Belles. You will have to convince the world that they should listen to you . . . respect you. Do you know what it's like to be a queen? Any idea?"

I push away the weight of her words. "I can learn."

"You've never struck me as someone who wanted power. Or needed it. Frankly, you didn't seem that interested in being a Belle." The Beauty Minister eyes me.

"You don't think I can do it?" I sit up straight, ready for a challenge.

"I didn't say that. Any woman who enters the Trials will have to rise to the occasion. Charlotte grew up around queens—from her grandmother to her mother—and thus had an advantage of seeing how things have always been done. Now the world will have to make new traditions and that is always difficult at first. Nostalgia becoming the biggest obstacle."

I consider this, imagining myself in Charlotte's place. Making decisions for the Belles but also everyone else in the kingdom. I think of the hundreds of people I passed just on the way to the palace. They would be my subjects. It doesn't exactly appeal to me, looking after them all. I want things to be true and just. If that is what a queen is responsible for, and I believe that it is, then it's what I must aim for.

"You think I can win?" I let the question ease out without looking at her.

"Both you and Camellia have the same stubborn streak. When you get your teeth into something, you don't let go. Your jaw locks. I'd never count you out." She pulls a newspaper from beneath her and hands it to me. "But everyone has a reason for wanting to be queen," she says. "What will yours be beyond wanting to protect your own? Queens have to look out for us all."

I take the paper from her and scan the headlines. Hundreds and hundreds of pages detailing every aspect of those who have put forth their names to the Minister of Games. As I comb through their profiles, they wink or smile, nod or giggle. A few blow kisses or scowl. Each profile details their bid for queen.

COMPETITOR NO. 56: LANA TRAVERS
HOUSE REIMS
All queens should care about every living thing—big or small— and I will ensure even teacup pets live incredible lives and have a say.

Lana's blond hair spills over with teacup sloths, and her portrait won't stop with its incessant giggling. I flip the page. The freckles on the next competitor's brown skin wiggle each time she smiles, and her zigzag curls flicker like fire in a hearth.

COMPETITOR NO. 98: ESTELLE LAMBALLE
HOUSE OF ORLÉANS, COUSIN OF QUEEN CHARLOTTE,
SISTER TO DISTINGUISHED FORMER LADY-OF-HONOR
GABRIELLE LAMBALLE
Queens should come from powerful bloodlines. House of Orléans will continue to be favored by Beauty.

The next one has cropped black hair so stick-straight it cuts across her cheek like an arrow, the gloss of it shimmering.

COMPETITOR NO. 387: FABIENNE LORD
HOUSE OF EUGENE
Queens should respect the will of the people and that should shape how they govern.

The next competitor tips her hat as she lifts her eyebrows, as if asking a question.

COMPETITOR NO. 980: BLAIS DENE
HOUSE OF MILLINERY
Queens are like hats, protecting us from the harm of the elements.

Calandre Segale is impossibly beautiful: skin the color of honey macarons, eyes like emeralds, and a mouth so perfectly pink it reminds me of a bow. I wonder who has done her beauty work.

COMPETITOR NO. 34: CALANDRE SEGALE
HOUSE OF LOTHAIR
Queens are divine instruments installed by the gods, and thus their rule should be ironclad.

"What will *you* tell the newsies?" the Beauty Minister asks.

A knock startles us before I can answer.

"You have a visitor," the servant announces.

My heart lifts.

Gaelle.

"Tell her it's about time she showed up," I say.

"Glad you're excited to see us," a voice calls out from behind the attendant. Camille, Hana, and Rémy sweep through the doors. Their teacup dragons land on my shoulders, pressing warm, wet snouts to my neck.

The Beauty Minister leaps off the chaise. "Camellia, my little doll. It's so good to see you looking so well." She kisses Camille and Hana and pokes at Rémy before slipping from the room—presumably to fetch the Fashion Minister for this impromptu reunion.

"What are you doing here?" I ask as Camille pulls me into a hug. She refuses to let go even when I squirm, and when I finally get free, she studies me as if searching for wounds.

She looks older. Her skin is still a flawless rich brown but somehow ... growing tired. I think of all we've learned, all the lies we've unlearned. I remember my maman growing old more quickly than other women. Will we, too? Will being in control of how we use our arcana prolong our lives?

Camille's eyes tell of questions and concern, as well, but I know hers are of a different type—she's thinking about the Trials.

Hana flashes me a sheepish grin. Her dark hair hits her waist instead of up in a Belle-bun, and her expression holds the message—*I warned you.*

I finally wiggle out of Camille's grasp. "She seems to be in one piece, Camille," Rémy teases, getting her to loosen her vise grip on me. "Good to see you." His long locs are pulled back from his grinning face. "How are you?"

"Surviving."

"You won't if you try to enter the Beauty Trials," Camille interjects. "Get yourself killed before it starts. They'll never accept a Belle as queen." Her eyes comb over every inch of me, like I'm a parchment letter she's desperate to decode. "Did you really think we wouldn't show up and talk you out of this foolish plan?"

"It's good to see you, too, Camellia." I use her full name to irritate her. "And thanks for the vote of confidence." I reach down for Fantôme, gathering her into my arms. The teacup dragons are about all I've missed of life at home. "Where's Padma?"

"She's looking after the Belle babies with Ivy. And the few Gris ones we've allowed." She walks around her old salon as if it still belongs to her—readjusting pillows, moving the set of hourglasses from the fireplace mantel to the center table, shifting the tea carts around.

Rémy sits on one of the couches and pats the spot next to him, luring her to come sit with him. I wonder what's happening with them now. They seem so at ease with each other. Are they in love? Do they imagine a life beyond all this?

"Attempting to enter those trials is a distraction. We need to focus on finding the few Belles who have left the teahouses. Make sure they are safe, convince them to come back. We have room at Maison Rouge ready for them." Camille stands and paces. "We should also put forth another teahouse plan. Make them take a look at all your clever experiments and consider putting them into production. Ask for higher wages or—"

"Camellia," I interrupt.

"Stop calling me that just because you're mad at me," she barks.

"Stop acting like you're Madam Du Barry then," I snap back. "And I've been trying to do all those things. I send you every plan I put before Charlotte's cabinet."

Hana steps between us, throwing her hands in the air. She sweeps her long black hair over her shoulder. "Can we enjoy one night without fighting? We haven't been to a ball in a lifetime. It feels like we haven't been together for even longer."

"That life is over, and we can't pretend that it isn't," Camille interjects.

Rémy stands and walks over to Camille, taking her hand and causing her to settle. He kisses it, then leans to say something in her ear. It makes her smile, and the angry wind goes straight out of her.

My chest tightens, and a question whispers—what is it like to be that close to someone? Beyond touch. A life, a connection. With everything else I must face, it feels out of reach.

Adele strides into the room holding my bathing robe. "Lady Edel, it's time—" She swallows the rest of her sentence as she spots Camille, Hana, and Rémy. "My apologies, my lady. I didn't know you had visitors."

"Not real ones, Adele," I drawl. "You can relax."

I note her smile—it makes me smile, too. It must be because my sisters are here. I've never liked events like the Competitors' Ball—but tonight feels different. What happens tonight might change things forever.

I turn from Adele back to Camille. "I suppose you're staying here with me."

"The Fashion Minister is sending our dresses. And I hope the other bedchambers will be made available to us. I doubt you have other guests after all. If you're going to be queen, we must work on the charm."

 # TEN

That night, the Grand Imperial Ballroom winks with light. Chandelier-lanterns cluster in the ceiling domes, bathing everyone in the most beautiful glow. Royal painters float above in carriage-balloons, erasing the old frescoes of the royal family and replacing them with rich blue peacocks trimmed in gold. Flower shrines to the gods line the walls: Belle-roses for the Goddess of Beauty, magnolias for the God of the Sky, black calla lilies for the Goddess of Death, adeniums for the God of the Ground, and blue hydrangeas for the God of Fortune.

Charlotte has sold all the papers on the Trials. The whole kingdom is in a frenzy: lotteries wagering on which competitor will triumph as victor, the newsies releasing special newspapers profiling each entrant on the hourglass as the names are sorted, celebrities and courtiers quick to endorse their favorites and send support. There are hundreds of competitors, and thus pages and pages of news. Just what Orléans loves most—excess.

We're all supposed to be happy. We're all supposed to be celebrating. We're all supposed to be excited about the Beauty Trials and the new start it could mean for the kingdom.

And yet, it's not truly a new start if a Belle isn't allowed to enter.

Contestants from royal houses are adorned in cameo portraits of their ancestors—some with slithering animated ribbons growing into the branches of family trees, others with glistening webs highlighting notable ancestors and dignified relations. Those from merchant houses exaggerate their wares—the Perfumers with their top-hat atomizers, the Spicers leaving trails of saffron and cinnamon, the Inventors in cog-and-gear corsets, the Milliners with their flying hats.

Many of the celebrities and courtiers don veils, too ashamed to expose their gray. A few proudly taunt onlookers with their illegal beauty work. Whispers explode through the space, everyone speculating where beauty work is being done and whether it compares to the past. The atmosphere is sparkling, a frenzy of excitement.

Parties like these always make me want to die. I'd rather be anywhere but stuffed into a too-hot dress, surrounded by frolickers trying to make small talk.

Rémy and Camille dance, their hands swallowing each other's. Hana talks to three of the Iron Ladies, admiring their spiderwebbed gowns and begging to try on their now-legendary iron masks. If Valerie were here, she'd be investigating every sweet pavilion in the room, tasting all the puddings and lemon tarts and chocolate flowers, dancing to every popular waltz, admiring all the vivant gowns.

The Beauty Minister and the Fashion Minister sashay from group to group, circulating as their duties require, but I can see how it thrills them, to be doing this again. Everyone around me marvels at the delights. Others saunter past, lifting their drinks to toast me on such an auspicious occasion. I catch snatches of conversation:

"This gives me hope. A reminder of the old days. Everything is just so beautiful again."

"I just want it all to settle down. My nerves can't take more of the stress. The rioting is giving me a rash. It's dreadful."

"No sign of Auguste Fabry, disgraced son of the former Minister of the Seas—are we sure he hasn't stashed his evil maman away?"

"I hear talk that Lady Georgiana is campaigning with the Jolie Society. I don't imagine he'd invite her for tea at this point."

I grit my teeth as I watch the Minister of Games and Queen Charlotte greet all the competitors and adorn them with trial pins—a Belle-rose whose stem curls around the four divine objects. I glare at them as they pass, knowing the sweetheart neckline of my gown should have one, too. Yet here I stand, and there they go, kissing cheeks with appreciation for their sacrifice and bravery. Theorizing about what the Trials might entail. Laughing together about the beauty of the night. Their musical chatter angers me, a melody I refuse to accept.

Charlotte's excuses drum through me.

"The peaceful transition of power is of utmost importance."

"The kingdom can only accept a certain amount of change."

"Be patient as people learn to accept the Belles' new role in society."

A fresh start.

A new dawn.

I hate it all.

I hover by a beignet pavilion and sip from a champagne flute. The snowmelon juice holds animated ice swimming about, morphing into replicas of teacup narwhals, whales, and fish, but even these jovial details cannot put a smile on my face. I can only see the stormy-evening clouds skate by the windows. These windy-season skies are always how I pictured the afterworld. A sunless sky, searing with heat and no source. In this room full of laughter and music, it feels as if I'm the only one who remembers that people will die tonight, that they will line up to drink from a chalice full of nectar that might—that probably will—kill them.

A warm hand slips into mine. "You're frowning—and impossibly beautiful."

I flinch and whip around, my frustration loose and ready to be unleashed.

Gaelle bats her eyes at me, the hazel ones I gave her before leaving for the Silk Isles. Her grin sucks all the anger out of me. My heart flutters a little. She's dusted her deep brown skin with glitter, and she resembles a cold night sky: cloudless and twinkling. Her zigzag curls are swept into a bun and filled with magnolia flowers. A violet vivant dress wraps around her large and beautiful body.

"Where have you been? A wedding all this time?" I try to hide my pout. "I've been sending you post-balloons!"

"Don't be mad at me." Gaelle puts a hand to her forehead like she's exhausted. "My cousin's wedding was in the Gold Isles; then Maman and I had so many appointments after. Everyone wants to know what's going to happen in the Trials. What the future holds. Business is thriving."

"You didn't write me back but once."

She pokes out her bottom lip, then lifts my hand to kiss it. "I missed you. I should've written. Anouk was so needy this week. I guess we're almost official, but Christophe has been begging for me to take him back."

"Everyone covets you," I say, and swallow a pinch.

"But I came to court tonight just to see you." She pulls me close and cups a hand near my ear. "See that pretty girl in the corner?"

We both look. It's Anouk, glaring at us with a jealous stare.

"So, no more pouting in this corner."

I force a smile and show her all of my teeth. "See? Smiling."

"So pretty you are." She makes it impossible to stay mad at her.

"Now, come. I want a wind cake." She drags me toward a pavilion where a man flips tiny pastries imprinted with gigantic gales.

"I need to tell you so much," I say as she breaks open one, exposing its sticky insides.

She pops it into her mouth. "Later. Let's have a little fun first."

She fills me with more champagne, and we stumble through the crowd. As we breeze around the room, Gaelle tells me all the sordid details of her clients' lives: who is having an affair, who is in trouble with the law, who is stealing, who is lying. I never know if what she says is true any more than if her cards in fact reveal the future. But she makes me laugh even when it's the last thing I feel like doing.

Everyone is trying to distinguish themselves. Dresses that move to the rhythm of the orchestra even when the wearer isn't dancing. A ball gown that appears to be made entirely of fake blinking eyes. A thin young woman, barely more than a girl and who I hear calling herself Cesarine, wearing a glittering green dress and holding several snakes, kissing them on their scaly snouts.

I bump into a young woman wearing a tuxedo dress that balloons in layers of onyx and cream. Her hat shakes and turns to the rhythm of the room's orchestra.

"Silly hat," I say, the champagne sharpening my tongue.

"Perhaps to someone with no eye for sophistication," she replies, eyeing my dress.

"Who are *you*?" I reply.

"I'm Blais Dene, House of Millinery."

"And I'm Edel B—" I start.

"Everyone knows who you are," she says, clipped. Her hat settles back on her head, and she disappears into the crowd. Throughout it, I catch sight of other Belles—Kata, Noelle. Under the river of champagne, my heart swells at the sight of them. All I want is for them to be fulfilled, happy, safe. Even Gaelle's levity can't lift me out of the sudden cavern I plummet into—anger at Charlotte, anger at this evening, anger at everything.

Glass clinking interrupts the joyful calamity of the ball. Voice-boxes drop like fat spiders from beauty-lanterns drifting overhead. Charlotte steps upon a dais with her father, King Francis, and her mother's other partner, Lady Pelletier. She speaks into a voice-trumpet, and her voice booms through the room, cutting all conversations off.

"These past three years have been difficult as we adjusted to new and startling realities," she begins. "Tonight, we come together for something momentous."

The room bursts with applause.

"As we embark on more change in our world, I know that my decision to invoke the Beauty Trials is the right one. There may be more troubles on the horizon. But letting our gods help us usher in this next part of our future will be worth it." She lifts her glass.

"I hope each one of you who has chosen to compete knows the divine service you are providing to our great kingdom. How your willingness to sacrifice your lives is what makes our world magnificent. To Orléans, the Land of Rising Beauty. Long shall it rise!"

The room joins her in taking a sip from their glasses.

"Bring forth the Goddess of Beauty's pomegranate nectar. Let our competitors begin the journey."

Attendants assemble with silver platters holding tiny bottles of deep red liquid. The huge room and its waves of people ripple into a new formation as competitors shuffle into lines, one by one, ready to receive theirs, to test themselves against the invisible eye of the Goddess.

Charlotte's smile has faded, and she regards the room with gravity. "Tonight you will drink, competitors, and let the Goddess of Beauty decide if you are worthy of entering the tournament to compete for the crown. It has been so very long since the Beauty Trials occurred, but we were all born here in Orléans—we all know the story. The nectar sometimes acts quickly, sometimes slowly. But no matter what, by tomorrow morning, the Goddess of Beauty will have selected her Anointed Eight."

The crowds of girls and women—some barely more than children, some stooped with age—press forward. I can hear the clink of the tiny bottles of nectar. My stomach drops watching all the hopeful competitors—they wear varying expressions of preparation: giddiness, determination, and the occasional hint of fear. But do any of them look righteous? Do any of them walk with the purpose of justice? I can't be sure. And the longer I watch, the line getting fuller with the bodies of those who are free to do as they wish, I feel the snap of my last shred of reserve.

I slip my hand from around Gaelle's arm and plunge into the crowd, moving toward the front of the line.

"What are you doing?" she calls after me in a whisper.

"What I must," I reply without looking at her. My eyes are on Charlotte, who hasn't yet noticed me, smiling benignly at the crowds of competitors. When I arrive near the throne, however, her eyes lock onto me.

They are filled with disappointment and a fresh bloom of irritation, and I expect her to call the guards, but she doesn't need to lift a finger or say a word—two guards already move to block my path. I clench my fists, glaring through the space between their shoulders at the queen. She warned them already. She planned for me. I try to reach around the guards, but one grabs my arm. A few guests turn in surprise.

A gentler hand touches me now, Gaelle spinning me around, away from the dais and the guards.

She leans close to my ear and whispers, "Don't make a scene. There will be another way."

But even though her breath is soft enough to make me sigh, I pull away, away from her and away from all this. I leave the ball behind, aimed for the night, ignoring her calls, and those of Camille, who I storm past on my way outside to the terrace.

The future is supposedly inside this ballroom, but so far it only looks like more of the past.

The wind slithers through the fabric of my dress as I stand at the huge arching windows, watching the last dozen competitors claim their tiny bottles of nectar. The buzz of the crowd makes it through the window: I see people with their heads tilted back, downing the drink, probably sending up prayers as they let the Goddess's nectar leak down their throats. The music lifts again—the dancing will resume. The party never stops.

Not even when people start dying.

It doesn't start at any particular place in the grand ballroom—I don't even know if the first woman to drop was actually the first, or just the first that caught my attention in the big glittering room. She's wearing a grand dress the color of a spring morning, and she spins to the floor like a blossom from the branch. Her friends laugh at first, thinking she's drunk, or teasing. I know better: before she even hit the floor, a ribbon of blood striped her chin.

Then there are more. They fall like leaves in a storm, crashing through dining tables, toppling from their partners' arms mid-waltz. They die and they die, and I watch and I watch, and apart from a few tears, no one even screams, at least not that I can hear outside. All I see are the women dying, and the gossip-balloons sweeping low like vultures.

ELEVEN

I don't think I'll ever forget the screams or the sound a body makes when it hits the ground. No matter how many times I dunk my head in bath water to block it all out, even between all the bubbles and water and rose petals, the memory of the ball finds me.

"You hiding from me?" Gaelle's voice echoes through the room.

Only she could pull me out of the bath early and make me smile a little after such a horrible night. Gaelle uses her long fingers to separate my wet hair. The gentle motion of her hands makes my eyes drift open and close. I could fall asleep right here, wrapped in the softness of her legs and the sweet vanilla scent of her gown.

"Why did you really want to enter the Beauty Trials?" Gaelle asks.

I sit up to look at her. Her eyes are the richest chocolate, like the sweet buns threaded with cinnamon our cook always made for tea at Maison Rouge.

Now they well with disappointment.

"I have to keep my sisters safe," I reply. "That's why I stayed at court these past years to begin with."

A frown drags down her pretty mouth. "But is *this* the only way?" she asks.

"You don't think I can win? You sound like my sisters."

"I didn't say that." Her palms graze the nape of my neck. Her touch makes my heart flutter. I squeeze my eyes shut.

"I think you can do anything you set your mind to. You're a force. A tide from the God of the Sea. I just worry," she says.

"I can't sit here and let there be a new queen who I don't know. What if this person tries to put us back in the teahouses? What if things go back to the way they were? What if she lets Sophia out? I've seen the edicts. Beauty work and the battle over Belles isn't going to end unless the right person is in power."

She takes a deep breath. "I don't want to argue."

"Neither do I."

"You always want to argue, Edel."

I grit my teeth. "I've tried to keep my sisters safe, and they don't listen to me. If I'm queen, they will. They have to."

"How can anyone ignore you?" she says with a laugh.

"You ignored my post-balloon," I scoff, then smile.

"Let's say you win the Trials and become queen," Gaelle continues, looking serious. "You won't have time for me.

You won't have time for anything but cabinet meetings and appointments and speeches and writing laws." She looks down. "And you'll have to get married."

The words hang between us like a series of fireworks ready to explode.

"Thrones are passed to daughters. You'll have to have children with someone. You won't be able to be with me anymore."

"That's not true," I whisper, then lean forward and nuzzle her rose-oiled hair. "I'd be queen, so I can do whatever I want. You could be in my cabinet or stay here with me. Official card reader for the queen."

She shoves me away. "Be serious."

"I am being serious."

"What if something happens to you?" Her eyes glisten with tears. "I don't want to be a queen. Why do you want to?"

"To protect my sisters," I repeat. The gravity of my statement becomes a storm.

Gaelle sweeps a hair off my forehead. "What if you die?" A breath catches in her throat, and her hands fumble into mine.

My heart thuds so loudly it's the only noise between us. Her eyes comb over my face. I feel her taking in every detail. Every time I look at her, I discover something new. A fresh freckle left by one of my brushes beneath her eye. More light baby hairs along the crown of her head.

"I have to take that risk," I say. "I could die now, after all. It's not a safe world for Belles."

She pulls back from me. "My maman thinks once the Trials are over, business will dry up. She wants me to get married. To secure the family."

I roll my eyes. "You always have someone chasing after you. It won't be hard."

She gives me an annoyed push. "No one I actually want."

"What about Anouk?"

"Too possessive. She holds me so tight I can't breathe. Worse than a corset."

"Christophe buys you all that pretty jewelry." I run my fingers along the diamond necklace on her collarbone.

"He just sits and stares at me."

"'Cause you're pretty."

"My best friend is a Belle."

That words *best friend* almost pop.

"We're best friends?"

"Aren't we?"

I've never really thought of it. I've only had sisters. All I know is, I don't ever want her to go away.

I hold out my palm. "Read it," I say. "Tell me what's going to happen."

She slides her hand in mine. "You know I don't like palms. Let me read the cards."

"Or look at the stars," I say. "Make a forecast map. It doesn't matter. Tell me what's going to happen."

She lies down beside me. A tiny gold ring glitters in her nose. Up close, you can see the honey tones of her deep brown skin. The beauty work I've given her only enhances her natural template.

"I think it's funny," she says.

"What?" I murmur.

"When we first met, you hated me."

I laugh. "I hate everyone at first. That's what my sisters say." I pause. "And you were trying to tell my fortune, remember?"

She turns my palm over. "How else was I supposed to get your attention? Get you to be my friend?"

"I didn't believe in those sorts of things."

"But you believe now." She bats her eyes at me.

"Then tell me what I'm thinking."

"I'm a fortune-teller, not a mind reader."

"But you must know things."

"What I do know is, you're going to still try to enter, aren't you? Even though they said no?"

I bite my bottom lip. "I have to find a way."

"They're going to try to keep you out. They will hurt you if they have to." She slides off the bed and pulls her cloak off the hook.

"Where are you going?" I ask, alarmed.

"I'm not going anywhere," she says, rummaging through her cloak pockets for a moment, then returns with her palm closed. When she opens it, a tiny bottle glitters up at me. My breath catches.

"Is that . . . ?"

"Nectar?" she teases. "Of the goddess variety?"

"How did you get this?" I breathe.

"You left me unchaperoned at the ball." She shrugs. "I did what you would do for me."

"Gaelle..."

"You cannot die," she says in a forbidding tone. "Did you...see tonight? All the death? People just kept dancing...."

She trails off and we sit in silence, and I know we're imagining the same thing. The number of people that died in the ballroom, and the many more that will likely die in their beds tonight. If I drink this nectar, Gaelle could wake up next to a corpse.

"I have to," I whisper. "For my sisters."

She swallows heavily, then hands me the bottle. "You can't argue your way into this, Edel. If you're truly so determined, take it. See if the Goddess of Beauty will let you in."

"Thank you, Gaelle," I say. The bottle warms in my grip.

I pull out the stopper and guzzle down the sweet liquid before I lose courage and change my mind.

 TWELVE

"Edel! Edel!"

Buried deeply in the covers of my bed, I roll over, clutching my head. Gaelle is shouting and jostling my shoulder, and my head pounds from too much champagne and staying awake until the morning star to try to keep from dying. "What *is* it?" I moan.

Gaelle drags me out of bed and to the long mirror in the corner of the room. She pulls back my mess of blond hair to reveal my face. "Look," she commands.

On my cheek is the unmistakable image of a small Belle-rose. In awe, I touch it gently, and its petals open and stretch as if turning to the sun.

The Goddess of Beauty selected me.

"You're one of the Anointed Eight," Gaelle whispers.

"I am one of the Anointed Eight," I repeat, then rub the

sleep from my eyes. I wet my finger with my tongue and trace it over my cheek.

It doesn't wipe away. This isn't some cruel trick... or optical illusion.

My whole childhood, I always came in last—never earning high marks on Du Barry's assignments or being even thought of as a contender to be picked as favorite. I never wanted to be chosen like Amber and Camille. I was content being in the shadows, watching everyone make fools of themselves. Content being underestimated. Discounted.

But for the first time, I feel proud to be chosen. Because it isn't about me, but about keeping my sisters safe.

The delicate petals on my flesh don't so much as tickle—it's as if I'd been born with a birthmark on my face. I run my fingers over them one more time, purpose strengthening in my bones.

"You could be the next queen of Orléans!" Gaelle shouts, wrapping me in a hug. I can feel the excitement humming in her arms right alongside the relief that I'm alive.

Adele and a guard rush in, alarmed.

"Lady Edel, is everything all right?" Adele asks.

Then she spots the mark.

She stumbles backward. "The queen must be alerted at once."

Camille and Hana burst through one of my chamber's side doors, and Rémy follows.

"What's going on?" Hana rubs the sleep from her eyes. Then she sees my face in the mirror.

"The mark appeared," Gaelle says, turning me around to face them.

Camille clasps a hand over her mouth in shock, then rushes to brush my cheek. "It must be some sort of mistake."

"It doesn't rub off," I snap.

Rémy touches Camille's shoulder. "She's been chosen. She must compete."

"I will alert the Minister of Games," Adele says, then rushes out.

There's a long moment of silence, and Hana disrupts it with a sigh. "Well, you've certainly done it now, Edel," she says.

In the Grand Dining Hall, a small table sits in the massive space like a solitary lily pad lost out to sea. Servants wheel carts around, offering tea and sticky cakes and fresh sliced snowmelon. Newsies with light-boxes shout questions at us, their navy story-balloons and black gossip-balloons floating along all the congratulatory post-balloons. These flood the ceilings and shower the floors with confetti and tiny wrapped wind-drop sweets. It is the Competitors' Breakfast for the Anointed Eight, all those with Belle-roses on their left cheeks.

I recognize only two of the ladies. The first is the girl with the flying hat and the tuxedo dress from the Competitors'

Ball. Blais, I think her name is. The second is Violetta—one of the Iron Ladies.

As I enter, all gawk. I turn my face to flash the mark on my cheek. No need for words.

They gasp, clutching hands over their mouths or scowling. A few whisper, sharing their shock and displeasure behind fast-flapping fans. Their angry glares feel hot. I clench my teeth and narrow my eyes as newsies' light-boxes flash and their portrait quills race to capture my image. The young woman closest to me snickers. I suck my teeth at her, then pluck a strawberry from a tiered tray on the table. I pop it into my mouth, chew, and make sure to flash them my prettiest smile. Violetta's frown stays steady, but the girl with the flying hat raises her eyebrow, as if half-amused.

The doors open, and Queen Charlotte sweeps in, followed by her father, the ministers, and the Iron Ladies. I scramble to bow with the other women.

"Welcome to the Competitors' Breakfast," Charlotte announces. "The Goddess of Beauty has seen fit to select you to enter her Beauty Trials." Her eyes find me, and I'm almost surprised by their coldness. Almost. "Please take a seat. We will feast; then the Minister of Games will explain all that is to happen next."

I sit as far from Charlotte and her ministers as I can, sandwiching myself between Violetta and another competitor named Minette. Everyone stares into their cups of parfait or drowns nervous words with glasses of snowmelon juice. Charlotte's most innocuous questions receive only clipped answers. The melody of cutlery scraping against porcelain and the whoosh of the celebratory balloons overwhelm any chatter. I'm uncertain whether everyone's unease is because of my presence or if my fellow competitors drank the nectar without actually expecting for the Goddess to choose them. What then? They expected to die? It makes me angry at all of them—toying with something this important, for what?

Finally, the Minister of Games breaks the silence. She stands and circles the room, her cold eyes finding each and every one of us. Her dress is deceptive—dark folds fashioned into billowy pants sweep the floor. "I will now meet with you all to validate your marks. Then I will review your parchments to ensure everything is in order."

Eyes drift toward me, confirming that at least some of the tension here revolves around my presence, and I sneer.

"We will proceed by last name. Edel Beauregard shall be first."

Suddenly, the table is filled with talk. "You'll let her compete with us? She is a *Belle*," a competitor wearing a House of Orléans emblem complains.

"She has advantages," another puts in. "Gifts."

"How can this be fair?"

The Minister of Games clinks a knife to her glass. "Settle, please. Quiet down."

"The Goddess of Beauty chose me," I blurt out. "Just like you. If you have a problem with it, take it up with her. I'd love to see how any of you accomplish that."

Charlotte clears her throat. There's nothing she can do. Beauty chose me. After reading through the Belle archives in the Imperial Library, I understand at least a little now: to debate the validity of the rose on my cheek, I think, would be to debate the validity of magic, including beauty work.

Not an option for a queen in Charlotte's position.

I can do this, I think.

"We will get to the heart of the matter," Charlotte says. "But for now, Edel will compete. She has the mark—just as you all do." She walks over beside me and places a hand on the back of my chair. "If we use their gifts, if we use their blood, then the Goddess must believe the Belles should have a say."

Her words startle me. Only days ago, she didn't want me to be a competitor. Why the sudden change? Perhaps it hasn't occurred to her that Gaelle or someone provided me with the nectar. Perhaps she thinks the Goddess chose me without me drinking a drop. It makes me want to laugh, this idea of myself as sacred. That isn't what's helped me survive. I have my wits to thank, and friends like Gaelle.

Another thought nags at me: Charlotte clearly doesn't like the idea of a Belle in the running. Does she think I'll die? Hope I'll die? Maybe she sees the tournament as a convenient method to get me out of the way. Sophia would have killed me outright, by her own hand—but that's not Charlotte's style.

"Edel, will you join us in the tea salon?" Charlotte asks calmly, and saunters out.

I rise and stiffly follow them. The salon is minimalist— just chairs and the table, no dining carts or other frillery. Nothing to distract from the matter at hand.

I ease into the seat farthest from Charlotte. The Minister of Games's eyes burn into me. I meet her glare and narrow my eyes to slits. I don't break eye contact until she does.

"This is highly irregular," Charlotte says. "I think you know that."

"I didn't make the rules," I reply. "And I've been chosen." I will not be run off. I will not yield.

"You understand our alarm," the Minister of Games says, pursing her lips.

Charlotte sighs. "I need a promise from you, Edel."

"What is it?"

"You are entering these trials with a gift that no other competitor has. The arcana. I must ask you not to use them."

"Many people have gifts. Someone out there is clever, or good at puzzles, or extraordinarily strong," I say. "I have the gift to make people beautiful. Though right now, it feels more like a curse."

Charlotte and the Minister of Games exchange worried glances.

The minister sounds reluctant. "You may go pack," she finally says. "The competitors' carriage leaves in two hourglasses. We're headed to the Gravier Palace, where we will await the first trial. It's one of the most central locations for where the challenges will take place, and therefore most convenient. Lady Gravier will be overseeing the competitors' visit there, and she is not to be trifled with, so try to get along, Edel."

I restrain myself from rolling my eyes—everyone is always concerned about my sharp tongue, as if a sharp tongue is all that's needed to take a life. It requires more than that, or Sophia would already be dead.

"You will follow the rules, Edel? Won't you?" Charlotte says as I get up to leave.

I nod and turn to go but look back once, just to make sure I remember the concern on Charlotte's face. Is she worried about the tournament being fair, or is she merely terrified that a Belle could win?

THIRTEEN

We are stuck in the competitor carriages for more than five hourglasses on the way to Gravier Palace. We cross what feels like endless land and traverse so much of the main island, much of it I've never seen before. Blimps and spectator carriages accompany us, like a vast flock of migratory birds. As I open the drapes to gaze out into the rain, the other competitors continue to speculate about what we will face: monsters, or underwater labyrinths, or perhaps things we don't even have names for. The buzz of their chatter has kept me awake the entire trip, but I'm too distracted by my own thoughts to be disagreeable. I keep thinking about Charlotte, wondering over her change of tune. If I had any doubts about winning this tournament, I reinforce my confidence and steel myself. Nothing like a little spite to drive one forward.

Down the length of the imperial island, I can see a golden bridge. It leads to the Gravier Palace, which glows like a sun trapped in a dark cloud. This is my first time ever seeing it. My very first time visiting the Isle of Minnate and the nearby city of St. Nanterre. The scent of the world is different down here. Just like in the Spice Isles. Jasmine and vanilla plantations cover this island, perfuming the air.

"We have arrived," an attendant announces as our carriages finally approach the gates. The blimps and carts of spectators have peeled off elsewhere—only the competitors will be housed at Gravier.

"I heard Lady Angéle had to be browbeaten into hosting us," one of the Anointed Eight whispers—I believe her name is Lana. She whispers it to Blais, who raises her eyebrows in interest. Gossip. It never ends.

Licorice-black spindles curl into rose-tipped railings along the face of the building. Window-boxes hold magnolias and jasmine and roses like carts of petit-cakes. Moss trees fight the winds to hang on to their sweet berries. Our carriage stops at the gate, and in the momentary lull, I finally notice how my heart is plunging ahead. This is it. We are here. This is where it all begins.

The gates open, welcoming the competitor procession. At the entrance, men wait in the rain with gigantic storm parasols covered in the Orléansian crest. They bundle us into the dry warmth of the palace.

The guards close and lock it behind us. No going back now.

The walls are violet and turquoise, like a sky tumbling

into nightfall. The ceilings bloom in pinks and tangerines, a fruit bowl of the gods. Doors inlaid with ivory and jewels dot the long corridor. Mirrors are studded with rubies and sapphires. Rich wool rugs stretch out beneath our feet. I can almost feel their warmth and softness through my shoes.

"File in! File in!" the Minister of Games orders. The eight of us have already organized ourselves into a line, as if sorted by confidence. Lana looks like she wishes the carriages had overturned on the way here.

"Welcome to the home of Lady Angéle, the sister of our dearly departed Queen Celeste," she booms.

Lady Angéle stands on a grand staircase and is like a reverse mirror of her dead sister—skin as pale as the magnolias, glistening with gold dust, and a hair-tower filled with sunset-pink flamingos. Her eyes drift over us. "I'm very happy to host the Anointed Eight, those chosen by our most beloved Goddess," she says. But I don't quite believe her. The faintest evidence of a scowl is etched between her eyebrows, and the brows themselves are too high, as if forcing herself into an expression of enthusiasm. Her voice is flat. "All your comforts have been anticipated. You may take tea in my Game Salon"—she gestures to the left—"while my attendants will get your rooms sorted."

We all bow our heads.

"One more thing," she says before anyone can move. "Gravier Palace is not accustomed to housing strangers.

Therefore it is required that you stay within the bounds mandated during the length of the Beauty Trials. Once your rooms are ready, you will be escorted to them, and we ask that you remain either there or the Game Salon." She seems to remind herself to smile, bright but strained. "This tournament is . . . rather unexpected."

Imagine that, I think. *The gossip was accurate for once. Lady Angéle most definitely resents our presence.*

"The challenges of these trials," Lady Angéle goes on, "are three days apart. I'm told if any of you are not present for the announcement of a challenge, you will be considered the property and prize of the Goddess of Death. Understood? Good. Now, you may move along."

I grit my teeth and know being in this house might be as terrible as the Trials themselves. I follow the group into the Game Salon. Many ooh and aah at the room's lavishness. The decor is enameled with the departed queen's favorite card suites. Tables displaying porcelain game boxes studded with precious gems dot the room. The ceiling arches in jutting curves and slopes. Chaises and high-backed chairs and claw-footed sofas circle game tables. Windy-season curtains flutter along the wall, exposing carved glass doors leading to terraces.

I'm intrigued by the strong floral scent that seems to permeate every room. Not jasmine or magnolia or vanilla— something flowery, almost too sweet to bear. Although it's a little weaker in the Game Salon, it's still heady. I catch other competitors sniffing, looking around for bouquets. There are none in this room.

This must merely be the scent of the isle.

I wander past the game tables to look for an old one I always play with Gaelle, Four Winds. I find it in a corner far away from the other women. Tiny red-and-black disks engraved with teacup peacocks and doves and elephants sit inside wells along the board's perimeter and a beautifully drawn square holds the symbol of Orléans, a fleur-de-lis.

"They don't tell us anything. It's ridiculous. How do they expect us to prepare?" Estelle Lamballe complains loudly. I read about her in the papers. She's a cousin of Queen Charlotte, and her sister is a former lady-of-honor to Sophia. She fiddles with the royal House of Orléans emblem around her slender brown neck.

Lana Travers cowers on a couch with her head in her hands. "Oh gods. Why was I even picked for this?"

Blais Dene, still wearing her hat, stretches along a chaise. She tosses the hat up, and it sprouts wings before fluttering down to her chest, then rises. She smiles at the stream of complaints.

I channel my nervous energy into restoring the disks on the Four Winds board, lining them up as if Gaelle were standing across from me. I think of how she always beats me, landing her ten disks in the pockets first.

Minette Caron skulks over to me, dragging a cane, wrinkles pressed deep into her skin. The newsies have been kind to her. "Care to play?" she asks.

"Not with you," I say back, uninterested in being social. Her face pinches. *Charm*, I remember Camille saying. "Sorry," I add.

Even though I'm not.

Across the room, Calandre Segale is leaning into the only mirror to add more powder to her honey-colored skin. "I heard that the Goddess of Beauty might reveal herself during one of the tasks," she says. "Ugh, these eye films hurt. How will I keep them in if we have to run? Or something equally horrid."

Cesarine Pompadour spritzes herself in what must be her family's perfume while pacing before a crackling fire. "My sisters said that the teeth of Beauty's comb will hold the key to understanding. It will have something to do with managing sharp situations."

"Put a pin in your speculations," Estelle grumbles. "No one knows anything." The two of them burst into a loud argument.

It stills as the door opens, and Queen Charlotte, the Minister of Games, and Lady Angéle enter.

"Our Gamekeeper has arrived," Charlotte informs. "Gather around."

A young man steps up. "May I introduce you all to Quentin Arnoux," the minister says.

His skin is bronzed, and he wears a wide, crooked smile. His eyes are beautifully curved, pinched by a smug grin. A vulture perches on his shoulder. The Goddess of Death's bird, flown straight from the black egg in the caisse to find us here.

That smile . . . those eyes. I've seen him before. My mind races through memories, agitating the arcana inside me. Then I remember.

"It's you," I say. "What are *you* doing here?"

FOURTEEN

Everyone turns to face me. He grins. I glare.

Charlotte looks back and forth between us. "Edel?"

It's the boy from the Grottos. The one who brought Camille and me food when the Iron Ladies had us imprisoned in their dungeons.

"You know him?" Estelle asks, her pitch peaking. "Another reason why she should be ineligible to compete!"

"Can someone explain all of this?" Estelle demands.

I scowl and open my mouth to speak, but Violetta cuts me off.

"Quentin lives on an island near the entrance to the Grottos where the Iron Ladies used to live," she says. "We hired him for many tasks."

"Like feeding prisoners," I spit.

"Good to see you, V," he says with a tiny bow toward Violetta. "I *am* popular."

She smiles. "May your threads be strong."

"So, how does an errand boy become the gamekeeper of the most important event in history?" Estelle crosses her slender arms over her chest. Her light brown cheeks bloom pink with anger.

He doesn't even flinch. Tossing back his hair, he says, "If you *must* know, my family—the Arnoux, of the fallen House of Arnoux—was blessed by the Goddess of Death. We are forever her servants—and therefore must protect her interests."

My tongue itches to pelt him with questions, to take him apart in front of this audience. But Camille's words keep echoing back—I need to work on charm. So I keep my mouth closed . . . and still glare at him instead.

He seems to sense that I'm holding back, because he smiles extra brightly and gives us all a cheeky wave. On his shoulder, the vulture shifts. He glances up, where the ugly bird looks down at him, then at us. "Oh, forgive my manners. Meet Encerclant."

The Goddess of Death's vulture. I feel my glare weaken in the face of the bird's intensity.

"Now that I've submitted to your interrogation," Quentin continues, "I will go through the rules."

He scratches the bird's head fondly, and it releases a series of disgusting hiccups. As everyone pulls back, it coughs up a tiny golden scroll, barely bigger than a thimble. "Revolting," someone murmurs.

I can't take my eyes off it. I can almost hear the pages

of Maman's book of fairy tales rustling, as if the creature swooped right out from them. *Ever the skeptic,* Queen Charlotte had said of me, but who can blame me after the rug has been pulled out from under my entire life? But now, deep under the ashes of skepticism burns the tiniest ember of faith—here is magic. Not everything was a complete lie.

I feel a sudden ache for my maman—I know if she were still here, I would find my way through all this.

Quentin unfurls the tiny scroll.

"I hereby call forth the first trial. This is a test of composure—the ability to remain calm and no matter the circumstance."

The words rattle in my chest, then settle. There's a long silence. I can feel the waiting in the room, the expectation. But Quentin merely stands there grinning, stroking Encerclant's throat feathers.

"That's *it*?" Cesarine whines.

"What does that even mean?" Estelle says, beginning to pace. "How are we supposed to prepare?"

"You will know," he replies.

"So you have no clue, is what you're saying?"

Encerclant squawks, expanding triple in size. It stretches its wings to their full span. We all cower, which is exactly what the vulture—and Quentin—wants.

"You either have the qualities or you don't," Quentin replies.

The room descends into chaos. Everyone attempts to decode whatever promise his cryptic message contains.

A pit burns in my stomach. How would he know the qualities it takes? And why is he even involved?

Without another word, he turns and departs.

The vulture darts back in the room, as if it somehow knows everyone is discussing it, the Trials, and Quentin. It caws and does a lap around the ceiling.

Lady Angéle watches him go, then takes a deep breath. "Well, that was quite the commotion!" she says. The scratch of a scowl between her eyes remains. "Let's get you to your rooms."

We follow, joining her train. The hallway spreads out like a river, and plush cream carpeting masks our footsteps. House servants shuffle behind, wielding gigantic peacock fans. The silky feathers catch a hot breeze laced with the scent of an approaching storm.

And of course, the lingering, heavy smell of the unseen flowers.

I count the doors. At least two dozen, stretching down the halls, and Lady Angéle has no children. What do they hold? Perhaps she has two dozen lovers. It's the sort of thing I might ask if I wasn't so focused on keeping my mouth shut as Camille and Gaelle advised.

One by one, the competitors are dropped off at our rooms, while Lady Angéle reinforces her rules. "I run a tight ship," she says, enough times to make me roll my eyes by the time we reach my door. But unlike with the other competitors, Lady Angéle pauses for a moment longer.

"Obey the rules," she says, staring deeply into my eyes. "And there won't be any problems."

I almost open my mouth to ask, *What does that mean?* But I glare back at her, meeting whatever challenge lingers in her words.

Then I'm ushered into my room by the attendant, and when the door closes, I can't fight the feeling that it's reminiscent of the Everlasting Rose. We've been told we can come and go as we please as long as we stay within bounds, but... the feeling of the door closing behind me says something else.

The room is overdecorated and looks like a garden vomited in here. Different flower patterns clash, and the colors feel violent and loud. It overlooks the ocean and the wide blue sky. The balcony stretches alongside the length of the palace, connecting to all the others. Below, ornate gardens stretch from wall to wall and staircases lead down into it. I can't stand the silence, and I step out into the wind rolling off the ocean.

Outside, it's empty of the other competitors—everyone is in their rooms strategizing, I'm sure. I still smell the strong floral scent, but the breeze carries it away. All my life, restriction after restriction. Bound by custom, rules, expectations. At least this is one place where we're allowed to be without being considered "out of bounds."

Movement on the rail startles me, and I jump. The hunched form of Encerclant sits on a black iron balcony railing, eyes fixed on the ground far below, as if looking for prey.

I remember vultures. We would see them at Maison Rouge sometimes, and when they weren't circling some unfortunate animal, they would dot the limbs of trees, hulking shadows waiting for death. They gave me the shivers then, and Encerclant gives me the shivers now.

As if hearing my thoughts, the bird turns to look at me, eyes catching the moonlight.

On impulse, I ask, "Are you really the Goddess of Death in disguise?"

It answers with a caw and a flap of its wing. Quentin suddenly appears on the balcony, standing at the top of the nearest staircase. "They could never be the Goddess, Edel," he says. "Encerclant is Encerclant."

Charm, I tell myself, but I have nothing to say to him that would be charming or queenly. So instead, I just say, "Good night," turning on my heel and stepping quickly back into my room.

I feel a draft, and the window rattles. I push the heavy curtains that fall on either side. One of the panes is loose. I make a mental note to ask for it to be repaired. All I need is one of the other competitors sneaking in during the middle of the night and strangling me in my sleep.

I toss my competitor's uniform from my bed. It's in eight pieces, symbolizing us, the Anointed Eight. I know the other competitors will be in their quarters busying themselves with trimming and trying on. I can't bring myself to care.

I throw myself down and look at the table sitting opposite. Four Winds game tokens stare back at me. The fire in the hearth leaves its orange streaks across the wooden floor, and night-lanterns cluster around the bed, fussing with their ribbons.

In this lonely place, I can't help but think of Gaelle. I wish she were here, holding my hand. I imagine Camille, somewhere far away, with Rémy's arms around her. Is there a future like that for me? Or will every season of my life feel like a different prison?

 # FIFTEEN

A soft knock echoes through the room. I hope it's not one of the other competitors—I don't want to discuss theories about the first trial or how they're feeling. The carriage ride and the game room were enough. I've been busying myself with Four Winds for probably three hourglasses and trying to keep my mind off everything.

"Who is it?" I call.

No one answers.

"Go away."

"Is that any way to talk to your best friend?" a voice replies.

My heart flutters as I pull Gaelle into my room. Just the sight of her calms me.

"Nice place," she says, examining the decor. "Oooh, they have a Four Winds board!" She grins at me.

"Your favorite." I lock the door behind us. I don't know if

visitors are even allowed, but I'm not going to risk it. "How did you get in?"

"You don't want me here?"

"Of course I do," I say, "but I don't know if you're allowed to be." I try to quell my excitement. Even if she's only here for an hour, it will be enough.

A cart rattles. "Evening tea," a servant calls.

"One moment," I call quickly. I signal to Gaelle to hide in the bathing chamber. After she has tiptoed off, I open the door, and an elderly servant shuffles in.

On the tea table, he sets out sticky dates, a fruit cup, a powdered beignet, and tea to wash it down. "It is tradition in the Minnate to take your tea with a bite," he tells me, lifting the hand-painted kettle. He pours the steaming golden liquid—thick with milk, scented with cardamom and ginger—into a jade tumbler. Then he opens the spice box and drops in scoops of poppy, fennel, and nutmeg. As he stirs, it becomes an inky black.

Gaelle peeks out from the bathing chamber, monitoring the servant's every move. I motion her swiftly to get back.

Finally, he is done. "That will be all," I say.

"Very good, my lady." He shuffles out.

"Now, what are you doing here?" I ask Gaelle.

"There are groups following the competitors," she says. "Surely you saw the blimps?"

"Of course, but that doesn't answer my question." I take a sip of the hot tea. It burns its way to my belly, and I hold in the cough that comes with scalding, sticky-sweet liquid. Instead, I burp to make her laugh. She does, the tinkling sound that I adore, as if magic itself had its own tone.

"I came with news," she says, shrugging. "It seems to me that all Lady Angéle cares about is that no one is wandering around her palace dirtying up her floors."

"What if you had come to kill me?" I ask indignantly. "Do they not care about my safety?"

"I assure you I was thoroughly searched."

"Not *too* thoroughly, I hope."

She rolls her eyes, then turns to the game board.

"Care to wager?" I ask.

"What kind?" She grins, revealing the tiniest sliver of a gap between her front teeth.

I extend my arm and invite her to the Four Winds board.

"Play with me," I say. I begin to line up the little chips on both sides, though I know she will land her ten disks in the pockets first.

"You're going to be mad when I beat you," she replies with a clever smile, revealing the set of dimples I gave her.

"Name your prize."

"A kiss."

I sigh. "What for?"

A kiss could be so simple, but it doesn't feel that way. Not lately. Without meaning to, I think of Camille and Rémy, their easy intimacy at court. How does it become easy? How does a kiss draw you out into the light from the shadows that feel so safe?

"You have dozens of women and men willing to do whatever it takes to get close to you," I add. "You don't need a kiss from me."

"Maybe." She grins. "But I want it."

I blush, the feeling so foreign.

"Do you accept?"

I look at the door, then back to her.

"Deal," I say.

She takes her place opposite me and motions for me to start first.

"Feel familiar?" she asks. "Setting up for the game?"

I snort. "The stakes are a lot lower here on this board. No queen of Four Winds."

I thump one of my chips easily into a near pocket and smile triumphantly.

"Lucky," she says. "I hope you keep that good fortune."

I frown, avoiding her eyes.

"You know it's possible that I could pocket all my men before you get to take a single shot."

"You're liable to get distracted," she says.

"I have an ironclad focus when determined."

"So do I," she replies. "As you know."

I cross my arms, confident this shouldn't take very long. Gaelle doesn't know that I've lost to her so many times I've stolen most of her techniques. And she's a master at this game.

I circle the board and shoot another disk into a pocket.

"Your turn *again*," she says.

I reach for another disk, and my fingernail throbs from plucking them. I pause to suck it.

"Need to forfeit?" She grins. "Or I can rub it."

"You wish." I shake out my hand and lean over the board again to study my next move. I thump another disk but miss the pocket.

She takes the next turn and easily lands another piece. "That's three to two now."

"I wouldn't get cocky," I reply. I swallow, then add: "Stay the night." By now, I shouldn't feel like walking on a high wire asking such a thing, tight and nervous. Perhaps Gaelle is one more rug I'm afraid will be pulled out from beneath my feet.

"You need your sleep," she says, and finally looks up at me, her eyes serious. "Aren't you nervous? It all begins tomorrow."

I scoff. "It's already begun. The first trial is just the first trial. I doubt it will even be over after the third."

She doesn't take her next turn and instead purses her lips and looks away at an invisible spot on the wall.

"They hate me," I finally say.

"I'm not surprised," she replies, always straightforward. "I pulled a card for you. I had a bad feeling. I want you to be careful. They're going to try to kill you."

Fear doesn't give me goose bumps anymore, but under my skin my muscles tense. I don't believe in fortunes, but I believe in Gaelle. I grab her hand and make her look at me.

"I'm more worried about the missing Belles," I say. "Have you heard any word? Any whisper?"

"No," she says, shaking her head reluctantly. "And I've been listening for news of illegal teahouses or anything of the sort. But nothing. It's like they disappeared. Perhaps they are lying low until everything shakes out with the new queen."

"Me," I say grimly.

"I hope so," she says.

"I will find them, queen or not," I growl.

"And I promise I will keep my eyes and ears open," she says. "I'll be doing a lot of fortune-reading in these groups that have followed for the tournament. I'll be listening, and you know the moment I hear anything, I will tell you."

The knowledge of having Gaelle on my side strengthens me. I flash her what I hope is a reassuring smile, then move to take her piece from the board.

Finally, she laughs. She clutches my hand. "Don't even think about it."

But we've already forgotten about winning and losing. When her lips meet mine, the noise of trials and queens fades to a hum. I hear only the rustle of her skirts.

 # SIXTEEN

Before sunrise, we set sail in the imperial fleet, their golden noses like a pod of gilded dolphins moving through rough water. We are headed for the Glass Isles. The location of the first trial.

My stomach mirrors the sloshing waves below, seasickness eager to sweep me under. Gaelle is right that they're trying to kill me ... even before the whole thing starts. But I can't figure out if it's only the motion of the boat or what lies ahead. From my tiny, luxurious cabin, I can hear the roars of laughter from the deck of the gargantuan boat. I had assumed they'd keep competitors separate from the spectators, but I should have known better—they'd sold deck seats to the highest bidder so they could be on the boat and gossip to their friends later about what they had heard, influence bets about winners based on what they claim they saw. Perhaps the rest of the Anointed Eight are on deck currying favor with the newsies. I'm grateful I have a room to hide out in, and try not to vomit.

There comes a tap at the door, and my reflexes are delayed by my nausea—but it's only Gaelle. I sit up as much as I can, surprised. Gaelle had slipped out in the early hours after our fifth round of Four Winds.

"They let you down here?"

"I was lucky. The attendant is the same one as at Gravier Palace. He knew my face and let me pass." She studies me. "You're as green as a pear."

"I hate ships. Why would anyone want to crest across the water? I'll never understand it."

"It's like a cradle."

"The cradle of death." I press a hand to my stomach.

She laughs and takes my hand. "It'll be a few hourglasses before we reach the isles," she replies. "And I have information for you."

She unfolds a newspaper—the *Herald of Orleans* boasts flickering pictures of the mirror from the caisse over the city of Nouvelle-Lerec, and then again near the Isle of Quin. "Could be a hoax? Or people trying to get in the newsies?"

She opens another paper, the *Trianon Tribune*. "There are so many articles about the arcana. Everyone's thinking it'll give you an advantage."

"Oh, do they think someone will need beauty work along the way?" I shove the paper away. She laughs. "Anything about the Belles?"

"Barely," she says. "I don't want to distract you—some of it will only make you angry. People hoping that a queen who wants a return to beauty work wins. But people are also wondering if the Belles are in hiding or if the Goddess of Beauty has called them back to the sky. The uncertainty makes them superstitious."

That almost makes me chuckle. If the Goddess of Beauty were going to call us back, she would have done it by now. All the belief I had in her magic crumbled when I learned the Belles were being hatched in pods.

"Your eyes are reddening," I tell her, to change the subject. "Let me fix them."

"You need all your strength for what's coming."

"I need a distraction." I coax her into lying down.

She sighs, pretending to be upset. "But you don't have your beauty caisse."

"I'll tell you a secret," I say. I cup my hand near her ear as she smiles. "The instruments are just for show."

She looks at me in shock. A shiver of pleasure runs up my spine. Putting magic out into the open like this—it feels scandalous, but also natural. The way it should be.

"Close your eyes."

"You love ordering people around."

The arcana awaken quickly, unused and full of power. "Especially *you*."

Gaelle's form appears in my mind like one of the competitor portraits: her luminous eyes, her figure an apple swaddled in the prettiest of dresses. I darken the brown of her eyes, add a few freckles to her nose, and deepen her dimples.

She squeaks with pain.

I open my eyes. Her forehead holds beads of sweat.

"Are you all right?"

"Yes," she pants. "But without the Belle-rose tea, I almost can't bear it."

I take her shaky hand and squeeze it. "I've forgotten how painful it is for you all," I say. "I'm out of practice. My arcana was probably too strong."

She clamps her eyes shut and takes more deep breaths.

"I apologize," I say. I cup her face in my hands, and she closes her eyes, relaxing. The arcana is quiet, but this still feels like magic.

"I've been so busy writing up laws and plans nobody would listen to," I say. "Not least Charlotte."

Gaelle's eyes open, and she places her hands over mine against her cheeks. "You will return from this competition, yes?"

"Yes," I whisper to her, a flush burning my cheeks. "I promise you."

There is a knock, and the door opens before I can answer. "Lady Edel, we are arriving," the attendant says.

The sun rises along the horizon, bathing the dark water in a kaleidoscope of tangerine and scarlet and marigold. The deck is illuminated with morning-lanterns and sky candles, floating over us like stars. My heart lifts with anticipation.

Other women glare in my direction. A blush rises in my cheeks, but I lift my chin. I flash onlookers the perfect haughty smile, stretch upright to display the best posture and tilt my head so my neck is at its longest and most graceful. I'm a giraffe from the animal menagerie in the Rose Quartier.

"Loved ones, find your seats," the Minister of Games calls.

Gaelle gives my hand another squeeze before slipping into the crowd.

At the far shore, I can see the masses crowd the market stalls and pier, watching, waving, throwing flowers into the sea. Children clutch tiny golden caisses to their chests or hold up dolls fashioned to resemble the competitors. I remember when it would've been Belle-dolls, complete with signature Belle-buns and flowers.

Midnight-black newsie boats follow close behind, and overhead air postmen lurk in their bulbous airships, their shadows stretching over the deck like an ominous storm cloud, ready to navigate urgent and immediate story-balloons to all corners of the kingdom.

"Welcome, competitors!" the Minister of Games booms. Beside her, Charlotte sits looking regal and benign. "You have embarked upon a mission not to be taken lightly—to determine our next queen. It requires sacrifice, and for that, I am grateful."

Small applause ripples out. I try to fold my scowl away. I think of all the people dancing and dancing the night we all drank the nectar—bodies falling and everyone still dancing.

The boats slow as they approach the harbor. As we round the bend, the glass-paned houses and shops and even water-coaches scatter light over the water.

We all gasp.

High above the cluster of the Glass Isles, as if supported by the clouds themselves, a brilliant maze stretches. Winding and curving like a topiary garden, its brass trees and shrubs are suspended in the sky.

"What in the gods is that?" Estelle asks, craning her neck up.

"Welcome to Beauty's Labyrinth," the Minister of Games says.

SEVENTEEN

"How will we even get up there?" Cesarine exclaims as the boat drops anchor. "And what are we supposed to do?"

"Obviously, it's a maze," Estelle says. "We have to make it through. That's what you do in mazes."

I can't take my eyes off the bloom of floating trees, as golden as the Goddess of Beauty's comb. They look like their needles are just as sharp.

The roar of newsies and onlookers greets us the moment we take our first steps off the boat. They pummel us with questions as we head for the square. My heart accelerates to their thunderous noise.

"What do you think is inside Beauty's Labyrinth? The *Daily Orléansian* has wagers."

"Share your theories of what lurks inside with our readers at the *Trianon Mirror*—most widely circulated on the imperial island."

"What are your plans to navigate the maze? Share with the *Orléans Globe* for an exclusive feature!"

Navy story-balloons swarm overhead like angry bees, and black gossip post-balloons try to fight their way closer to us. The hissing cuts through the whistling and cheering. Against a bright sky, golden paper lanterns are bright with our names: *Cesarine, Blais, Estelle, Calandre, Minette, Violetta, Lana.*

Edel.

Guards have created a long tunnel through the masses leading from the dock to a platform just under the expanse of golden trees. As we snake through it, people reach out through the locked ranks of guards to touch us. Some are shaking good-luck signs. Some hold up newspapers. Many are sporting monocles to see us more closely. I smile and wave, wanting to impress them, wanting to be good enough to be remembered as worthy to be queen.

"The *Orléansian Times* endorses Estelle Lamballe," a newsie hollers. "Let the House of Orléans continue to rule!"

Banners and blimp screens sparkle with her picture. Estelle basks in the cheers and raises her chin, waving her arms about as if she's already been coronated.

"The *Glass Isles Inquirer* picks Minette Caron of House Merania, a royal family from the Glass Isles themselves!" another newsie shouts.

The crowd chants her name. She sinks into the collar of her cloak like a teacup turtle hiding from poking fingers.

"No Belles!" someone shouts.

I flinch, then search for the culprit.

"No Belles! No Belles! No Belles!" the chant begins. The agitated crowd joins the chorus. Someone tries to throw a tomato, and a guard wrestles her to the ground.

Heat claws its way up my neck. I thought that nothing could be more overwhelming than the Beauté Carnaval, but no one was shouting "No Belles" that night.

"Eyes ahead!" the Minister of Games directs.

I watch the labyrinth in the sky to avoid looking at the crowd. Shadows circle it—seabirds skimming the breeze. It makes me think of Quentin and Encerclant—where are they?

As we finally emerge from the tunnel of bodies, the noise of the crowd intensifies. Onlookers ring the square, perch in royal boxes high on stilts. They lean out with eye-scopes and spyglasses, their ear-trumpets like elephant trunks. Their faces are filled with wonder and anticipation.

In the shadow of Beauty's Labyrinth, I can still hear the sea lapping twenty paces away. I try to focus on the sound of the ocean and not the shouts of the crowd, but when I look up, all I can hear is the wind in my ears. I imagine finding my way through the sky to the labyrinth.

"I still don't see how we get up there," someone says. I'm wondering the same thing.

Then the ground begins to shake.

A shiver at first, growing into a tremble. The onlookers

all back away instinctively, but the Minister of Games barks: "Stay where you are!"

And so the Anointed Eight stand motionless as the ground beneath us begins to buck. It takes all my courage not to scream when it starts to rise, a small mountain growing beneath our feet. A crater toward the center drops out of sight, and Estelle screams, and I would, too, if it wasn't for the sight of Quentin coming into view. He and Encerclant emerge from the hole as if stepping through a doorway. And all the while, the ground rises under our feet, lifting us into the air toward the floating labyrinth.

The Minister of Games must have anticipated something, but not this. She tries to stay grim-faced, but I see her fright. A stone stairway is carved into the side of this newborn mountain, and it takes everything inside me not to flee for it.

But then the ground grinds to a stop, and there's the far-off rumble of the earth, as if its stomach is settling after a belch. Quentin stands in the center unruffled, Encerclant on his shoulder leaning into his hand as he rubs her plumage. Above us, the labyrinth and its glittering foliage is close enough to touch, like a low-hanging chandelier.

I dare not.

The Minister of Games attempts to busy her shaking hands by swiping dust from her cloak. She nods at Quentin. "Please welcome our gamekeeper."

Quentin comes to stand beside her. Encerclant gives

Quentin a magical quality himself, with his dark hair thrown back from his face.

"Gather around," the Minister of Games orders, and we obey—some of the last obeying we will ever do, whether it is because we will be queen or dead.

Quentin steps into the middle of our circle. When his eyes find mine, he winks. I scowl in return. His pink mouth curves, letting loose a whistle, and he takes the scroll from Encerclant's beak, unrolling it.

"There is a beginning and an ending to a queen's reign, and she must forever remain composed throughout her tenure—a quality not all women possess."

"I don't understand how making it through a maze will show what it means to be composed, to lead a kingdom, to be a queen," Violetta complains.

Suddenly, Encerclant lunges off Quentin's shoulder and zips into the opening, her black form disappearing like a cloud of smoke.

"Where is she going?" Calandre demands, panic running through her voice.

"I read that there was a guide during the last trial," Cesarine reports.

"There won't be any help for us when we enter that maze, you fools," Blais replies. "The Goddess of Death has allegiances only to herself."

"We are *not* fools," Cesarine counters. "I read—"

"And, of course, you would believe everything you read." Blais unsuccessfully tries to hide the smile playing across her lips.

"Enough," the Minister of Games says.

Encerclant bolts out of the opening to the labyrinth with another scroll in her beak.

"You will make your way through the Labyrinth of Beauty, and it will show you its exit when you prove that you are worthy. Be careful not to lose your head," Quentin says.

"What does that mean?" I ask before I can stop myself. Quentin only smiles.

The Minister of Games signals to a guard, who yanks a lever. Slowly, the labyrinth lowers a narrow staircase, made up of eight steps. "I will draw names. This isn't a race, so the order does not matter. Step forward onto the platform when called." She lifts a velvet pouch.

I'm again reminded of the night of the Beauté Carnaval when my sisters and I were paraded up for all the world to inspect and to see us display our talents. Set on a glittering dish like a sweet tart, ready to be devoured.

I take a deep breath as she reaches her hand in and yanks out a name token.

"Cesarine Pompadour," she says.

Cesarine leaps with surprise. "Me? First?" A blush sets into her graying cheeks as the name is repeated into a voice-trumpet for the crowd to hear.

"No, your sister," Blais says under her breath.

"I hope you die immediately," Cesarine shoots back at her.

The Minister of Games shushes them. "This endless fussing won't help any of you." She reaches out a hand to help Cesarine onto the first step. Once up, she curtsies smugly, then ascends the stairs. We watch her disappear into the labyrinth.

The Minister of Games pulls another name.

"Calandre Segale."

I'm aware after a moment that Calandre has not moved. She stands staring at the minister, her mouth opening and closing like a fish washed ashore.

"Calandre Segale," the minister repeats, frowning.

"I . . . I can't," Calandre says, softly at first. Then louder. "I can't. I can't!"

The minister's eyes widen, and around me the remaining Anointed competitors shift. I'm as shocked as the minister— if anyone were to lose courage, I expected it to be Lana, who had done so much shaking and weeping at Gravier. But Calandre looks drained not just of courage, but of life. Her skin is sallow, a fine sheen of sweat coating her face.

"I can't!" she says. Her voice rises into a scream. "I won't do it! I won't go in!"

"Do you understand what this choice means?" Quentin says gravely. From his shoulder, Encerclant tilts her hideous head left and right as if asking Calandre the same question.

"I don't care!" she screams in reply. "I can't do it!"

Quentin goes on staring for a moment, and to me, his eyes look sad. But Calandre isn't changing her mind—her screams only echo louder, and she begins to hit Minette, who blocks her blows unsuccessfully.

"Take her," Quentin says.

With a horrible thunder of wings, Encerclant is off his shoulder and growing before our eyes, her shadow seeming as great as the labyrinth. She gains air, grows huge, and swoops toward Calandre, whose eyes clear of terror for the brief moment it takes her to understand what is happening.

The talons close around her, and Encerclant darts off the mountain. Far below, we hear the rise and fall of the crowd's shock and horror as they realize what has happened. By the time I look again at Encerclant, the enormous bird is far off, winging toward what must be the Grottos. Toward the Goddess of Death, where Calandre will be delivered.

"I supposed someone had to get cold feet," Blais says carelessly. I want to slap her.

Yet the show goes on. In a voice that sounds hollow, the next name is called. "Estelle Lamballe."

Estelle goes to the edge of the mountain, waving down at the adoring crowd, blowing kisses and bowing, before nearly leaping onto the staircase. She does a curtsy before disappearing into the opening.

"Edel Beauregard," the Minister of Games says.

My name is a firework. The crowd below is suddenly

silent. I had expected more jibes, but somehow the silence is even worse—they don't care if I live or die. On the platform, I focus on balance. "I chose this. The Goddess of Beauty chose me to do this," I whisper over and over until the rhythm of the words erases my fear.

As I take the first step up, the newborn mountain and Quentin and everyone disappears. The darkness of the labyrinth looms above me like a gigantic mouth ready to swallow me whole.

I climb carefully, heading toward a golden darkness above. As I rise, an expanse of trees and shrubs and bushes and massive flowers emerges. I see rusty, sharp needles poking from each. A breeze pushes through, and they clink and clang in a rippling, eerie echo.

I hold my breath until it all stops.

I take my first step inside.

EIGHTEEN

Paths curve in all directions, and I feel the temptation to plunge straight ahead—a direct line from start to finish. But I remember the Minister of Games saying this isn't a race. *It's not a race.* But if it's not a race, then what is it? A test of composure? Navigating through a bunch of spiky-looking trees? The arcana hum beneath my skin, agitated. Their presence reminds me: I am a survivor. I will get through this. I can do this.

It's not a race. Well, then how does one win?

As I walk, I see this is a topiary garden. Each golden tree or shrub is in an intricate shape despite its spiked edges—some are turrets and towers, others teacup pets, many replicas of the splendors of the Orléansian landscape. Their color makes me feel I am walking through the inner workings of a gilded clock—which only reminds me of the time.

I imagine the other competitors already on the other side, betting leas on how long it will take the Belle to complete the challenge. I've been imagining myself uniquely suited for this task, but what if it's the opposite? Not special, but inferior, as Sophia had sneered in the Rose?

I shake the thought out of my head before it can find a foothold. I can make it. I will make it. Even if it means walking past the same golden shrub a thousand times.

No matter how firmly I remind myself of the nature of labyrinths, I still question myself: Have I passed here before? Or are the corridors of this strange, sharp place changing directions the moment I turn my back? I turn and turn, trying to imagine the God of Luck leading me on a path that is different, a path that will carry me toward whatever ending is in store.

I pause to study a tree, trying to remember if I have seen it before. At the base of its long needles are delicate golden orbs, like empty pincushions. I root the image of them in my mind.

But as I approach the next corner, I see the pincushions again—the golden needles, terrible and shimmering, exactly as they were. I swallow a growl, desperate impatience mounting inside me. But another step closer and I see that, although they are nearly the same, something is different. A metallic stain on the tip of the needles is unmistakable.

Blood.

But . . . whose blood?

I reach out slowly, carefully, to feel whether the blood is wet or dry.

The pain is sharp and immediate. I hear myself gasp before I am aware I made the sound. I stare down in shock—how? I had barely touched the stamen, and yet a tiny pearl of blood appears on the tip of my finger. The pain is like a brand.

And then I hear the rustling.

All around me, the gilded trees and bushes are swaying to life, as if blown by an invisible breeze. The breeze becomes a wind. And the wind becomes a gale. The limbs and their many golden needles begin to sway ferociously—all, I realize with creeping horror, pointed toward me.

The topiary garden is gone—in its place are a hundred thousand swords and daggers. I back away, then gasp at the wall of pinpricks against my back. The hedge bristles toward me like an army.

I turn and run.

But where to hide in a sea of swords? The needles are long and short, all of them seeking my flesh, stems lengthening in the moment I pass by, missing me by a hairsbreadth. No amount of speed will matter, I realize.

Then I hear screaming, close enough to make my eyes dart for the source. I know better than to run toward it, but I don't have to—as I skid around a corner, I crash into Lana, who is spinning back and forth to avoid the hedges bursting with glittering points. It sounds like the opening and closing of an army of birds with steel wings.

I back away in horror as they lengthen to pin her. There's no escape—they pierce through her back and protrude through her skin like icicles. Lana tumbles forward, gasping for breath, and I hear the wheezing sound of a punctured lung. Blood races down her shoulder blades. Another needle pierces her directly through the throat. A third, larger than the others, plunges in her middle and lifts her toward the sky.

I grab her legs, trying to pull her down, but the spears push her higher and higher, out of reach. My breath rattles as blood drops sprinkle down like rubies.

Then, suddenly, it all stops. In the labyrinth floor opens a hole perfectly sized for her to pass through. The needles release her, and she plummets, down toward the city below.

I hear her body thump against the cobblestones.

The hole rapidly closes. My stomach feels like the ocean: swelling and swirling and churning. I fight the desire to close my eyes. And then I see another figure, strolling calmly along a corridor parallel to mine.

Blais.

She pauses for only a breath to glance down at all the blood. Then she smiles at me, one corner of her lips curving up. Right before the needles from the hedge plunge into my arms.

They sear me, hot pokers traced along every part of my body. I squeeze my eyes shut, knowing that if I see the needles pierce me, I will be sick, I will be lost, I will not be able to do this. The arcana flood through me, and my skin fights to close those pinpricks. The pain surges beneath.

And then so does memory—a memory so jarring and sudden it's like being struck by lightning.

I'm walking in the graveyards behind Maison Rouge with Amber and Camille. It's the windy season, but we still wander among the tombs, knowing we shouldn't be here, knowing we've been warned, but drawn to the death and gloom like it's something we can actually see.

And I remember stepping directly into a snare.

We'd been warned to avoid the graveyard. Told all sorts of scary stories; though we'd never fully believed it—perhaps even then, we sensed we were raised surrounded by lies. But the trap was real, and my skin grew redder and angrier, then finally blue, as the blood failed to find its course.

I fought to get loose, and it wrapped itself around my calf, only digging deeper into my flesh as I struggled. *"Be still!"* Camellia shouted, crying because she couldn't think of any solution but this, and Camellia always had to fix things. *"If you keep moving, it will take your whole leg off!"*

And Amber just stood there, useless as always, repeating, *"We never should have come, we never should have come."*

But my maman saved me. I remembered her having

warned me that a snare would only tighten if you struggled. That to be free, you had to relax into it. *"Fear is a mighty
opponent,"* she had said, *"and it can only be beaten in the mind."*

Memory had saved my leg. And it would save me now.

I take a deep breath and think of her. I try to forget that
I'm caught.

My muscles soften, the adrenaline draining slowly from
my body.

And suddenly, the needles relax like a teacup porcupine
that has been fed milk. The golden spines slide out of my left
arm, then the others from my right.

The pain leaving my body takes my strength with it. I
collapse to the ground, and a breath later, the ground dissolves. I slip through a hole, out of the labyrinth and back to
the world outside. A scream echoes out. Just before the hole
closes, I watch the quivering needles turning in the direction
of someone else's pain.

I pick myself up off the ground, barely having felt the
fall. Though my legs shake, I move forward. My breath has
already returned. I think of Gaelle. Touching her face the way
I did after her beauty work, when she laid her palms over
mine. Breath. Hers. Mine.

More than queendom on the other side, there must be
Gaelle.

Ahead, the path from the mountain back to shore is
obvious—a tiny golden bridge leads me out now that the

weight of fear has left me. I can see through the path. On the other side is the platform for those who succeed. Blais, Estelle, Cesarine, and Violetta are waiting.

No one else comes out.

NINETEEN

I don't remember the journey back to the Gravier Palace. I don't remember the sounds of competitors sniffling and crying as we sat in the battered competitor's carriage, two dead women in boxes between us. My mind fights the images of gold teeth piercing their bodies, blood pouring out like red wine. And, somewhere, Calandre presented like a gift to the Goddess of Death.

I don't remember standing before the long dressing mirror in my room. I can't feel the servant's touch as she fits a crinoline around my hips. I can't feel her pull my arms through the wide sleeves of a white dress and yank it down over me. I can't feel her tie the pink sash around my waist. I can't feel as she slips my feet into the little wooden shoes that will prevent me from sinking into the graveyard's soft earth.

When our mamans died, this is how they dressed us. When Camellia, Hana, Padma, and I buried Valerie, Amber, and Arabella this is what we wore. Even the day Du Barry buried my mother and I shattered into a thousand pieces. This is customary for Orléansian funerals.

And here we are again. Death another thing to dress up for.

I didn't know these two dead competitors well. I don't even know if I liked them. But the reality that they are no longer in this competition with me, they will no longer be at the dinners, and they will no longer be in the carriages reminds me that this trial has consequences that cannot be undone.

The servant walks me to my vanity. She opens the drawers of my beauty caisse and points. I know she wants me to put makeup on, but my hands and fingers shake, and I can't seem to hold anything. I don't recognize my reflection dressed in the mourning clothes.

"You must finish getting ready, my lady. Everyone will be waiting for you to attend."

"I can do it myself," I reply.

She lets out a little exasperated sigh before leaving me there to stare at myself. The skin around my eyelids is puffy, more pink than white, and too sore for eye shadow. I can't grip the rouge pot, and my bottom lip trembles.

Get it together, I tell myself. *You have lost people before. You have lost so much more. You will move on to the next trial, and you will be fine.*

My door slides open with a pop. In the mirror, I see the Minister of Games and her assistant trudge in. I don't face her.

She comes up behind me. "Make up your face, and finish getting ready for the funeral," she says. "As a competitor, you are required to attend."

"I need a moment."

She stands there as if counting.

The day Du Barry came to get me for my mother's funeral, I told her I didn't want to go. She said all my sisters had been through the same thing, and I was spoiled—the last to lose my mother. The most coddled and spoiled. She said, *"The Belles' journey is different. Like a flower. Gentle and delicate. Unable to last forever."*

Lies, lies, lies.

"The newsies will want to interview you afterward," the Minister of Games informs me.

"I don't want to talk to them."

"We are documenting this for the world to see. All citizens of Orléans will know each competitor's story. It's the only way to ensure the transfer of power is successful." She glares at me. "People must get to know you. Fall in love with you in order to follow you, to root for you."

My fingers tingle. I'm covered in an angry sweat. I want to punch the feathered hat off her head and shove her into the mirror. I let my eyes burn into hers, vowing not to look away until she does.

She breaks first and jerks me around. I smell the tea biscuit she's just eaten.

"You're here to become queen, yes?" she asks, and grabs

a rouge-stick from my open caisse. "Blais said Lana ran, and that's why she died."

"If that's what she said happened," I say. I will away the flush of anger climbing up my neck.

"We'd like to get an accounting. For the families. So they know how their loved ones died."

"Or so you can sell it to the newsies for a nice bag of leas," I grumble.

She raises her eyebrow with irritation. "I've spent the past several months combing through every document that exists about the Beauty Trials. I have found the Goddess of Beauty's divine orders, and I am familiar with what she would want. I will enact my authority if you don't cooperate."

I take a deep breath and say, "Please leave so I can finish getting ready."

She storms out in a huff. I manage to put on a tiny bit of rouge-stick and mascara. This was a tedious ritual as a child, but the older I get, the more I despise it. I wasn't allowed to ask: *Beauty? Why does it matter at all?*

I smooth the front of my dress, ready. The servant walks me to the open lift, where Blais is waiting. Her neck and arms blend into the white fabric, making her look like a spirit.

"Why do we have to do this?" she complains.

The doors close, and we descend to the first floor.

"Everyone loves a show," I answer. It's the answer my maman would have given. "Especially a sad one."

We walk through the main hall, where servants and

attendants race about. The chandelier-lanterns burn white in honor of the dead. A servant kneels, then opens the doors to the outside. Storm clouds block the moon—a thick forest stamps out the remaining light. Lanterns illuminate the dark branches, and poles hold candles high above rows of chairs. Newsies flash their light-boxes as we walk forward. I feel eyes drift over us as we walk. My feet become heavier, as if they're filled with sand.

Far ahead, I see a fire. It's stretched along a platform like an oven grill ready to roast a chicken.

The Minister of Games stands on a small platform. She's added more peacock feathers to her hat since harassing me in my room. The Minister of Beauty puts on a show, too. She turns in our direction. "Girls!" She sucks in a huge breath of air. Her brightly painted lips quiver. "So good to see you, and very sorry that we are here to send off these two competitors. They depart now to the caves of the Goddess of Death."

Newsies release their story-balloons over our heads.

The Minister of Beauty pulls me first, then Blais, into her arms. I stiffen and feel each stroke of her long nails down my back and almost choke on the scent of cinnamon and clove tobacco. She turns her attention to Blais, who has begun to weep. It feels rehearsed. The newsies race over to her, asking how she feels and how close she was to Minette and Lana.

I'm supposed to be sad that Calandre and Minette and Lana lost their lives this morning. I didn't even know them. I cannot perform sadness when what I feel is so much more complicated. I can't fold into the minister's arms and cry for the light-boxes and newspapers. I won't.

Blais and I take our places on the podium behind the minister with the other competitors. One glance tells me I'm not the only one whose makeup was ineffective—I see bruises, cuts, pinpricks. But the wounds are only the half of it: their eyes are haunted. Even Blais—smirking Blais—looks faded, like a flower cut and left to wither in the sun.

Behind the podium, the fire spits and rages. I follow the flames. They're long fingers reaching for the bodies perched above it.

On beds of rose petals, the women rest. All but Calandre, who has already been taken to the Goddess of Death. Their arms are folded across their chests, their house emblems resting at their heads. They're dressed in their signature colors. Their makeup makes them look like sleeping dolls. One empty bed sits symbolically, representing Calandre's final resting place.

An attendant takes us from the Beauty Minister and walks us in front of the Minister of Games's podium. We are given prayer beads and have to kneel. Our white dresses hang away from our bodies like curtains.

The circular beads press into my palm. "I will not lose this trial," I mutter. "I will not end up burning."

The Minister of Games pulls the voice-trumpet to her mouth. The fire at her back gives her an orange glow. "We are gathered here today to say good-bye to three worthy competitors fallen in the Beauty Trials. They are now at peace in the afterlife, gone to the Goddess of Death."

She turns to the families, who cry out with sorrow, their wails sharp and piercing.

Facing the fire, the minister bows her head and lifts two fingers in the air to show respect for the dead. Everyone follows suit as two servants work to turn a huge lever that slowly lowers the bodies into the fire.

The pulley creaks. I wince with each turn.

"We will now have a moment of silence while these new souls find their way home."

I hold my breath as the platform nears the flames.

The fire engulfs the dead, burning up the roses and tearing through their silk dresses, and then their skin and bodies. Tiny sparks flicker like fireflies as their bodies disappear.

In three days, the Beauty Trials will begin their second round and more will die.

 # TWENTY

I sit in the tearoom at the Gravier Palace, watching embers crackle in the small fire and reading the *Orléansian Times*. Post-balloons drift above my shoulder like angry red wasps. I think of Minette and Lana. Every time I close my eyes, I see their bodies turn to ash. Hair burned like ribbons set aflame, flesh and bones incinerated into a dust as fine as bei powder.

"You going to open those?" a voice asks.

I glance over my shoulder to find Quentin and his insufferable grin.

"They'll be fine for a few more minutes." I turn back to the fire.

He drops down into the adjacent chair.

"Did I say I wanted company?" I glare at him in hopes he won't get too comfortable.

"The room is big, and the fire is warm. You can ignore me like you usually do," he spits back.

"Why are you like this?"

"Why are *you* like this?" He smiles, and it makes me scowl because I almost laugh and I don't want him to make me laugh. "After so much death, you shouldn't be left alone," he adds.

I sigh with frustration.

"You don't like me?" he asks.

"Don't take it personally—I don't like anyone," I tell him. "At least not at first. And especially not strangers."

"I'm not a stranger," he replies, putting his hand to his chest in mock upset.

"I don't know you."

"The definition of a stranger is someone you've never met. We met in the Grottos."

I look up, my annoyance growing. "And we had tea and dinner and a nice walk and talked about our favorite colors and dreams, right?"

"Point taken."

To end our conversation, I snatch the tails of one of the crimson post-balloons, pulling it down into my lap. It's from Camille.

Dear Edel,

You don't have to go through with this. I can't bear to lose another sister, and especially not you. Please consider forfeiting before you end up dead.

But I write to you about other matters. While you're in Gravier

Palace, I sent Hana to check in on the Belles in the teahouses. *More illegal beauty work is happening. Many of the Belles are struggling, and more have left. One Belle was killed in an illegal teahouse. The people she was working for dumped her dead body in the street.*

Charlotte's cabinet has new "Belle dogs" to hunt us down. They've trained them to sniff out our blood in case we try to hide.

I got word that St. Nanterre has one of these teahouses hidden in a candle shop. You're only ten miles away—I need you to go check it out. Please, Edel. On the back of the letter is an address.

Be careful.

PS We buried her in the Belle graveyard.

I jump up as if burned. Belle dogs. Damn them. Why would Charlotte go along with something like this? This sounds like a thing Sophia would do.

"What is it?" Quentin stands.

"I need to go into St. Nanterre. Right now."

"Why?"

"No time to explain."

"I'm coming with you," he says.

"I don't need an escort."

"Everyone needs an escort into St. Nanterre. It isn't like Trianon or any of the other capitals. It's a place where people know when you don't belong. And as the Gamekeeper, it is my responsibility that you return for the next challenge."

I hesitate. It's true: I don't know the area at all. And on a mission like this, having a member of the family chosen by Death may not be such a bad idea.

"Fine," I relent. "But leave your vulture here."

"Encerclant has more important things to do than take a ride to St. Nanterre," he says.

As it turns out, bringing Quentin was wise. Though I'd never tell him this. He prevented me from choosing a carriage that he claimed would draw too much attention, instead hailing us a rickety-looking wagon heading south. As we hunker down, he asks, "Aren't you glad you left your cloak?" Quentin had pulled down gardening smocks from the servants' wardrobes for us instead. Mine is itchy and smells like earth, but I know he was right.

"I'm just glad we got out of the city quickly," I say, keeping my eye on the driver. He doesn't seem to recognize me, but I trust no one, and all along the road to St. Nanterre, I turn my head away from the many strangers on foot.

"Anything you might want to clue me in on before we arrive?" Quentin says, tossing his hair off his face. "You flew out of the Gravier Palace like a teacup bat from the Grottos."

"Such as?"

"If we're going into battle, for example, I should like to know."

"If you're waiting for a trumpet to sound the start of the war, you're too late."

"Better late than never," he quips, and I roll my eyes,

then turn back toward St. Nanterre, growing larger on the horizon. But even with my gaze turned elsewhere, I can feel him studying me.

"What is it?" I snap.

"You're beautiful," he says. It lands more like a diagnosis than a compliment. "I am concerned that if your goal is to stay concealed in St. Nanterre, you may have some difficulty."

Something about his indifference makes me blush. It's better, somehow, than being fawned over. He's not a fool, therefore bringing him was not foolish.

"I don't plan to be recognized, and you're wrong," I say, and he frowns. He points to the place on his cheek where the Belle-rose blooms on mine.

"Really?" I say. I put my hand to my cheek and feel nothing. But why would he lie?

In my mind, I hold the image of a Gris woman. One far between beauty appointments, gray seeping through her skin like a storm. I feel my scalp tingle as my fourth arcana, Glamour, is summoned from deep in my blood.

When I open my eyes, I am transformed. The expression on Quentin's face does not change, but he leans backward a little, seemingly satisfied with my temporary illusion. It must hide the mark enough. I'll have to trust his reaction, as I don't have a mirror.

"It's a glamour," I say. It feels similar to telling Gaelle about the beauty tools: one less lie in the world. There is the tiniest bit of weight off my chest.

"I have heard about many of the Belles' gifts," he says, studying me. "But never this."

"You know more of my gifts than I know of yours," I say.

He casts me a sidelong glance. The wagon jolts over a bump in the road, and we jostle together.

"What does it mean for a family to be blessed by Death?" I ask.

"Nothing so interesting as a glamour," he says, gesturing toward my face. He turns his eyes toward the city. "You should put on your veil. I don't think the mark of the Goddess can be hidden, even by a Belle."

I curse, throwing the veil over my face as the wagon we travel on passes under the archway that leads into St. Nanterre.

The noise is immediate. The air buzzes like hornets and shatters like dishes. Shouting, arguing, fighting—pots are being emptied through windows, doors slamming, rugs tossed out to be beaten. So much talk: even the friendly conversations shouted, laughter loud and impolite. It's enough to make my head spin, overwhelmed with scents and sounds.

"It smells like..." I start, but can't put my finger on it.

"A far cry from your delicate chambers," Quentin says, and his mouth only begins to become a sneer when I look at him.

"It smells like olivestone," I say, glaring. "The same stone they used to build the Everlasting Rose. It's a dry smell. Like old sand." I pause. "I was there for weeks. I got to know it well."

"Olivestone is what they used to build many of these buildings." He nods, his sneer gone. Something like respect glistens in his eyes. I look away, drawn into the sounds of St. Nanterre.

"It will be easier to find what you're looking for if you tell me," he says.

He's right, of course, but after Amber, trust is a frail concept. I reluctantly hand over the letter, choosing against my better judgment.

He reads, and I watch his eyebrows rise. He lifts his gaze to my face. "Why does your friend know about this?"

"Why do *you*?" I say. "Can you take me there or not?"

He rolls his eyes, pressing the paper back into my hands. "Of course I can."

I go on watching the streets, my body tensed. The headlines are different here, too. They shimmer and flicker only in spurts over shop doors and the mouths of alleys. They have a decrepit feeling, as if they could sputter out at any moment.

QUEEN SOPHIA'S CRIMINAL TRIAL SET TO BEGIN

SOURCE CLOSE TO TOURNAMENT COMPETITORS
SAYS BLOODSHED HAS ONLY JUST BEGUN

"Watch yourself," Quentin mutters near my ear. I jump at the tickle. "We're almost at the market your friend wrote you about. It gets a little rough, so keep your wits about you."

"My wits are never anywhere else," I reply. But I think, *Rougher than* this?

Quentin tosses the owner of the wagon a few leas, and we step down into the dusty street. There are Gris men and women everywhere—some barely trying to cover the gray. Many wear wigs dusty from the street. I pat myself on the back for choosing a Gris glamour, even as my head buzzes with the effort of holding it. Quentin was right: I would've stood out like a sore thumb.

Quentin guides me without guiding me—nudging me imperceptibly here and there to keep me going in the right direction. Every moment that passes feels like burrowing deeper into a stone onion—the city is layered in circles of stone. The streets twist and turn—he could only know this path after having traveled it well. Later I will need to press him for the answer of why he knows the way to an illegal market so well.

"Any idea who we're looking for?" he murmurs as we walk.

I'm beginning to lose patience, when we take a sudden sharp turn into the darkest of alleys. Something presses against my veil, thick and sticky like a curtain of spiderweb. I claw at it, but from somewhere in the dark, Quentin's hand reaches out and stills me.

"I should've warned you," he says. "Relax. Don't make a commotion. We're about to enter the market."

As I continue through, every part of my body wants

to continue clawing—not just at the strange material, but at Quentin, too: anyone within arm's reach. But I think of Camille's letter. If this is the market, then I might be close to the Belle who needs my help.

When we break through to the other side, we are in the market as promised. It's smaller than I expected—a few dozen stalls and shops, ragged banners hanging from crumbling stonework. I look over my shoulder to see what we passed through—a mesh of spiderwebby material hangs glimmering and dusty.

"Keep moving," he says, and I do, because the market is much quieter than the rest of St. Nanterre, and I can feel eyes passing over me.

"Look forward," he whispers, but he didn't need to tell me. I move through the marketplace without glancing at any of the stalls, even as I burn with curiosity about what's so illegal about any of their wares. I don't see any sign of beauty work—only fewer gray hands exchanging coins. I scan the walls, trying to be surreptitious.

Finally, I see it. The oily windows are old and smudged, but the flicker of a hundred wicks glows through. Strong incense wafts out. "Candle shop," I murmur.

"Stay close," Quentin says, but my steps are quicker, and I enter the shop first.

Inside, the shelves and floor are as oily as the windows. Behind a listing countertop stands the shopkeeper, cleaning his nails with a bit of glass. His eyes wander over me in a familiar way, but his posture remains languid—he's hoping for a slip of my blouse or dress.

Quentin steps in beside me. The shopkeeper stands a little taller. "I'm about to close."

Quentin ignores him and heads straight to one of the filthy shelves, confidently plucking out an assortment. "Eight of these, nicely wrapped."

I pretend to look around at the shelves as the shopkeeper reluctantly takes Quentin's leas, eyeing him. As I finger tiny perfume cones and hold them to my nose to inhale sweet plum and spiced nutmeg, I feel the shopkeeper looking at me.

After several tense minutes, he turns to the back of the shop to wrap Quentin's purchases. I peer desperately around, looking for any sign of a Belle. Only shelves and shelves, many of them empty. A curtained doorway, the edges dented and chipped. Through the incense, the smell of burnt bread and cheap syrup.

Yet something else is underneath—a familiar fragrance that calls to me. I shoot Quentin a look, hoping he's as smart as he thinks he is.

"Wait a minute!" he says, raising his voice. "I said nine! What are you, trying to swindle me?"

The shopkeeper whirls, his eyebrows low and heavy. "Nine?" he says. "You said eight, clear as day."

"I said nine!" Quentin shouts, and moves closer to the off-kilter counter. I take my chance and slip through the ragged curtain.

Away from the clouds of incense, the scent is much clearer. It's metallic, wrapping itself around me, snaking up my ankles and calves.

There are only two doors: one is propped open to the back alley—an escape route, no doubt; the other door is closed firmly, only the barest glow escaping under the crack.

I can still hear Quentin and the shopkeeper arguing. I step forward, grasp the doorknob, and twist.

The smell of it washes over me. It's as much a part of my memory as my maman's lullabies.

Blood.

A woman is slumped over at a table, her thick hair snaking down her back in a fat black braid. Needles poke every part of her body. There are tubes, endless rows of vials. Blood bags hang over my head like glimmering red stars. Moss fills the bricks, the smell of death and decay.

This place is already a tomb.

I dart over to her and lift the woman's chin. It's Kata, from Chrysanthemum Teahouse. I shake her shoulder. She doesn't open her eyes or even twitch. I yank one of the needles from her arms, fury rising in me.

I hear voices barking, getting closer. A blink later, the shopkeeper and Quentin burst into the tiny room. "What do you think you're doing?" the shopkeeper snarls, trying to struggle past Quentin, his eyes on fire. I'm a mouse cornered by a hungry cat.

"What have you done to her?" I rage.

"What's it to you?" he says, his voice loaded with threat. "You're trespassing in my store."

"You can't keep her here against her will!" I shout.

"She came to *me* to work," he growls. "Her blood gets two thousand leas per bag. Now get out—the bags need changing."

He reaches for one of the blood bags above Kata's head, twisting the opening.

"Get away from her," I scream, watching the fresh bag fill up like a red balloon. Vertigo hits. Suddenly, I see myself sitting there, the endless tubes of crimson clawing their way into my veins.

The shopkeeper reaches for a knife in his belt. "I'm getting my last penny's worth. Now get out of here before I—"

The arcana surges.

Dead.

She's dead.

All along the walls, the moss shudders and then balloons, slowly at first, and then faster. The man's eyes are wide with terror and confusion—he looks everywhere but at me. He doesn't understand that it's me doing it, that it's me who will take his life.

The moss begins pressing him between the green swells, crushing his chest, crawling up over his face like a film. His arm, constricted by the growing plant, twitches toward my veil. I bind him tighter and tighter and tighter. The man gasps for breath. His face has begun to turn purple.

"We need to go," Quentin says, grabbing my arm. I shake him off. "*Now.* We won't be alone for long."

"I won't leave her," I say through gritted teeth.

"Then let's take her," Quentin says. The gentleness in his voice pierces my fury. "But we need to go. NOW!"

The moss releases the man and drops him to the floor, unconscious. I see him through a haze as red as the blood everywhere.

"One more thing," I say. I snatch the bags of blood, and, using the knife in the shopkeeper's belt, slice them like organs. The blood runs through the cracks in the floor, turning the moss crimson. When the man wakes up, he will be in an ocean of blood he'll never get to use.

I turn away from him to find Quentin wrapping Kata gently in the thin sheet that had been draped over the table. While I was ripping the bags, he had removed all the tubes.

"It's time to go," he says.

Part of me wants to stay here in this cold, damp room. She died here alone.

And I couldn't save her.

TWENTY-ONE

My fingers can barely keep up with my mind as I write Camellia about what happened.

> *Dear Camellia,*
>
> *I was too late.*
>
> *Kata is dead. The Gamekeeper was with me when we found her—he has arranged to have her body sent to you at Maison Rouge.*
>
> *I know when you were at court, Sophia was experimenting with Belle blood, but how would others know? What are they doing with the blood?*
>
> *We have to find all the Belles that have left the teahouses. We must warn them and see if we can get them to return. Or perhaps you can make room for them at Maison Rouge.*
>
> *They can't get away with treating us like this.*

A knock interrupts.

"One moment," I holler, quickly signing the letter and popping it into the back of one of the Gravier Palace's post-balloons. The marigold and peacock glitter when I light its candle. I swallow my anger and upset, then turn to the door.

The knock sounds again, urgent.

"Who is it?"

"Caron Bisset. The Minister of Games," she reminds me.

"Come in," I reply. What could she possibly want? I open my terrace doors and set the post-balloon afloat. It gets caught in a windy-season gale and glides off.

The Minister of Games is followed by a small procession. "You've been summoned to the palace," she announces.

"What is it?" I fill with dread. "Is it one of my sisters?"

"No. You will testify in the criminal trial of Her Majesty Sophia. They would like you to speak to the crimes of which she's been accused."

"Sophia's trial has begun?" I cry. "Surely it would have made more sense to wait until the tournament selected a new queen."

"The Minister of Law has brought many people to speak before the court. Your sister Camille gave a detailed report and submitted her Belle-book to provide even more information." She steps aside as a guard and attendant enter. "You are to tell the truth of what you know."

"She's guilty of every single crime, every accusation

lobbed at her, I can assure you. Murder, abuse, generally being a disgusting person," I rattle off.

The Minister of Games purses her lips. "The carriage is ready," the attendant informs her.

"I have to leave right now?" I ask, looking down at my nightgown. "What about the second challenge? It's tomorrow!"

"I assure you you'll be back in time. Queen Charlotte believes the proceedings will be brief." She turns to the attendant. "Help her pack."

I sleep as the carriage whisks us along, and fall in and out of wild dreams. A ballroom filled with balloons of blood, so engorged they wobble and sway. My maman and sisters dancing in circles below. Outside the window, the moon also a red balloon. The haunting music of a violin rises and falls. I find Quentin in the shadows, his vulture swaying to the melody, eyes glinting crimson. The violin begins to screech, and Quentin to sing: *In the caves, in the caves, come to the caves, in the caves you all die....*

"Lady Edel," the palace attendant says, pulling me out of the tortured dreams. "A glass of snowmelon juice to refresh you? We will be arriving soon."

We cross the golden bridge into the city. As we plod through the streets, Trianon feels as if it's settling back into its old rhythm. There are no protestors. Instead, the billposters shout about which competitor is favored, what the next challenge of the competition will be. The carriage turns left, moving through the Rose Quartier before arriving in the Royal Square. Courtiers spill out of gilded carriages outside the most beautiful mansions and shops. Manicured trees and windy-season flower boxes hold small perfume blimps.

It's almost like nothing happened.

"The minister says you will go straight to testify this morning. Then you may rest in your Belles apartments before returning to the Gravier Palace," the palace attendant replies.

I wonder about the haste—in the middle of the tournament? I would have thought Charlotte would allow the new queen to preside over the criminal trial. My belly shifts. I worry Charlotte is listening to whispers, still trying to please everyone.

The Receiving Room has changed since Charlotte took the throne—all baubles and trinkets removed; puffery replaced with elegance. Everyone is layered in gauze and gowns as if the court proceedings are one more glamorous spectacle. And in a way, it is: newsies hanging from columns, gossip-balloons clogging the air. I'm glad I chose to wear only a traveling dress. Simple and comfortable.

Charlotte and her ministers sit gazing at the crowd as the attendant leads me to the speaker's box, where I settle myself on a cushion embroidered with gold. Etched into the mahogany are the words THE GODS ARE WATCHING.

But are they?

"Queen Sophia," an attendant with a voice-trumpet bellows, and the buzz simmers to a near silence, people shifting to get a better view as the doors at the far end of the room swing open.

Sophia steps inside. Her hair is blond today, and her dress is silver. In an instant, the newsies and spectators burst into conversation and questions fire off like arrows from bows. Order isn't restored until Sophia takes her seat across from Queen Charlotte, her lips closed in a ghost of a smile. I wish my eyes were poisonous, that my glare could kill her. Preferably excruciatingly.

"Lady Edelweiss Beauregard." Queen Charlotte's voice rings out across the stretched silence. "You have come to offer your truth in the criminal trial of Sophia. You understand that what we ask you today is what you have seen and heard yourself? Nothing told to you or that you have inferred?"

"Everything I know I have witnessed myself," I say, keeping my voice steady. "I was tortured by Sophia and her court. I was thrown in jail with nothing but rotten food to eat. I was beaten and manipulated. She has killed animals, people... anyone she cares to murder."

Singe, Sophia's teacup monkey, moves slowly along the edge of the table, venturing near her hands. Sophia's eyes twitch from the animal to me. They look watery, as if she could cry, or vomit. One of her long fingers darts out, pushing the monkey away. He hides beneath the table. *She must be nervous,* I think. *Perhaps she finally knows her days in power are over.*

They ask me more questions, questions Charlotte already knows the answers to.

Did you ever see her use her power for evil?

Did you ever hear her admit to her plans?

It needs to be said out loud for everyone to hear. But as I answer, detailing all the ugly things Sophia has done, I can't help but think it won't. The newsies are going to print what they're going to print. The Jolie Society will believe what they want to believe.

Nothing will change unless it's forced to.

Queen Charlotte and her cabinet nod calmly, quills scratching. I fight the rage that sparks in me. Will Charlotte ever do the right thing, or will she continue to strategically please the isles? Is "right" even an option?

"Sophia has inflicted incalculable wounds on the future of this kingdom," I say. "The only way the wrongs can begin to be set right is if she is held accountable for her crimes."

"Sophia," Queen Charlotte calls out. She sounds tired. "Would you like to speak against any of the matters brought forth here today by Edelweiss Beauregard?"

Sophia is looking at her fingernails. Charlotte calls her name again, sharply. Her head snaps up, eyes flying over the faces of those in charge of the court.

I realize her eyes are red not from anything so human as crying. It's simply the Gris affliction seeping through.

"Oh, no," she says, merely glancing at me. Her voice is indifferent, not filled with her usual hatred. When she speaks, I see a flash of red, her teeth and gums. Still drinking the tea she brewed in the Everlasting Rose it seems. I want to leap out of the speaker's box and tear her hair from her scalp.

"Lady Edelweiss Beauregard, you are released," Queen Charlotte says formally. "The court and the crown thank you for your time today." Then she adds, "The gods are watching."

The newsies and courtiers froth with gossip as I make my way out of the giant courtroom. I know my face will be on the cover of the newspapers, with headlines about how today's testimony will weaken my chances in the tournament. They are so accustomed to gossip having sway, controlling someone's reputation. They haven't caught on yet that the only person that can weaken my chances is me.

I'm offered my old Belle apartments to rest in, but I refuse—I'm back in the carriages headed for Gravier Palace before they've even finished oiling the axles. Bumpy road or not, I sit down immediately and begin to write Camille a letter:

Camille,

You must find out who is bleeding the Belles—Kata isn't the only one. Find out, and put a stop to it. Now.

I will do what I can from here.

Edel

TWENTY-TWO

The next day, I stare out at the sight of the next trial. The Coliseum is as large as the Gravier Palace. Half domes the rich red of Belle-roses, trimmed with gold, curve over the onlookers. The sky flashes stormy afternoon clouds. The windy season here feels perpetually like evening—a sunless, searing sky. It's how I picture the Goddess of Death's lair.

Fat blimps float about with portraits of the remaining competitors.

Blais.

Violetta.

Estelle.

Cesarine.

Me.

As we stand against the wind, I remind myself that I am doing this for the Belles. Sophia and her red teeth flicker through my thoughts again; a tele-trope reel stuck on a loop.

As awful as it was being in the same room yesterday, her face has filled me with purpose. She looked beaten down, her hateful energy flagging. Now all I have to do is win. If I succeed, I can ensure she's gone forever.

And if they choose not to execute her, I will handle it myself when I am queen. I will collect her head and preserve it so all will be reminded of her evil, and what happens to those who harm others.

Whispers rustle through the crowds as the ceremony begins.

Gaelle's mother, the royal astrologer, marches down the aisle, followed by her female disciples, including Gaelle. The sight of her makes my heart backflip. I surge with happiness. I didn't know she would be here. Why didn't she tell me?

Her eyes find me, and she winks, relishing in the surprise.

The whole Coliseum holds its breath as she ascends the stairs.

The large headdress she wears twinkles with celestial shapes—the moon, the stars, the sun. Her rich brown skin glitters, and her gown trails her like a dark wave of stardust. Disciples carry two massive star maps draped between two poles. Two blimps carry a map of the stars stretched between us. The celestial bodies twinkle like eyes. The crowd gasps.

Charlotte kisses both of her cheeks after she bows. "Madam Symone of the House of Fortunes."

"I am honored to be brought here today to read the fortunes of our noble competitors—now the Favored Five," she says, her voice smooth and powerful. She turns and nods at us, and her hazel eyes fix on me, as she searches through them like a room with a hidden treasure. I wonder what she sees—if she can look through my skin and see that Gaelle is one of my treasures.

"The stars first require blood," Symone tells the assembled.

One of Symone's veiled disciples presents a golden knife. Another holds a chalice. "Palms," they whisper in unison, and take both my hands. One gouges the point into the center, drawing a perfect pearl of blood, then repeats it with my other palm. I try not to wince.

The other disciple holds the chalice beneath my hands. A small red stream trickles into it. Satisfied, she takes the cup to the royal astrologer. The majestic woman sticks her nose near the rim, as if it's a cup of tea she's about to sip.

I look quickly about for Gaelle. She's holding her chalice under Cesarine's dripping fist. All of us giving our blood—I imagine there will be more before the next challenge.

"Dust," Madam Symone orders.

A box is brought forward and opened. Madam Symone rummages through the bottles, raising a midnight-blue one in the air. "I will ask the stars and the God of Fortune for their favor."

Symone pops the cork from her bottle. She pours the contents into her hand. The dust sparkles like pulverized jewels.

"The blood," Symone booms.

Disciples hands Madam Symone the chalices one by one. She sprinkles a pinch of the dust inside each, then pours them into the air. The dust and blood mixture creeps out of the chalices like writhing slugs, then five red clouds float before her.

Five clouds filled with our fortunes.

Madam Symone pokes at them with a long finger, and each twists into a sizzling orb.

"The candle," she says. One of her disciples has one already lit. She holds it for seconds beneath each pulsating sphere, mumbling something I can't decipher.

Then a platform is brought out and she steps onto it, lifting higher and higher until she's eye level with the star map and perched far above us. The orbs, our fortunes, follow. Suddenly, they unfold in multiple directions, each of its own accord, and splatter themselves across the star map. Our blood is fiery red as it travels through the map's veins. The God of Fortune buries his secrets deep inside stars, the stories say. Our blood is tying sets of stars together, knitting our specific fortunes.

Symone's attendants pass her a basket. She shouts a word I've never heard before, then the star map illuminates one last time before the five gigantic orbs fall into her basket.

Symone descends from the platform; her eyes are full of new knowledge.

"Contained inside these orbs are your fortunes, bestowed by the God of Luck himself. I will read them to you. They are not secrets, unless you'd like them to be."

Blais elbows me to the side, moving me into last place. I want to punch her in the jaw, but Gaelle shoots me a warning look. I give Blais a poisonous glare instead. I look over in time to watch Madam Symone hand Cesarine her glowing pearl. It cracks open like a glowing egg, revealing three fortune cards.

"Eyes on the teeth, dear. Always the teeth," she says, her voice deep and haunting.

Cesarine looks puzzled, looking down to consult her cards, but Madam Symone doesn't pause to explain.

For Violetta, Madam Symone says, "You require more than threads. A spider awaits you." Violetta looks shaken.

I can't hear what she says to Estelle. To Blais, right beside me, she says: "Two faces. Know the risks." I try to see her cards, but Blais holds them close, her face pale.

Then Symone's gaze falls on me. Her eyes narrow to a squint. She turns her icy gaze to the basket in her arms.

Only one pearl left. My fortune.

Symone drips with sweat, as if she'd been caught out in the windy-season rains without a proper parasol. She extends the massive pearl to me.

Merely touching the pearl causes it to open slowly and gently. Inside are my three cards. I pluck them out carefully. Meanwhile, the crowds of watching courtiers lift ear-trumpets to try to catch any word they can. Symone smiles, cups her hand beside her mouth, and whispers, "Your fortune is not for the masses." She inches closer to me, smelling of cinnamon and frankincense and far-off places.

She flashes the first card—a moon hidden by silver clouds. "First, darkness. You have many unanswered questions, many unknown memories."

"Yes," I say.

"Two, death." This card features a waning moon. "You feel like your old self might be dead, or dying."

I nod.

"Three, rebirth." A sun rises in the card's background. She twirls it between her fingertips and bites her bottom lip. "A change has already begun." She touches my face, and I feel held by her warm gaze. Questions flutter through me like the shuffling of her card deck.

"The queen who wins will bring fire to this kingdom," she whispers, although no card is left. "But you must wait for the *real* fire."

She turns abruptly. Gaelle and the disciples follow solemnly. I want to shout after her to wait, to be clear, to explain. I don't understand what she means, and I have no time to decipher riddles.

"It is time," calls Quentin from the farthest edge of the Coliseum. Standing with Encerclant perched heavily on his shoulder, he looks like a mage. The entire room is caught in his trance.

"Prepare yourselves," he says.

I brace—for what, I don't know.

A scream fills the air, so loud and blood-curdling that everyone present writhes in pain. Even with my hands pressed tightly against my ears, the sound seeps in. I look around for the source, and see the Goddess of Beauty's caisse at the center of the Coliseum. It is flipped open with the sound emanating outward. The bloodied filigree pulses, then bleeds together. Beauty's chalice emerges, hovering just above. The box's edges disintegrate, melting like a brick of chocolate set on a chafing dish, into a puddle.

Not a puddle—a chasm. The chalice spins, then falls into the gigantic hole in the ground.

Encerclant rises off Quentin's shoulder, careens into the sky, and then nose-dives into the black hole in the ground. The world is immediately silent again. The crowd sits in stunned silence, many rubbing their temples.

A gaping hole stretches between us all.

The Minister of Games rushes closer to the chasm and peers down. At that moment, Encerclant sails out, sending her crashing to the ground. Quentin tries to hide a chuckle as the vulture drops a scroll into his hand, then dives back into the dark pit left behind by the melted caisse.

A voice-trumpet floats beneath Quentin. He clears his throat, unrolls the scroll, and speaks:

"With the blessing of the Goddess of Death, the Gamekeeper will accompany you into the caves for the second challenge." He looks up at us. "I will not help you. I will not guide you. My role is as a keeper of record. Without my presence, no one will ever know what happened to you." He looks down again. "You each have something the others need. Your death is your own." He folds up the scroll. "The second Beauty Trial has begun."

The entire Coliseum is silent. All I can hear is my own heartbeat.

What awaits us in that darkness?

TWENTY-THREE

Quentin steps forward, leading us toward the pitch-black of the pit. I feel the terrified tremors of Violetta's arms as we walk side by side. I find Gaelle in the room; her eyes filled with worry as she nibbles at her own fingers. I wink at her and try to pretend that I'm not afraid of walking headfirst into an abyss of nothingness.

I hold my breath as I step into it. I feel as if I've been swallowed. My insides tugged left and right, my skin stretching and burning. I can't even scream. My mouth shut tight as the world around us, the Coliseum, the people, the light, dissolves in a blink and is sealed from us. The darkness consumes my sight, and everything becomes nothing.

I hear Quentin's voice. "Hold on tight. Only a moment longer."

A soft light appears, and this new world begins to sharpen around us. The whole place has a fearsome beauty—glittering stalactites and stalagmites and the roiling texture of fossils in the walls.

The Goddess of Death's caves. It has to be. Fairy tales say monsters lurk here, bodies decomposed but spirits still lodged inside, stalking the tunnels in search of flesh.

I squint as I take in the rest of the space. My eyes struggling to make out every single element of my surroundings.

"Be patient. Your groundsight will conitnue to sharpen," Quentin says as he sees us looking around. "It only occurs under very special circumstances." He seems comfortable in the caves, at ease. However his family's magic works, this must be part of it.

Violetta murmurs in admiration, turning this way and that to admire the tunnel we stand inside. I keep my eye on my fellow competitors but look, too, still grappling with the fact that every story, every legend, every fairy tale was true.

"Each of you has a piece of a map," Quentin says. "You will know the endpoint when you see it: through the Goddess's teeth. Sometimes you may see me. Sometimes you may not. I will not help you, even if you beg. I cannot even if I wanted to." He pauses. "Until then, I wish you luck."

And just like that, he's gone, the wall as smooth as sand blown by wind. We all stare at the place where he stood just a moment before. Blais rushes forward to touch the spot where he disappeared.

"He said we have a piece of the map," Cesarine says. "I don't have a map."

"Two eyes and one mouth," Violetta says benignly, and leans down to pick up a small sack at her feet the same color as the ground. There's one in front of me as well, and I snatch it up, my mind leaping ahead.

I turn my back on the other competitors, moving toward the rise in the stone where Quentin disappeared. I need a moment to focus.

A piece of parchment rolled into a narrow tube tumbles out of my sack. My eyes fly over it: it's a pathway marked in golden ink. Even with groundsight, it's hard to make out— the pathway curves, opening into a bowl-like shape before the parchment stops, the line cut off. Someone around me has a piece that connects, that shows what's next.

I shake out the bag. There are also two vials of medicine, thin-spun bandages, and a knife, which I immediately secure at my hip.

I glance up just in time to see Cesarine pounce on Estelle.

"Oh gods," Violetta says, panicking. She rushes off as the two girls claw at each other, her sack dangling from her hand. I watch with my mouth open as she disappears into the dark mouth of a tunnel. She didn't even consult her scrap of map. Does she know where to go and what to do?

Meanwhile, Blais leans against a wall, watching the other two fight. A smirk haunts her lips. "Good shot, Cesarine," she calls into the fray. "Don't let her get you on the ground, Estelle. Did that hurt? Hold her tighter, my petit!"

"Stop instigating," I spit back.

Blais's smirk turns to a frown. "Why?"

I don't have time to spar with her, instead I turn my attention to the others and try to convince them to stop shoving and kicking each other.

A spill of blood turns the sand under the scrabbling feet a dark brown, and Cesarine stumbles backward, clutching her face. A red ribbon spurts from her nose. As she pants, I can see she's missing a tooth. Estelle, on the other hand, has lost nothing but gained a new piece of map.

"Aha," Estelle says, holding it up triumphantly. "Good try, little Cesarine. But not good enough."

Blais pushes off the wall to join her.

"Together we have three pieces," she says. "Shall we form an alliance? Maybe we can track down old Violetta— convince her to let us take a peek."

Estelle casts a glance in my direction as Cesarine spits blood into the sand. I give them my blankest stare—I will them to feel the cold. Even from this distance, they must.

"Let's go," Estelle agrees, and they make their way down the tunnel where Violetta disappeared.

"Are you all right?" I ask Cesarine when they're gone. "Did she get anything else?"

"I still have my food," she mutters, not making eye contact.

"If you have food, you can stay with me," I tell her.

Even with blood dripping from her nose, her temper flares.

"I don't need you," she spits. "I can just follow them. And when the time is right, I'll get my map back. Plus theirs."

She spins away, stalking down the tunnel after the others.

"I don't like those odds," I say to myself, and slide down from the stone rise.

There are many tunnels to choose from, but several look short, like I would only be able to walk ten paces deep. Instead, I choose the tunnel next to the one my competitors disappeared into. Perhaps I will still be able to hear them if I stay close—I don't want any surprises, especially down here.

But the caves are full of surprises anyway. Tiny winged creatures intermittently burst from nowhere, screeching sharp-toned songs. Like everything else, they're the color of sand. I think about trying to catch one to examine it, but it's the kind of thing Gaelle would chastise me for. Stay focused, stay alive.

The groundsight changes up ahead, thins. "Space," I say out loud, just to hear something besides the sifting sound of my shoes through sand.

"Correct," says Quentin. I jump.

"What is that up ahead?" I say, recovering. "A cavern?"

He doesn't answer. I don't need him to—I'm closer now, and I can see by the way the tunnel opens up, the way the ground begins to fall away.

"What are the creatures?" I ask. "The tiny ones with shrill songs."

"They're sand bats," he says. I can almost hear him smiling. "Have you been bitten?"

"No."

"Good. You would die."

"Oh."

I lean backward to keep my momentum from tipping me forward as I descend the sandy incline. My foot strikes a rock, and it clatters into an opening that had been hidden by shadows. I go to the edge and peer down—stalactites extend toward the ceiling, their sharp points reminding me of the needles in the labyrinth. I tell myself to be more careful.

"A pity," Blais rings out. She and Estelle are some distance away, hands on hips. "We had hoped you'd fallen already. Estelle almost did," she adds.

Estelle shoots her a toxic look. They're both smudged with sand, and at a distance, I can see a bloody scrape runs across Estelle's knee.

"We can only wish the others did. Or got lost somewhere down here, never to be found," Estelle says. Her voice echoes off the soaring cavern walls.

"Sorry to dash your dreams," Violetta calls. We look—she stands in the mouth of a tunnel far across the cavern, next to something flat and sparkling.

I can't believe we've all ended up in this same place. The odds feel impossible. Perhaps the Goddess of Death brings travelers together, hoping for blood.

I wonder if Cesarine is dead.

"Shall we compare maps?" Violetta calls.

"We don't need your map to find our way," Blais calls back.

"You wish that was true," Violetta says. "Don't you?"

Estelle and Blais exchange looks.

"Only way I'm letting you look at my map is if you offer something," Blais says.

"And vice versa," Violetta replies, her snort echoing. "I have a proposal. We will agree to a glance. We put our pieces together, and someone counts. When the time is up, maps away." Violetta smiles. "If you want to fight after that, you're welcome."

I see Blais stiffen. She's a clever weasel—clever enough to know she'll lose to Violetta in a fight.

If I can glean any knowledge from a quick look at their maps, then I can get away again as soon as possible. Is this what a queen would do? Find allies only when necessary? Or is my distaste for allying with these dangerous fools a mark against my queenliness?

"Fine," calls Blais.

Estelle looks annoyed. "Who will count? Not me."

"Quentin," I say.

In a swirl of sand, he appears near the apex of a huge, pointed rock.

"Yes?"

"I wasn't exactly calling you," I say, surprised but pleased that he arrived so quickly. "More seeding the suggestion. But since you're here . . ."

"I cannot assist you," he says.

"We don't need assistance," I drawl. "We need you to count."

He hesitates.

"You can stay where you are," I say. "In case the Goddess of Death needs proof."

He stares impassively. I take it as assent.

"What's that over there by you, Violetta?" I call.

"A tiny pool," she answers. "Dripping from nowhere."

"Let's meet there."

Violetta begins to descend immediately, but Blais and Estelle hesitate. I ignore them, moving along my own path that curtails their position. My eyes shift from the ground to the air, and back and forth. The tunnels, though dim and winding, felt safer than being out here in the open. But I have offered a plan and must stick to it.

When I get to the pool, Violetta is already there. Estelle and Blais slip and slide down a rocky embankment.

"Think Cesarine is dead?" Violetta asks.

"Probably not," I say. "Yet."

She nods, lips tight. Blais and Estelle arrive, panting, on the other side of the water.

"No covering things with your hand or funny business,"

Blais says when she catches her breath. "Hold it up, clear as day, and Quentin will count."

"Will I?" he calls out, still watching from his boulder.

"Yes," I holler back. "To five."

"Ten," says Blais.

"Ten!" whines Estelle.

"Five," says Violetta.

There's a long moment of silence until Blais makes a sucking sound that signals agreement. I touch the edge of the parchment where I've stowed it away in my camisole. I'll be able to see Estelle's the clearest. But Blais and Estelle each have their own maps, plus Cesarine's. I grit my teeth, readying myself.

"On three," Quentin says.

Everyone takes a deep breath. "One," Quentin begins. "Two..."

Someone mutters something, and a scream echoes out.

Quentin stops counting. I can't see his face clearly from here, but he doesn't look surprised.

"Cesarine," Violetta says without emotion.

My mind flits to the sand bats. They looked so harmless, but Quentin said they could kill. Was he joking? Perhaps Cesarine...

The screaming gets louder. Every muscle in my body tells me I should run, but the echo is disorienting. I might run directly into the danger.

I stuff the map back into my camisole—there will be no comparison now.

"Where is it coming from?" Blais says in a low voice. I glance at the pointed rock where Quentin was perched—he's gone.

I turn to the pool. Ripples vibrate out from its edges. I slowly back away, moving toward the gloom in the tunnel to my left. I can hear that it's Cesarine now—shrill and ragged, coming this way. Whatever is following her must be right on her heels.

"What do we do?" Estelle cries.

Violetta is already gone. I know I should be, too. But instinct keeps me rooted—I need to evaluate what I'm up against.

It doesn't take long.

"Oh gods," Blais says. For once, the smirk is out of her voice.

The creature is made of stone and sand, with four-fingered hands grasping at the air. Its single bulbous eye is lidded with strange wrinkly flesh, its body wizened and dry as parched earth. It crumbles as it walks but never gets smaller, and its mouth is wide and round and full of stalactites. It staggers after Cesarine, fifty times her size.

I'm running before I feel my legs move.

I sprint headlong toward the tunnel and dive, the thunder of the creature's footsteps knocking loose pebbles and sand on top of me. I don't stop to cower. Scrabbling for balance as the ground trembles, I take off, not caring where the tunnel leads. My blood thrums with a chant: *Survive. Survive. Survive.*

As I run, I don't look back. I only look forward. So I don't see what's behind me, what grabs my ankles and pulls me down.

TWENTY-FOUR

I kick using every muscle and clawing for the knife at my hip. The arcana thrums in my blood—but this is the land of Death, not the land of Beauty. I alone can fight, with a knife, like anyone else.

"Stop fighting, you fool! I'm trying to save you!"

It's Violetta. The words find my brain but take a moment to reach my body, still struggling and scraping at sand.

"I said stop fighting! You're going right toward the nest!"

She hauls me up from the ground, shoves me against the wall.

"Listen."

I shake with adrenaline but finally stop thrashing. I press myself against the wall, away from her hands. I can hear the sound of breathing—not my own.

"Do not move," she whispers. "They're coming."

My heartbeat hammers in my ears, but I obey.

It's not the sound of breathing, I realize. It's the sound of slithering.

It's worms. Masses of them, all dry and scaly—worse somehow than wet maggots. A tidal wave of writhing bodies. I should be used to these sorts of creatures, having been bled my whole life using sangsues, but it takes every bit of control not to flail, to scream, as they pass over the tips of my boots. Violetta is as still as a statue, watching them calmly. A group of sand bats bursts from the wall. The worms roll over them, pulsing, churning. When the mass passes, I see tiny skeletons scattered around.

Gods.

As the wave of worms surges toward the cavern, more screams echo. I don't know whose. I can't care.

"I hope she dies before the worms get there," Violetta whispers.

"How...how did you know?" I pant, finally daring to breathe.

"I'm of the Grottos, remember? I spent my days down here after losing Claudine. I am an Iron Lady. I have faced this darkness before," she says neutrally. "I passed them on my way to the cavern. When they have the space, they fill it, assembling into something much larger. Let me see your map."

I glare at her, wanting to argue. But her look tells me what I already know: I owe her. I stand out of arm's reach, then withdraw the piece, holding it up for her to see. Surprisingly, she does the same.

"There will be a river," she says, pointing to a corner of her map. "That bowl on yours? A basin. Aim for it. And for gods' sake, avoid the cavern."

Then she's gone, trotting down the tunnel in the direction of the nest she'd warned me about. I almost call after her until I realize, of course, it's empty. I hate the idea of tailing her, but the only other direction at this point is back toward the cavern, where I can still hear the pulse of the worms—and no more screaming.

I will turn at the first juncture, I think.

It doesn't take long—the caves are a honeycomb. Interconnected chambers, tunnels short and long, smaller caverns that could fit many times inside the one I just escaped. Even with Violetta's portion of the map inside my head, there's no telling which direction will lead me toward an exit.

I think I trust myself to find drinkable water, but there's nothing to eat but sand. All I have is medicine—no food. There's no telling how many hourglasses it's been, how many wrong turns I've taken, what new monsters await.

So when I hear the sound of weeping, my first instinct is to turn and run the other direction. I may not be from the Grottos, but I remember the tales from my maman's book well enough—the way ghouls can imitate the sound of a human child, the way mind and matter can be manipulated. But my mind flashes back to Kata, her lifeless body in the back room of the candle shop. What kind of queen walks away from suffering?

I round the corner and find Cesarine sprawled out across the sand, bathed in blood. Whimpering, so small in the huge tunnel, she looks like a child. She practically is one, I suddenly remember. How has this tournament made me forget what a child is?

"Maman..." she whispers. Her voice sounds like water dripping in a well. My heart wrenches.

I have dedicated my purpose to protecting Belles, and she is not one.

Still, I reach for the medicines in the sand-colored bag. I strip her of the ridiculous layers of fabric they gave us to craft a uniform. One of the vials in my bag is a rinse, and I flush all the wounds I can see. Most of them are scrapes; some deeper gashes.

I can't help but think I could use my arcana to heal her. *But you have medicine*, I tell myself, thinking of Charlotte and her cabinet. They wanted to keep me out of the tournament because of the goddess's "gifts." But what about my other gifts? The ones I gave myself?

I will win this tournament, and no matter how I win it, it will be because of me.

I crouch, cleaning and binding Cesarine's wounds, making sure the worst one by her collarbone is clean and dry. Her eyes flutter open.

"Water," she whispers.

Her bag is strewn several feet away. I retrieve it, then withdraw the canteen, pressing it to her lips. She drinks deeply, sputters, lies back. I take a long drink as well, then nearly drop the canteen when Cesarine's open palm cracks across my cheek.

"That's *mine*," she croaks.

My anger rises. She's so close, so helpless. I could kill her right here. I put the cap back on the canteen and drop it to the sand, flexing my fingers, considering.

Her eyes widen.

"I'm sorry," she says, squeezing her eyes shut. "I'm sorry."

I reach for her bag—inside, dried strips of some kind of food. I eat, staring at her, daring her to speak. When her hand reaches for some, I allow it.

"I was so close," she says. "I could hear their voices. I was hidden in the sand—I saw their maps. Blais and Estelle. I know the way now. But the rocks started falling and they ran, and I had to run, too. Then I ran right into it. That giant. Its one eye."

"You're alive, though," I say, still surprised by that fact.

"I wedged myself under some boulders," she says. She takes a deep breath and whimpers from the pain. "But then it started picking them up. It got me here." She points at her clavicle. "And then it stopped. And the giant was fighting something, something that looked like snakes. . . ."

"Worms," I say.

"I got away," she says. "But I'm just so tired, and everything hurts...."

"You need to rest," I say matter-of-factly. "None of your wounds are bad. You're just exhausted."

"I can't rest here," she moans.

"Probably not."

"There's another cavern that way," she says, pointing behind us. "That's where they were headed. There's water there."

I frown, thinking about sharing space with Estelle and Blais. I don't want to be near *anyone*, but perhaps it's better to be close and know where they are than staying in the dark and wondering.

I have no idea where Violetta is.

"How far?"

"An hourglass."

"I'll help you." I sigh.

And I do. I carry both the sand-colored bags and their remaining supplies while Cesarine leans against my shoulder muttering on and on angrily, wondering how any of these trials are truly showcasing what it means to be a queen. She limps along, and I barely notice her weight. She's brave for starting the fights, I think. But when is bravery stupidity?

I know we've arrived when I hear Blais's laugh. It's high and melodious, and it might be pleasant if it didn't always come with a smirk.

When Cesarine and I limp into the small cavern, the laugh is cut abruptly short.

"Look who's here!" Blais says in the tone of a host. "Make yourself comfortable. If possible," she sneers.

I decide spontaneously to limp along with Cesarine. Let Blais underestimate me—think we're both wounded.

The two of us collapse on a flat boulder, Cesarine whimpering, refusing to look at Blais and Estelle. *Toughen up*, I want to tell her. But this isn't the place for advice.

"Did you see the worms?" Estelle calls. "I captured one, see?" She holds up a jar. Inside, a small worms writhes and sticks against the glass. I shudder, it reminding me of all those sangsues hanging on to the sides of pretty porcelain bowls, ready to reset my arcana.

"They leave nothing but bones," I say.

Blais grins. "My kind of creature. When I'm queen, perhaps I will bring some of them to the imperial isle. I could use them in the Rose. The perfect torture instrument."

I stare at the sandy floor so she doesn't see the look on my face. I would love to put my hands around her neck.

"When *you're* queen?" Estelle says petulantly. "My family is already of the royal house."

I glance at Blais just in time to see a look of hot anger cross her face.

"Interesting," Blais says. "I wonder if the kingdom feels the same way."

"Didn't you see the newsies?" Estelle sniffs haughtily.

"They endorse me. They say I have the template of a natural queen."

"Is that so?" says Blais. I dart my eyes between the two of them. Cesarine is focused on her own pain, but I know what I hear—danger.

In a flash, Blais breaks the jar against the rock and flings its contents at Estelle. The blood and screaming are immediate—shards slice Estelle's face as the single worm thrashes its dry wrinkled body against her skin. I don't remember standing up, but my whole body is poised either for fight or flight or something in between. My heart feels throttled as I watch Estelle shriek and claw at her face.

"So much for that natural template!" Blais howls. Cesarine looks on in horror, her hand pressed against her chest.

Estelle gets the worm off and flings it against the wall. It makes a sickening sound, then falls to the sand. We all think it's dead until it starts pulsing, growing, and making its way across the floor, headed for me and Cesarine.

I don't wait. I pick up the largest stone I can handle, then stride toward the worm, dropping it like an anchor right on top. Maroon blood bursts in all directions, dotting my boots and the wall.

"Good aim," Blais says, sitting primly upright. Estelle stops screaming, and her eyes widen as she clasps her hands over the wound on her cheek, the blood running down between her fingers.

"One little worm," Blais says scornfully.

"She's in shock," I say quietly. "She needs medicine."

"She still has hers," Blais says dismissively. She tosses one of the bags in Estelle's direction.

Estelle doesn't move away, even when I come close. Taking the medicine from her bag, I gently pull her hand down away from her wound. The mouth of the worm has left purple blisters all along the edges, and the blood bubbles.

As I rinse the wound, black flecks pour out—something the worm left behind. For all I know, it's poison. She might not last the night. I glance over at Cesarine. She lies with her eyes half-open. Blais kneels at a small nearby pool. She fills her canteen, her face calm. Beyond them, I think I see Quentin's face, blending in with the sand. He's both there and not there. The look on his face is soft—too soft for me right now. When I'm done with Estelle, the bandage winds around her skull and bulges at her cheek like a white egg.

I return to Cesarine, take my bag, and move off the sand onto another rock. *You can sleep,* I tell myself. *But not too deeply because you must keep watch.*

Suddenly, I wonder if this is how a queen always has to sleep.

TWENTY-FIVE

I startle awake, unable to breathe. Something squeezes my throat, thin and slick, and part of it trails down my chest, choking me. I reach for my knife. My fingers graze empty space against my hip. Someone has taken it.

I roll down off the smooth rock, flailing, gasping. The thing around my neck tightens. I try to get my fingers under it, but it's pressed too deeply against my skin. I feel my skin start to burn and threaten to rip open.

As I stagger back and forth, still clawing, Quentin appears. He has the same soft, curious look on his face— but this time, it is etched with sadness. As he stands with his arms at his sides, I try to choke out, *Help me*. But he only shakes his head. I am beginning to lose vision.

Then I see the knife at his hip. He stares across the cavern quickly, then shifts sideways, one arm angled slightly behind his body. It leaves the knife free and clear.

I lunge at him, almost knocking him over. I yank the knife from his hip and fall against the rock. *Be calm, Edel,* I tell myself. *Be calm.* I try to control my hands, but calm isn't a choice. My body is overriding my brain. If I could just breathe . . .

Then, as my maman taught me, I relax, will myself to believe this isn't happening to me. My fingers comb over the thing, trying to identify it by touch. Is it a wire, a rope, or something worse? My brain can't figure it out, and I start coughing. I bring the edge of the knife to my neck. I slip the tip under the rope-like item. I wince, feeling the blade bite in, but I can't cut it without almost cutting skin. I take a deep breath and do it anyway.

As I hear whatever it is snap, air rushes into my lungs like a gale. I take great heaving breaths.

I glance at the ground. It wasn't a rope. It was a ribbon. It glitters in the sand, silver and shiny, then twitches. I've seen them at court: enchanted ribbons that can slither through hair like a snake. And apparently squeeze like one, too. But they're only supposed to ensure hair buns stay in place.

My vision gradually clears, but my head is pounding. Blais and Estelle are gone. So is Cesarine. One of them—probably Blais—set the ribbon on me and slunk off into the shadows, headed back to the surface. I pat my chest, where my piece of map is still rolled up safely. I wonder if they looked for it, or if their focus was killing me.

Would I count as dead if I never made it up?

I realize this isn't like the labyrinth in the sky. That was just a matter of surviving. This is a matter of getting out first.

"You're alive," Quentin says.

"Yes," I say, pulling myself to my feet. "Somehow."

He holds out his hand for his knife, but I fix it at my hip.

"This is mine now." I shrug. He raises his eyebrow and almost laughs. So do I.

"Careful with that," he says, looking mysterious. "Not your ordinary knife."

"I'm not an ordinary girl."

I aim for the big tunnel on the other side of the cavern. I pause to drink my fill at the pool of clear water, then begin to walk. Cesarine was right about there being water here, which I think means I'm close to the basin Violetta pointed to.

"Breathing will be hard tomorrow," Quentin says, falling into step beside me. "Your throat will be bruised."

"Perhaps I'll be dead tomorrow."

"You don't want to die down here," he says. "Dead flesh but living soul? Wandering the passages?"

"Yes, I've heard the stories."

"You don't believe them?"

I twist my mouth to the side. "Yesterday I would have said no. Today . . . well, I've seen quite a lot."

"Well, you don't have the believe that one," he says with a grin. "It's made-up."

I gape, pausing. "So, you were what, teasing me just now?" I can't help it—I laugh so loudly it echoes up and down the tunnel.

"You're awful," I say.

As we walk, neither of us leads. I let my feet guide me, making my way through the almost-dark sand coating every inch of my skin. Quentin never seems to sink into the sand— he floats along its surface.

"How old were you when you first came down here?" I ask.

"I was born in these caves," he says. "All my family was. Female lions find an isolated place to give birth. So do our mothers. I had groundsight before I saw the world aboveground."

"Were you happy down here?" I ask, thinking of my own childhood.

"I can barely remember," he says. "Being part of an immortal family is strange."

I consider. "So, are you hundreds of years old? Thousands?"

"It's complicated. You and I exist on two different units of measure." I glance over at him, and he clarifies: "I am many years older than you, but time works differently for people like me. My childhood was longer than yours."

"I see," I say, frowning. "I think."

"Belles have very short childhoods, don't they?"

I shoot him a look. "Not many people know that."

"I wasn't sure if it was true or not. It sounds like it is."

"Yes," I say. "It's different for us. But I don't think it was always this way. I'm still sorting out truth from lies."

"I know how that feels," he says, shaking his head. "Sometimes I wonder if my ancestors cheated Death or merely made a deal."

"Does it matter? If the outcome is the same?"

"The details always matter," he says. "Don't they? A deal has terms. I never know what the terms are."

"Can't you just ask?"

He gives me a wry look, enough to make me laugh again.

"You don't just ask the family Arnoux for information. In my line, information is dragon's treasure."

"Meaning there's a lot of it?"

He rolls his eyes. "Meaning it's closely guarded."

We walk in silence for a while.

"Binding the wounds of someone who wants to kill you is very brave."

"Or very stupid."

"Sometimes they're the same thing."

Silence settles over us again, and then he adds: "I wanted to help you."

"You did."

"I didn't. Not the way I would have." He pauses. "There is honor in the way you move through the world, including these caves."

I'm grateful for the dimness, because there are tears in my eyes and I don't know why. Maybe it's the exhaustion? Maybe it's the fact that these challenges are more than I anticipated? Maybe it's because I miss my sisters—and Gaelle—so deeply that I'm bone weary? Maybe it's because no one has said that to me before? We walk in silence for a long time—I don't trust my voice to speak. Instead, we watch sand bats flutter before us, and a few smaller sand worms, pulsing along alone without a mass. I try not to shudder.

"Do some travel alone?" I ask eventually.

"Until they find a swarm. We send wormers down here to break up the big ones—if they get too big, they come aboveground."

"A whole world below our feet that we know nothing of," I murmur. A whole new monster to worry about.

Then the ground seems to fall out from under me, sliding down into darkness that groundsight can't penetrate. It's not a straight drop, but I'm sliding fast—I flail desperately, trying to find a hold. Just in time, my foot braces me against a narrow shelf of rock.

"Gods," I gasp. I look down. Below me is nothing.

"It's an earth vent," Quentin says from above. "Don't lose your grip. The fall will last several hourglasses." His voice is so calm. I strain to look up at him where he crouches above on the path. He could reach one arm and help me to safety.

I know he won't. I know he can't.

"Hourglasses. How many?" I shout. My swollen throat is already sore. My feet are firm, but my grasp on the rock feels sandy and loose.

Quentin's eyes are sad. He presses his knuckles together, jaw tight.

"I cannot help you, Edel," he says. "But you are strong and courageous. You can make the climb."

I fling one arm up for a hold I can't quite reach, then the other. "I . . . can't," I mutter, adjusting my grip.

"You'll die," he says. "And you have work to do up there."

We lock eyes. The emptiness beneath me is nothing compared to the emptiness I feel when I think of Blais or Estelle— or even Cesarine—on the throne. What will happen to the Belles?

I may not become queen. But I must at least make it home. I promised my sisters. I promised Gaelle. I promised myself.

I dig my fingers into the sand, feel it fill up the space under my nails. It hurts. If we were higher up, there would be roots. Here there is only sand and rock, sand and rock.

I flex my muscles, pushing with my one foot. A couple inches higher.

"You don't need me," Quentin says.

I heave myself up from the vent and feel like a cork being pried from a bottle, then lie panting on the ground, barely able to move. Quentin backs quickly away, all the way to the wall. He wants to help. I can feel the need rolling off him like a scent.

I drag myself to my knees, then to my feet. He goes on watching me. My fingers bleed. But I'm alive. Again.

"I don't think this tournament deserves you," Quentin says softly, sitting beside me.

I close my eyes and then kiss him.

TWENTY-
SIX

"You're warmer than anyone I've ever touched." Quentin eyes me closely.

"I'm the only Belle you've ever touched," I whisper.

Quentin's face turns to sand, then falls away. In a moment, he's gone—there aren't even footsteps.

"See you later," I say to the air. I walk carefully, disappointed that Quentin's pleasant company is gone, but also relieved—I need to focus and probably rethink what I've just done, kissing him. I didn't think that through and it's probably against the rules. I step carefully around the vent—even now that I know it's there, the sand and shadow blend in perfect camouflage. I look at what almost swallowed me. Endless nothing. I wonder what would have happened if Quentin had fallen in. Can someone who serves the Goddess of Death die?

I hear whispering.

I pause, listening intently. It sounds like wind blowing sand, far off. Ahead, the tunnel is widening. The whispering is at my back, louder now. There's no wind underground, is there? A question I will ask Quentin when I see him next. I don't need Violetta or the map to confirm it—this is the basin. It must be.

I see Cesarine first. She's at the edge of another tunnel, peering across the basin. It's shallower than I thought. Her bandages are brown with dust. I follow her eyes, and I find Blais and Estelle. They are no longer together. Blais is climbing a rocky outcrop, and Estelle sits at the edge of a tunnel, her legs hanging over. Her face is still bandaged, and her shoulders are slumped. She looks defeated.

I don't see Violetta anywhere.

"Blais," I call. The cavern makes my voice enormous. "How's it looking down there?"

She turns, sees Cesarine, then me. I watch with satisfaction as she jumps and trips. If only she tripped in.

"Well, well, well," she calls back. Her voice lacks its usual bite. She goes back to climbing, getting closer to rim of the basin.

"Do you hear that?" Cesarine calls to us.

The whispering again. It's louder than it was last time— impossible to ignore. I look over my shoulder, searching. Something far off in the dark is moving. I can't make it out. But if I've learned nothing else in the caves, I've learned one doesn't wait and see.

I move.

I'm lucky: the area down into the basin is mostly sand and gravel, nothing as rocky as what Blais is struggling up. I wrap the sack around my hands to protect them from sharp rocks. Not for the first time, I'm glad I had the sense to fashion a uniform with pants.

The sound is no longer a whisper. It's turning into a roar.

I pause, panting. Blais has frozen, too—she hears it. We all hear it. But we don't know where it's coming from. Or how to get out of the way.

Is this Violetta's trap? I suddenly wonder. But then why wouldn't she have let the worms kill me?

The water comes all at once—like a hand the size of a mountain reached down and turned the tap. It booms from every tunnel, deafening me for a heartbeat, exactly the time it takes to grab Cesarine on its way down. Estelle is already gone. The roar grows louder. I think I catch sight of Blais being pulled toward the center.

Then I'm swept down into the deep.

TWENTY-
SEVEN

There's no point in swimming, in pushing against the tide. There is no tide. There is only chaos, water throwing itself against itself. It rolls me in circle after circle—I feel like the moon going around the earth. Drowning, I realize, feels almost peaceful. *If Quentin is watching*, I think, *he must be very sad*. And I thank the gods that Gaelle isn't here to see.

But someone is.

As the water spins me in its dark cocoon, light comes from below. And I see my maman's face.

At the bottom of the maelstrom, her smile is the rising sun over gentle waters. With her float Valerie and Kata, and all the Belles I've lost. Their hair and bodies sway as their faces call to me in the glowing darkness. I stop going against the tide. The water is helping me, I realize: helping me down toward those I love. I close my eyes.

My chest feels tight. My throat constricts. Just like the ribbon around my neck.

And I realize this feeling isn't peace, even if it has my mother's face.

This is death.

My eyes snap open. With my eyes truly open, it is as dark as the bottom of the world. And I see the silver, drifting form of Violetta, a fish down in the depths. She doesn't swim. She doesn't move.

This is where she was. An emptiness swells inside me.

I strike out with my arms and legs. There's no sense in going up against the pull. Instead I swim sideways, across the roiling spiral. My body is too tiny to break its pattern, but I am made of powerful material. I swim away from my mother and away from the dead.

When I break through the surface, the whirlpool has quieted to placid waters. My ears still ring and churn as if the maelstrom is inside my head. Finally, it stops, and I only hear one sound: the dip and slap of oars.

A boat. It skims across the stillness of the basin toward me.

A skeleton holds the rudder. Alongside is Quentin, eyes as sad as ever. As the skeleton stares down at me, I think how Quentin always jokes aboveground, out of the caves. I see why now.

I hear coughing—Blais. Estelle. And, incredibly, Cesarine. Inside the boat, the three of them shiver and retch.

"I cannot help you," Quentin says, but I just shake my head. I use the last of my strength to haul myself inside.

"This is the Ship of the Dead, on the Goddess's river," says the skeleton as it steers the boat into a black archway that opens like a yawn. "You are alive. Rest."

TWENTY-EIGHT

In an unspoken truce, we all sleep, lulled by the sway of the boat, the bends of the Goddess's river. It goes on and on, and I lose all sense of direction. The gentle jostling still makes me nauseous, but I try to focus on sleep despite it. When I wake, the only thing I can sense is Quentin nearby, dry and hot. He would say like the sand. To me, he smells like the sun.

"Is Violetta dead?" Cesarine asks. Her voice sounds like she's still underwater: weak and soggy.

"Yes," I answer.

"Good," Blais says.

I'm too tired to curse her, even after my sleep.

I don't notice right away when the boat pushes up against gritty sand. The river goes on lapping against us, rocking us gently.

"There are four of you left," Quentin says. "You must

decide among yourselves which two will leave this place and which two will stay."

He nods up at the ceiling. "Now it is midnight. At dawn, two doorways will open. Only one person may pass through each. If you attempt to follow another, you will be delivered directly to the Goddess."

He looks at us all. "Here, the future queen will find wisdom," he says with finality.

When the skeleton orders us onto the sand, I'm the first to go. My legs shake on solid ground. Cesarine falls. I don't bother helping her up. My bag is gone, I notice. Estelle is the only one that still has hers. My body yearns for food. But dawn is only six hourglasses away. I can eat at Gravier Palace.

If I make it.

When I make it.

The boat disappears into the blackness. The ceiling seems as far as the sky. At dawn, it will open and two of us will leave.

I can hear by Estelle's ragged breathing that she's not doing well. I meant to ask Quentin about the worm, whether it's poisonous. I'm not concerned about Cesarine. Blais sits far in the periphery, leaning against the wall. By the way her shoulders hunch, I would bet that her ribs are cracked.

"I'm not dying here," Blais says, her voice ragged but strong.

"You can all die," Cesarine says. "I'll go up alone."

Estelle doesn't speak. I have nothing to say. I stare at the beds of stalagmites that ring this wide stretch of grainy rock. We are all silent as sand.

I'm in a dream garden, barefoot in the soil. I smell the grapes that hang all around me and pause to twist my finger around a ripe bunch, feeling its gentle green grip. Somewhere nearby I can hear Camille laughing, and Gaelle, too.

No more sands, no more caves. Only sky and more sky, and rolling mounds of grass.

Edel, I tell myself. *Wake up. EDEL. WAKE. UP.*

The snake is curled asleep on my chest. A length of its body drapes down, encircling my fingers and wrist. Like a grapevine. The vine I was twisting in my dream.

With our home surrounded by gardens, Du Barry had taught us all the signs of snakes. Some liked to mimic their more dangerous sisters. Some were as dangerous as they looked. This one is smooth and golden—like all the creatures here, the color of ivory and sand. Its scales are pearls. It shifts only slightly when I breathe, enough to reveal the red bands of pigment on its long belly.

I know those red rings. One bite and I'm dead.

I turn my head a fraction, holding my breath. Estelle is sprawled ten paces away, her face turned toward me. Poison distorts her features, and her lips and throat are hideously swollen, her skin bruised, like rotten dough. Two thin lines of blood run down her neck. The bite.

Did this snake find Estelle? Or did someone lower it gently on her sleeping form?

Like a flash, I remember Cesarine at the ball. There, she had grinned and kissed her serpents. Had she found this one? Or brought it with her on the journey? Either way, I underestimated her.

But Cesarine doesn't know about Belles—how the Goddess put the sun in our bodies to keep the arcana warm, like an egg. Even now, I can feel it under my skin, ready and roiling. I could stop the snake's heart.

But I won't.

Gently, as if beginning beauty work, I lift the pale snake, its heavy tail unlooping from around my fingers, relaxed. Without knowing why, I hum a melody. It's not until I'm placing the snake on the soft warm sand that I realize the melody is the lullaby my maman used to sing to me. It slithers away as if uninterested in me any longer.

I stand and look at Estelle.

"She's dead," Blais calls. She's crouched over by the river, calm as always.

Cesarine sits in the shadow of a boulder, her knees curled to her chest. She has survived time and time again when she shouldn't have. Bravery or stupidity, I can't be sure.

Does that make her a queen?

I stride toward her. Her eyes widen as I get closer, and then she scrambles to her feet.

"Waited until I was asleep?" I say, livid. "Coward. Don't you know how to fight?"

"A queen doesn't need to know how to fight," she snaps, scrambling away from me. "Strategy is everything."

"Violence has nothing to do with strategy," I rage. "Haven't you been paying attention? There is only chaos!"

"A queen masters chaos," she spits. Her eyes are on fire. "Including those who cause it."

"There will be no mastering me!" I roar.

She stumbles, then flings herself forward, shoving me back. "Where did you find that knife?" she screams.

"The ribbon," I say. "You? You used the ribbon?"

"You thought it was Blais?" Cesarine says. "Of course you did. Another mark of a queen: let them underestimate you."

I jerk my head toward Blais, who has the audacity to look impressed. I don't tell Cesarine that she's right. That I underestimated her—felt sorry for her, even.

"I helped you," I said. "I bound your wounds."

Cesarine lifts her chin. She looks just like Blais now: haughty, proud. "Assisting the queen is the only role for a Belle," she says.

Anger flares inside me. I throw all my weight forward into my hands, all my strength, all my anger. I shove her the way I would the whole world if I could.

She flies backward, her face haughty until she falls. The bed of stalagmites pierces her, stabs her body, protrudes through her chest, now dripping red. Her head jerks forward, trying to look down at her mangled body. Blood chokes out around the sharp stones.

I can still feel the warmth of her body against my hands. The shock of it makes my heart skip. What have I done?

"I...I..." A dizzying ache fills me.

"Just us two," Blais says. She doesn't sound proud or sad. She simply is waiting for the doors to open. When they do—one and then two—we each climb our rope ladder in silence.

I hadn't meant to kill Cesarine.

I add my name to the list of people who should never be queen.

I am a murderer now.

TWENTY-NINE

Encerclant caws outside my bedroom window in Gravier Palace from her perch on the balcony railing. She begins to clean her dark feathers. I watch her from my bed, through a crack in the curtains, wondering if she's just returned from leading the spirits of Cesarine, Estelle, and Violetta to the Goddess's own cave.

I would have joined them if not for Violetta. And for Quentin, though I won't say it out loud.

Quentin didn't help me, he said. But how does the Goddess of Death define help? He didn't offer his knife, but he showed it. He didn't pull me out of the vent with his body, but he did with his words.

The kind of distinction to make if one is a queen, I think.

But my fire to win has gone out. A just queen wouldn't do what I did to Cesarine. Every time I close my eyes, I see her fall. I feel myself shove her. I feel that rage all over again.

Watching Encerclant, I think a just queen wouldn't be in this tournament at all.

The Beauty Trials aside, who am I really? I'm lying in bed when I should be figuring out where the missing Belles are.

Up, Edel. I throw my legs over the edge of the bed, haul myself out, and throw open the balcony doors. Aches surge through my body.

Encerclant lifts her wings and swoops in, startling me. She jumps from bedpost to dressing table as if inspecting the place. Her beautiful wings catch the night-lantern light.

"Do you have a message for me?" I ask her. "Like the stories used to say?"

She caws in response.

"She only sings the songs of Death" comes Quentin's voice from the balcony. "May I come in?"

A cool breeze rustles the folds of my nightgown, and I pull a robe close around me. The windy months have an icy tail. "If you must."

"Catching up on sleep?" he asks.

"Have you?"

"I don't sleep."

He settles himself in a chair by the hearth and gestures at the seat across from him for me to join. There's no fire, but he stares into the fireplace anyway. Encerclant flies over to perch on the back of his chair, as if to protect him.

I can't imagine him as a little boy. He's all hard angles and rough edges.

"What's it like being a half-dead boy kissed by the Goddess of Death?" I say, quoting one description in the newsies.

"I thought I explained. Unclear whether my family made a deal or merely got away. Either way, I am not half-dead. I am . . . not killable. Except by Death herself."

So that answers my question about the vent.

As if on cue, Encerclant lifts her wings and flies back out to the balcony. Quentin rises to follow—I wonder if it's magic that binds them together or duty. My heart sinks a little, watching him go.

But then he turns back to me. "Are you coming?"

"Well, we never did get an official tour," I say.

"You can almost see the entrance to the Grottos if you squint," he says as we stand on the balcony, pointing to the left. "So many sailors miss it because they're not paying attention."

"I'd like to miss it for the rest of my life."

He turns and watches Encerclant sailing over the palace grounds. At least Lady Angéle doesn't restrict us outdoors.

"This place is bigger than it looks, and Encerclant seems to love being out of the Grottos."

"Some of these pavilions house courtier families from the south—special guests of Lady Angéle—and a few other princes and princesses of the blood who don't want apartments inside the main palace in Trianon."

"Must be nice to have options," I say pointedly.

"I suppose." He walks ahead down the balcony. "A

fortress wall guards the perimeter. There are four guard tur- rets, and two small gate entrances, and two main ones." He pauses. "Can I show you my favorite place?"

I've never had a favorite place.

"Unless you're busy . . . but you don't seem to be."

"Give me a few minutes." I step back inside to put on a proper dress. Then we walk down the main palace stair- case, passing servants and attendants, ignoring their curious glances. He gestures, and servants hold open an imperial rickshaw's purple brocade and help me inside.

"Where are we going?" I peek through a small window to the front of the rickshaw. Two imperial runners take their places. Both have long, single braids, interlaced with gray. Their graying hands are a stark contrast to the black lacquer of the carriage handles.

"The God of Fortune's Temple. On the outer grounds of Gravier Palace."

The rickshaw runners' braids slap their backs as we race across the Golden Water Bridges. My teeth chatter from the cobblestones. The palace gates open, and we zip through gar- den mazes and topiary, past fields of jasmine. It's been a full day since Blais and I climbed from the sandy shadows of the caves, and the world still feels too bright, too loud.

When the rickshaw parks at the white-roofed temple, Quentin helps me down. My legs still vibrate with the motion and my head feels light.

"We can't go inside at this late hour," he says. "But we can walk the Gardens of Fate."

They spread out before us, a maze of orange and red-gold flowers, fit together in perfect arrangements that soar over our heads. I take in the view beside him. Each pavilion and temple and shrub, the river and late-night rickshaws, and guards at their posts. We are both alone and exposed. Only three night-lanterns drift over us.

This, they say, is a place that could end up changing our fates.

We meander along the gravel paths in perfect silence, dipping in and out of the shade. Peace, just for one moment. Gazing into a fountain of koi fish, Quentin lingers. "Want to play?" I find him lifting a box of Four Winds tiles from the stone shelving that surrounds the pond.

I arch one of my eyebrows, looking forbidding.

"Don't want to take the risk?" he says, unintimidated.

A voice inside tells me to turn around. Go back to the Gravier Palace, back to my bedchamber and my bed. Instead, I laugh. My feet move toward him. I remember his kiss in the caves, smooth and dry, before he disappeared.

"Are you afraid of me?" he says, closing the distance between us.

"I'm not afraid of anyone." I turn away from him.

He pulls me around by the waist. The warmth of his fingertips seeps through my dress. His scent wraps around me, and I inhale. I let him take my hand. "Your skin really is warmer than other girls'."

Despite myself, I think of Cesarine's snake in the caves. My heart sinks, despite the welcome nearness of Quentin.

"Do you like being a Belle?"

The question surprises me. I let it roll around in my head.

"I hated all the preparation and all the rules and not being able to do what I wanted to do."

"If you win the Trials, you'll have even more people telling you what to do."

"But I'll be a queen," I reply, the word thick and foreign on my tongue.

"What will you do about the Belles and beauty work—and this whole kingdom's obsession with it?"

Here is a question I can answer. "I would have Orléansian scientists study the Gris affliction—see if there's a way to use medicines to help manage it. I was getting somewhere with an elixir before this ridiculous tournament was announced. A tincture that bonds with a person, attached to the tiny pieces that make them who they are."

He nods with approval. "Not what I would do, but that might work."

I scoff. "And what would you do, since you know so much about it?"

"I would leave," he says simply. "If there are no Belles, there's no issue. People would have to live with their gray."

"That would mean—"

"Yes." He finally touches me. Fingertips drift over my forehead, my cheeks and lips. "I don't understand why I like you. I shouldn't like you."

"You're the insufferable one," I say.

His lips press into mine. Soft at first, then harder. My skin warms, and my heart flutters. All my worries drift off like post-balloons, and all I want to feel is this, over and over again.

But Gaelle's face appears in my mind. I pull away, catching my breath. This has started to feel like a betrayal, and I can't make sense of the weird tug I feel in both directions. What is happening between me and Gaelle—and is it real? What is happening between me and Quentin—can it even be real?

"We shouldn't," he says.

"I know," I say, still breathless.

The crunch of footsteps interrupts us. "Lady Edel!" an attendant calls. "Urgent mail." The young girl holds a post-balloon—it bears the violet House of Fortunes insignia.

Gaelle.

She hands it to me, and I take it, my hands wobbly with guilt and confusion. I scramble to open it, reading so fast my eyes almost can't make sense of the words.

Dear E,

I'm at a beauty party right now, and I just discovered something so shocking. They have several Belles here and they're collecting their blood in a vault. They're locked in there.

This woman has so much stored up. The address is on the back of this letter.

Come in disguise.

Love,

Gaelle

 # THIRTY

This time, I refuse to let Quentin accompany me.

"It could be dangerous," he says, standing just close enough to my door to keep it from closing.

"More dangerous than the caves?" I snap, then sigh when he raises an eyebrow. The truth is, I wouldn't mind him coming...if it wasn't for Gaelle. Already I wish I had something to freshen my breath—I'm afraid she'll be able to smell his kiss on me. She has said we're best friends. Still, this feels like I betrayed her.

"I must go," I say, and give him a light push out into the corridor. No sooner does the door close than I rush to my wardrobe, grabbing the same veil I wore to St. Nanterre. My hands tremble. *Blood vaults.* What will I find at this "beauty party"? Another dead Belle? Or worse? I'm already out of breath, sweat pooling in the long sleeves of my dress and in the small of my back.

I snatch Quentin's knife from the drawer where I stowed it when I returned from the caves.

As I sweep out, I startle the two guards closest to my chamber. They look alarmed at my sudden appearance and watch as I walk toward the arching front doors of Gravier Palace. When I request a carriage, the doorman looks reluctant. I tell him the queen has sent me on Belle business.

"It has nothing to do with the tournament," I assure him, smiling sweetly. "The next trial isn't until tomorrow. A girl needs a little private time."

He blushes and calls the carriage. The sky growls overhead with the threat of rain. A prickle races across my skin.

As the carriage rumbles down the streets, mansions and petit-palaces blur together, sparkling like multicolored macarons lined up in the patisserie stalls in the bazaar. Some have golden spires, others glittering arches and buttresses. Glass domes catch the dying moonlight. Delicate, rich, expensive.

This mansion is all stone and turrets, winding and curving, and it sits on a three-acre plot upon a man-made hill. It's not the fanciest estate I've seen, but it must be home to an important family. I drape the veil over my face in preparation to use a glamour, and instruct the coach to wait around the corner, in case I need to make an abrupt exit. As I arrive on foot, the watchman at the gate looks at me warily.

"Useless carriage," I grumble. "How late am I? Let me in quickly before she thinks me rude!"

It's just women here tonight, and the center of the room is bare except for thick carpets. The vast interior is like countless others in the Aristocratic Quartier—endless red velvet settees for people to chat, carved tables of teak and orange blossom wood, flowers covering every possible surface: Belle-roses and jasmine, ubiquitous and heady with their rich scent. The merchant insignias are sparkling.

Around thirty ladies sit cross-legged on the carpets in all their finery, sipping on Belle-rose tea and reviewing beauty boards. A servant pushes around a cart overflowing with tarts and treats. They don't notice me slip in, most of them already drunk. I note with relief that some of them wear veils to hide the gray. They are also terribly thin, with bony hands holding their teacups, and collarbones like curtain rods. It's because they're spending all their money on illegal beauty work.

These are Blais's kind of people. I need to be very careful I'm not recognized—I'm not sure what would happen if word got back to her that I was here, but the smirking witch is creative.

"Hopefully all this nonsense will be over soon, ladies," says the woman who must be the host. She sits at the head of the group, elevated on a stack of cushions. "We'll have our queen, and it will all get back to business as usual."

"Feels so good to be *normal*," another says, sprawling backward on a cushion and giggling.

"Suppose the new queen makes fun illegal," one woman hiccups, laughing. "Then what shall we do?"

"She won't be my queen!" the hostess says, her laugh braying.

"We deserve a little treat," one of the veiled women slurs. "It's been so long."

I edge closer to the group. Despite my veil, I'm relieved Gaelle immediately spots me. "Ah, welcome, Bastina!" she calls, raising her voice. "I'm so glad you could make it. I know your gray has been bothering you horribly."

I try to make my voice sound like a Bastina. "The invitation was most welcome, darling. You can't imagine my excitement when I heard the news."

"Are you a merchant?" the hostess slurs, staring.

My cheeks fire up under the veil, and I freeze.

"Oh, you must be *very* drunk, Joseline!" Gaelle laughs loudly. "You've met Bastina!"

Luckily, when servants appear with silver trays holding oil canisters, the guests are distracted. They begin to chatter with excitement. Supposedly, the oil makes beauty work last longer. Servants begin to rub arms and legs, offer me spiced tea. I shoo them away, trying to hold my temper in, and my dread. Where is the blood vault? Are the Belles still alive?

A beauty work table is brought out and set on a bed of pillows. I stare at the tiers of jewel-colored bottles, all their glittering stoppers. I think of my elixir that Charlotte wasn't interested in hearing about, and ball my fists. Her servant carried it off to the queen's quarters—and it probably still sits there, gathering dust. I stare as hard as I can so that I stay rooted to this cushion—so that I don't get up and send the whole display crashing to the floor.

"There's two new facials," Joseline says. "Georgiana dropped them off herself. Guaranteed to keep the gray away for longer. You can watch how they're mixed."

Georgiana Fabry—the mother of that foolish, disgusting boy that held Camille's heart for a moment. If I ever cross his path again, he will get my fist in his eye. But his mother? Hearing her name here makes me feel murderous.

"Do you see why I say there is only one true queen?" the hostess says. "Imprisoned, and still serving her people!"

They must be talking about Sophia.

A woman wheels out a cart, on which she begins to open one slim silver packet at a time, upending spice and then mixing it into a bowl of deep, rust-colored blood. She swirls it into a thick, pungent paste, then packs it into a cone.

I want to scream. I want to froth at the mouth. Even if I have never met her, that blood belongs to one of my sisters.

I'm too nauseated to stay in this room.

The servant cuts the tip of her cone and begins to cover the courtier's face in the bloody paste. I bite my tongue until I taste my own. As if sensing how close my rage is to boiling over, Gaelle stands up casually, then glides past me. "Second floor. Third door on right," she murmurs.

"Oh, Gaelle, have you had your turn?" the host says, pulling her away. "Let's see how you look with this. . . ."

With Joseline occupied, I slip into the hall, then up the stairs. The guards don't even take notice. I am just another drunk and foolish guest in this small palace. The hallway spreads out like a river. Plush cream carpeting masks my footsteps.

I count the doors.

One.

Two.

A guard opens the third door from the inside and steps out into the hallway.

Quickly, I pull down the neckline of my dress, waving as if I am hot. I make sure a little of my brassiere shows.

"What are you doing up here?" he says; then his eyes wander down to the little bit of cleavage. "I was told the tours were finished for the evening."

"I got here late and missed my tour." I make my voice sound breathy and helpless behind the veil. I close the gap between us before the door closes behind him. I wedge my foot in the door to stop it.

"Can you help me?"

The scent of chilled blood escapes the room.

He looks down. It is enough. I pull my dagger from its sheath and stab his shoulder. The feeling of the blade entering his flesh is terrible—but in a blink, there is no flesh. Right before my eyes, the man wrinkles, then crumples into a pile of dry bones and sand.

Not your ordinary knife, Quentin said.

My plan was to wound him, then issue a blow to knock him out cold. Not make him disappear, without even a body to burn. My pulse hammering, I tuck the knife carefully under my cloak. *Gods,* I think. *What magic is this?* I use my foot to scoot the bones into the vault as I enter.

Inside, it feels like I've stepped from the windy season into the cold season. Night-lanterns wash a row of cold-machines in blue. My breath creates little clouds in front of me. I open one of the cold vessels. They're full of vials of blood, marked by the date. The breath feels sucked out of me, my stomach churning with bile and hunger and something I can't quite figure out. I count the machines. There are thirteen.

I follow a door into the next room. It is filled with empty beds surrounded by trays of vials and needles.

A long treatment table cuts through the center. There, a woman lies underneath a lace cloth. Her hair is fashioned into a beautiful Belle-bun. Tubes snake down and around her arms, extending into a massive version of our arcana meter. Red liquid churns in towering, clear vats.

I can't tell if she's alive or dead. I rush to her side and lift the cloth, when a voice stops me.

"What are you doing in here?" a woman asks.

Noelle.

Her one-of-a-kind turquoise eyes are as bright as ever, and they glare at me in suspicion. The one glamour she always maintains to blend in more erasing the amber brown eye color that always connected us as Belle sisters. I haven't seen her since the tournament ball, when she stood arm in arm with Kata, drinking champagne. Now Kata is dead. And Noelle is here.

I yank off my veil. "What have you done to her?" I ask. "And why are you *here*?"

She gasps. "Edel!"

"Explain what is going on here," I say. "Immediately."

"This woman is a former Belle," she says. "I am caring for her."

"No one is a *former* Belle," I snap.

Noelle pulls back the lace covering to reveal the woman's face. Her skin is a collage of colors—gray, white, and shell-beige—and wrinkled like a paper bag. Her lips balloon unnaturally, and all her five eyes have drifted toward the corners of her face.

I lurch back in horror.

"She had been doing illegal beauty work—and has been abused. Her arcana are forever unbalanced. The proteins unable to regenerate to keep her beautiful, or enable her to transform others."

I can't look away, thinking of all the swaying bags of blood in the back room where I found Kata. Noelle walks to the large blood-churning machine. She clicks her fingers on the glass case. "See them?" She points at little floating disks that resemble crescents from a Four Winds game board. "Her blood proteins are sickle-shaped. Attacking one another. The arcana net is broken."

I gaze through the glass. The proteins drift around without purpose or direction. I stare down at the comatose woman. Whether her arcana are balanced or not, she is a Belle to me.

"What did they do to her?" I ask. "What did *you* do to her?"

"She's sedated and comfortable."

"You're *helping* them?"

She shrugs. "I'm safe. Sometimes you have to cooperate."

"Who has been doing this? Who is damaging Belle blood? Is this all for *Sophia*?"

"She didn't listen. She didn't follow your rules. This is the consequence," Noelle says, covering the woman's hideous face. The finality of it plunges me into a familiar grief—my maman, Valerie, Kata. Even Violetta. Belle after Belle, gone.

Noelle looks into my eyes. "I won't let this happen to me."

"They'll do the same thing to you, Noelle. They will set their sights on you as soon as it's convenient." Urgency rises in my voice. "Come back with me to Gravier Palace. We can figure out what to do."

"No," she replies, and it feels like a slap. "Don't you

understand, Edel? I don't want to go back. You've always talked about freedom. *This* is freedom. Choosing to do what I want."

"You shouldn't be here," I say, pleading. "You should be at the teahouse."

I stare at Noelle, feeling empty. "Is she the only one here?"

"Yes."

"Can she ever be fixed?" I ask.

"Never." The word drums through the room, and we're silent for what feels like a full hourglass.

I could kill her for what she has done. But could I kill a Belle? End her life, spill the blood that everyone wants so much?

I feel the desire burning in my heart as brightly as the grief.

No. I turn away. I don't stop by the parlor or seek out Gaelle. I simply walk out into the night. The rain had lulled when I first set out for the mansion, but now it returns with a vengeance. Just as I was beginning to dry off in the cool night air, it comes crashing again, soaking me through.

I rush along, mumbling and frustrated, my head full of Noelle's words: *Freedom means choice.* Why would she want to stay there? Why wouldn't she want to be with her sisters? Is proximity to power really more valuable than those who hold her best interests at heart?

THIRTY-ONE

I weave in and out of the winding streets looking for the carriage. I pass shops and salons—all closed. Posters about the Beauty Trials and current beauty politics freckle glass windows and walls. One catches my eye: WE STAND WITH THE BELLES. There's a spiderweb drawn around its letters. It must be someone sympathetic to the Iron Ladies, and perhaps us. Ordinarily it would lift my spirits. But tonight I am too full of rage and sorrow.

Before these trials, I was never this afraid—not even when we were on the run from Sophia and her madness, before Charlotte's return. Now the whole world feels like it's crumbling. Sinking down into an ocean of my sisters' blood.

I'm so caught up in my thoughts that I don't realize someone is following me until I see bits of their shadow. My skin goes clammy, like someone's too close, breathing down my neck. My hands feel for Quentin's dagger. I never thought I'd want to use it again after watching the guard's flesh turn to sand, but I've just seen vats full of bubbling blood—anything is possible.

I whip around. A young man stands grinning, stark-white teeth against smooth bronzed skin, a tattered shirt over oil-stained old pants, and a battlement jacket with half-worn medals.

It's the cocky grin that gives him away. *"Quentin?"*

He is as dry as ever, as if the sandy shelter of the caves is his own personal umbrella. I feel guilty again in my affection for him. Gaelle has my heart. But there is something about him that makes me fond—he understands the strangeness of being . . . not quite human.

"I saw you leaving your little party, and I thought you'd like to know that Sophia's sentencing came in. . . ." He pauses for dramatic effect. My hearts stops. "She's to be beheaded tomorrow. An invitation arrived for you to attend the execution if you wish."

I freeze, stunned in place.

He hands me a paper bursting with headlines about the news. The rain smears its ink. "This is good news."

"This is *excellent* news," I reply.

"Then why aren't you acting like it?"

I think back to seeing Sophia in that prison cell, so confident, so assured she wouldn't be in there for long.

He rests his hand on my still-drenched shoulder, the

touch of his fingers burning through the thin chiffon of my dress. The flecks of light in his eyes, amber in chocolate, catch me off guard.

"Let's get you back to Gravier."

Quentin waits beyond my dressing divider while I shiver out of my wet clothes and into a dry robe. I come out toweling my hair, hiding a smile at the way he looks at me, widens his eyes, and then looks quickly away.

"You're angry," he says. "That your sister wouldn't join you."

"Of course," I say grimly. "I just don't understand why she could feel safer standing next to the wolf than with the people who want to defeat it."

"An idealist," he says, raising his eyebrows. "Unexpected."

My temper ignites.

"Why is that so unexpected?" I snap. "Everyone is always saying *Edel, calm down.* Maybe I don't need to be less angry. Maybe everyone else needs to be *more* angry."

"I don't disagree with you," he says calmly. "I'm angry all the time."

That surprises me. "About what?" I demand.

"About death as a bargaining chip," he says. "My ancestor cheated death—and now my parents get to do whatever they want? All their decisions go toward making their own lives comfortable."

I stare at the fire.

"You complain about your long life," I say. It feels like the rain has followed me in from the street. "You should be grateful. Some of us are doomed to an abbreviated existence."

"You misunderstand my complaint," he says, raising his voice. I almost flinch, but instead I snap my head in his direction, glaring.

"Get out," I order.

"With pleasure," he replies, already standing.

"And don't forget your knife."

I point at where it lies on the table by the door. He stares at it for a moment as if he might refuse. Then he scoops it up. I expect the door to slam behind him, but it closes as soundlessly as sand through an hourglass.

I'm ready to fling myself on the bed and scream into my pillow, when I notice someone has placed a small box, like a gift, on top.

Something from Gaelle, I think immediately, and reach for it, glad that I threw Quentin out.

But when I open the box, it is not from Gaelle.

It's the bloody mass of an eye, yanked from a socket and dropped directly inside the package in my hands. I gasp so violently I almost choke, and drop the box. The pulpy eye stares up at me from the floor.

Its iris shines bright turquoise.

 # THIRTY-
TWO

Blais and I were given separate carriages for the journey to Trianon. A small mercy. The ride to see Sophia beheaded is long and silent, and the emptiness of the carriage matches the emptiness in my heart. Is Noelle dead? I can only assume she is. I blame Blais. Who else would it be? She must have followed me and, while I walked leisurely back with Quentin in the rain, beaten her and taken her prize.

In Trianon, the protests have resumed. Even without looking out the carriage windows, I can tell that the kingdom is divided—from one side of the road I can hear the calls for Sophia's head, and from the other chants of "One true queen! One true queen!" It's impossible to tell if one side is louder or more numerous than the other. And it doesn't matter, I think. I used to think that if Sophia was dead, all the problems of Orléans would die, too. I see now that what was harvested during her brief time as queen was sown long before she took the throne and will linger long after she loses her head.

I am surprised and pleased to see that it's Adele who opens the door of my carriage. "Are you sure you want to do this?" she says, looking right in my eyes. She has dropped all the deferential tones of an attendant. "Will it do any good to watch one woman die?"

It's as if she read my mind. But torture. Imprisonment. Cruelty. I need to see Sophia eradicated from the world.

"It's something I must do," I answer. Before she helps me out, I hold on to her hand for a moment. "Thank you, Adele."

She nods once, stiffly.

Those invited by the queen are brought behind the stilt-boxes at the Royal Square, hidden from the streets. I wave off assistance as I climb the long, carpeted staircase. I see above me that Blais has already arrived. My eyes burn into her back. I would've taken her for the Sophia-supporter type, but if I've learned anything about her, it's that she's hungry for power. Even if it's for a different reason, she is happy to see the former queen ruled out once and for all.

As I take my seat—far from Blais, who doesn't look my way—I take deep breaths. I can't help but think of Sophia. She must be in shock. She barely said a word at her trial, ignoring her beloved teacup monkey, Singe, even. I imagine all the Belles at Maison Rouge going about their day, ignoring Sophia's death rather than witnessing it. That feels suddenly more wise.

I'm just starting to rise from my seat, when the trumpets blare.

Sophia is dressed in her signature look—blond hair-tower full of jewels and ribbons, milky-white skin dotted with freckles, and the decadent white dress she has chosen to be killed in. Chains loop her wrists like pearl bracelets. Blimps crest overhead, some with newsies and their light-boxes, and others hold guards with massive elongated eye-scopes, watching every movement.

Guards flank her as she moves to the very center of the Royal Square, like a ship across a still sea. In front of the hourglass is a block, and aside it, a ramp for the guillotine. Attendants hold flickering candles and burning incense as she steps up onto it. The few final protestors and their banners are ushered away.

A blanket of eerie silence engulfs the crowd. A few in the court wipe at red-rimmed eyes. There will be no rescue mission for Sophia today. I study the faces in the crowd, recognizing no one. I imagine the faces, living and dead, touched by this woman's life. Sophia's mother. Noelle. Valerie. Camille, who suffered so much.

Then I glimpse a man whose face I know—from where? The Everlasting Rose. The one with the bronze butterflies. Was he there for a rescue mission that day? If so, he failed.

The Minister of Law walks alongside the team of guards towing the guillotine. Behind them, in a grim procession, walks a man holding an ax. I feel like I'm dreaming. I've wanted her dead for so long that I'm overwhelmed by the finality of it all coming true.

"I can't believe Her Majesty is actually doing this," someone says.

No one answers. Our eyes are all on the glinting blade hanging from the guillotine's sturdy crossbar.

Then Charlotte appears. The ministers follow her, solemn as tombstones. The lump in my throat can't be swallowed. It doesn't hit me until this very moment that she has sentenced her sister to die. Her *sister*. I can see, even from this far away, the smoothness of Charlotte's skin, how her features look ironed. I wonder if she'll cry later. If she'll cry now.

I allow my eyes to rest on Sophia. The guards have removed the chains, and she's gazing down at her hands, picking at her fingernails. She sways a little. I wonder if she's drunk on blood. Would I go to my death sober? I don't know.

There is another platform for the speakers. The Minister of Law unrolls a parchment, and his voice rings out over the silent crowd.

"On this day of the windy season, the royal house condemns former queen Sophia of Orléans to death for the crimes of murder, torture, conspiracy, and regicide. Queen Charlotte will now announce the penalty."

I look at Sophia, seeing if she will raise her face now that her sister moves to the voice-trumpet. Even the protestors in the distance go silent.

"Her penalty," Queen Charlotte says slowly, "is death by beheading."

The crowd roars pointlessly. People around me rise to their feet as the guillotine is rolled up the ramp. I keep my seat, eyes roving the Square. Perhaps this is why I came—I thought there would be one more fight. This can't be over. But the guillotine has come to a stop just ahead of Sophia, and she barely acknowledges it, still swaying.

"Kneel," the minister booms. Sophia stands motionless. Attendants move to position her body. She seems as pliable as dough. I expected a wildcat. Still, I can't help but think if she were any other prisoner they wouldn't be handling her nearly so gently.

Around me people weep, shout, pray, cheer. Maybe I am praying, too. I pray for my sisters.

Sophia's neck is angled over the lunette. As it closes around her, my heartbeat thrums in my ears. The blade drops with a screech like an eagle's. The red floods out and soaks through her hair where her head rests on the platform, rocking it almost imperceptibly.

I didn't expect so much blood. But then again, Sophia led a bloody life—no death could be bloodier than hers.

THIRTY-THREE

I'm dreaming of Sophia's blood and how it swept along the ground in rivulets when my attendant wakes me the next day.

"I think you'll be pleased, miss," she tells me conspiratorially. "I'm told that you and the other contestant are traveling to Maison Rouge for the final trial."

I sit straight up in bed. "My home? *Maison Rouge?* Are you sure?"

"I heard the carriage attendants talking," she says, nodding. "I don't know what you'll face, but the location has been revealed."

She may not know what the challenge is, but I feel it in my gut.

This tournament has been a balancing act between the Goddess of Death and the Goddess of Beauty. It only makes sense that the final trial would take us to the place where death and beauty intertwine. The dark forest. Where I played with my sisters. Snuck in on my own when I got older. I found Camille there at times. We were never supposed to be there—Du Barry would drag us out. But how could we stay away from the place where Belles were supposedly from?

Now I know they just didn't want us to know the truth.

And it all makes sense—why the tournament would call me back there now. I refuse to believe that everything happens for a reason. But some things do. A Belle was meant to be in this tournament. And that Belle is me.

Blais and I again are transported in separate carriages. The attendant that rides with me sits by the window, silent, shooting me glances every few seconds.

"Does it feel strange?" she says. "To be going back home for the tournament?"

"No," I answer.

She pauses then finally says, "They say the forest is haunted."

"No more than the caves," I say.

"The Belle graveyard is right there," she says. "Lucky, I guess."

We meet eyes, and hers widen.

"Because you believe I will die," I say flatly.

"N-no, Lady Edel!" she stammers. "I just...I heard...that you draw power from your dead."

"Sounds like cheating to me," I say, raising my eyebrow.

She frowns. "Perhaps. But they say Belles..."

"Who is they?" I say impatiently.

"The newsies," she says quickly. "They say Belles are witches."

"Funny how we were divine when they could control us, and witches when they can't," I say. Suddenly, I feel goose bumps. Camille would nod at this kind of thing. *See? When you control your temper, Edel, you arrive at real insight.*

"I see the ceremony smoke," the attendant says, peering out the window of the carriage. The road has gotten bumpier—the cobblestones of the roads to Maison Rouge. I know every crack by heart. "We must be close."

"Yes," I murmur. "We are."

The attendant was right—the ceremony smoke swirls above us, thick and gray. It makes Maison Rouge look haunted. Standing outside the carriage, I feel like it's been a lifetime since I last stood in front of this place. Things have sharpened—even from here I can see the headstones in the Belle graveyard, the way they look like thumbnails pushing through black soil. The trees remind me of a skeleton about to fall apart.

"Where is everyone?" I hear Blais mutter from several paces away. I am wondering the same thing—the crowds that have gathered for the last two challenges are nowhere to be seen. The air, which is usually filled with the shouting of newsies, is eerily silent. And that's when I notice Quentin's absence, and Encerclant's as well. Impossible that he would forego his duties as Gamekeeper simply because of our argument. Where is he?

"The Gamekeeper has yet to arrive," the Minister of Games announces, looking uncertain. Clearly, I'm not the only one who is confused. "So I will lay out the final trial. You will go into the forest empty-handed. Unlike in the other trials you've faced, the final object—the Goddess's mirror—is inside, waiting for the next queen of Orléans. The competitor who finds the mirror will be crowned." She pauses. "Keep your wits about you as the forest awakens. Only knowing your true self, which a queen must always hold fast to, will ensure your success."

She looks around at the empty grounds one last time for Quentin. As if answering my and Blais's thoughts, she says, "The final trial is competitors only. After Sophia's execution, Queen Charlotte and her cabinet believe it is best to not allow for onlookers."

My heart sinks. I hoped that I could embrace my sisters. I look up and can see the faces of Belles peeking through the curtains. Do they know Noelle is dead? I have no idea where her body ended up— or even if she's truly gone. Mutilated and no doubt tortured. It makes me irrationally angry at Charlotte. She must have known that being this close to Maison Rouge would be hard for me—and now to not even embrace my sisters? She who put so much weight into this tournament—this deadly tournament—can't even be bothered to attend the final event.

Blais wears a small pillbox hat, pinned neatly to her hair. Her expression is casual, and I almost don't blame her—with all the newsies absent, the stakes feel low. Perhaps she thinks this will be a stroll through the greenery. And now, as the minister says, the forest is "awake." It has never been a particularly friendly-looking place, but now it seems to stare back at us, hungry.

I hear Encerclant's caws before I see Quentin. He appears from between the carriages, slightly sandy, as if on a puff of cave grit. It seems like something he would be capable of.

"My apologies," he says to the minister. His face is a storm cloud.

The minister ignores him, too, looking snooty. She motions me and Blais toward the forest.

"Nothing is as it seems," Quentin says loudly. He addresses us both, but his eyes are on me. Blais looks at him curiously, but by now his eyes are on the sky, watching Encerclant circling overhead. I think that all dying things must feel this way, looking up and seeing her.

I grit my teeth and say to myself, *I will not die today*.

"The final trial has begun," Quentin says quietly. "You may enter."

We are so near the edge of the thick trees. We step forward at the same time.

And then Blais is gone.

THIRTY-FOUR

I know Blais and I crossed into the trees at the same moment, but inside the forest, I am utterly alone. Just endless trees, green-black, and night sky. Maison Rouge is gone. Quentin is gone. The minister is gone. I see my breath in the air ahead of me, gray bursts like the smoke ceremony. Once it is out of my mouth, it takes its own shapes: a bird, then the wolf that ends its life with a snap of smoky jaws. I shudder.

Outside it was midday. Now I look up and see the moon.

Find the mirror, I think. *Find the mirror, and then all of this is over.* But where, in this endless black and green? Unlike the caves, where one must at least decide on a tunnel, there is no real choice to make here.

I take a step forward, almost flinching. Sticks and leaves crunch under my feet, but the sound they make isn't normal—instead the crunch is like nests of millions of bird bones.

I wander endlessly, and find no one and nothing. I almost sit down to try to make a plan, but then ahead, I hear a rustling. When I crane to look, there's a person.

A woman stands far off in the trees. She glitters in the moonlight, but when she steps through shadows, the silver flickers. Not a ghost. A person. She walks easily, as if she knows this land like her own.

"Hello!" I call out. I don't know what makes me do it. Outside, I never speak to anyone if I have the choice. But this place unsettles me—makes me feel scraped raw, like after the long baths Du Barry forced us to take as children. Maison Rouge is so close—isn't it?—but feels so far. Part of me wants to abandon this challenge and race inside my home and hole up in my old room. I taste something like desperation on my tongue.

She pauses and turns slightly. I still can't see her face. As I walk toward her, I have the strange sensation that my body has grown without me noticing. That what feels like bones under my feet aren't bird or mouse, but human. I am a monster crushing their remains.

"Can you help me?" I ask, still making my way. Is this what a queen would do? Make alliances?

The girl takes a few slow steps toward me, curious, confused.

"Have you seen a mirror?" I ask.

"A mirror?" the girl calls. We're ten paces apart, and I can't see her face. Shadow and moonlight conspire against me.

"Yes," I say. And what I feel isn't hope, but that bitter desperation. Something clawing at my insides.

"I have it right here, Edel!" she says, and her sudden hoarse laugh stops me in my tracks. "Can't you see?"

She steps out of the shadow and directly into the moonlight, her chin raised high.

I stare at a mirror image of myself. Her face is my face. She has my neck, my shoulders. My arms. My lips, my teeth, my white skin, every detail exactly mine.

Except her smile is wrong. It's the smile of a wolf—all gum, too much teeth. Her nostrils are constricted, as if permanently inhaling. Her eyes are blank.

I turn and run faster than I ever have. The desperation has hatched in my stomach now—it doesn't want to find the mirror; it doesn't want the crown. It wants out. I want out. Out of the tournament, out of this forest. I want to run until I reach Maison Rouge, fling open the door, and hide in my maman's skirts.

Instead, something catches my ankle, and I fall, hard. Mouth full of dirt. Blood between my teeth. I try to stand, but whatever grabbed my ankle still has me. I whip my head around, trying to wrench free.

It's a hand. Reaching out of the ground, skin as white as fungus, coated in pink slime.

"Camille!" I scream. Her name rises out of my mouth as if it's always been there.

"Don't be frightened, Edel! It's our sisters, being born!

Welcome them! The Goddess has delivered them here to die! That is, be born! We die and we die and we die!" a voice calls out. The words echo all around me as if getting tangled up in the trees.

I can't kick out at the hand—something in my body is frozen, heavy with something like grief. *We die and die and die.*

"I will not die today!" I finally pull away, my ankle sliding out from the slime.

I claw to my feet, thorns catching my hands and tearing the soft webbed skin between my fingers. I ignore it, running again. And then I hear more screaming. At first, I think it's my own—my mouth is open like one unending scream.

It's Blais.

She barrels headlong through the forest, snapping through twigs and vines. Walking resolutely after her is another Blais. Somehow the other Blais is keeping up with the running Blais—the stride is so strange and long and ... wrong. I don't know if my doppelgänger is after me the way Blais's is after her—I don't dare look back. I dart away from the hands and the face that looks like mine but isn't.

Everything in this place is wrong. And everywhere I look hands are reaching up through the cold soil.

"It's just you, Edel!" that face screams after me.

But she's wrong. It's not. Blais is real, and I chase after her. We came here empty-handed, as the rules dictated, but we came here together. I feel the death in this place. I feel that it won't let us go, not until the mirror is found. But I don't care about the mirror. I don't care about being queen in this moment. Blais and I can help each other.

Blais is limping, I realize. She barely clears a log in her path, and when she trips on the next one, I've caught up with her. Her doppelgänger roars with laughter, and I don't dare look back at her face. I don't want to see the wrongness there, too.

"Get up!" I shout. "Come on, get up!"

Blais grasps my arm, and I haul her to her feet, and together we take off through the trees, still stumbling.

"I saw something glowing," Blais pants. "That way. Then it started chasing me.... I'm trying to loop around...."

I feverishly look from side to side. I don't see a glow anywhere—no stars break through the canopy. Just night and more night.

"There," she says. "It comes and goes."

She's right. I see it. I look back and catch a glimpse of my doppelgänger—her eyes are impossibly wide. Inhuman. The face is my face, but the eyes are something else. Not even eyes. More like two empty, black pits. And Blais...her doppelgänger isn't a doppelgänger at all. A long lithe body like Blaise, but with the face of a wolf now. Its eyes as red as rubies.

"It's the mirror, I know it," Blais heaves. "I feel it. Don't you feel it?"

My feelings are a mess. I feel terror and deep sadness. I feel a wave of shame. That I risked my life and the mourning of my sisters for this. To be here.

Blais lets go of my arm, trying to get a burst of speed. I don't want to be queen. But what happens if she gets the mirror first? Am I left here? Does this forest go back to sleep, and me with it? I imagine an eternity with the hands reaching from the wet earth. The hideous not-Edel, laughing in my face through death and beyond.

The wolf-faced Blais howls. If sound could wound, it would tear through my spine, pull it out through my flesh. The howl reverberates down the length of the bone, trembling my skeleton. Over and over in my head is *This place is wrong. This place is wrong. I will not die today.*

Blais was right—it is the mirror. I see it now, its silver glow. It rests on a tree stump as if waiting for us, a halo of light around it. I run faster. A distance to go, but my hands already outstretched. The desperation is in every finger.

Then Blais falls. I hear her gasp before her body hits the ground—disbelief. Victory and safety shoved from her lungs. The wolf-faced Blais howls again, and all my teeth chatter. I look back.

Blais, her face blank with fear, her hands reaching out for me.

"Take my hat, Edel!" she screams. "Take it to my family. Let them mourn me!"

I hate this place. I hate every drop of blood that has been

spilled for a game of lives. I turn away from the mirror and sprint back to Blais. I don't want her hat—I want her hand.

I skid to a stop, falling to my knees, latching on to her arms and hauling backward. She rises to one knee; she's reaching the hat toward me, and I'm reaching for her body, trying to pull her after me. The mirror is five paces away.

The wolf howls.

"Run, now!" I yell.

But she is so calm. She taps the top of the hat once, then thrusts it onto my head. The last thing I hear isn't the wolf—it's her voice:

"Long live the one true queen."

THIRTY-FIVE

They tell me I was asleep for three weeks. Now, six days after waking, my body and head ache as if I've been resurrected from the dead. My recovery feels so slow and far from over. I touch the bulky white bandages swaddling my head from clobbering it in the forest.

I watch as a nurse adds more sangsues to my arms to help rebalance my damaged arcana, and I fight sleep because I keep falling in and out of dreams where I'm screaming at Charlotte, telling her that I told her that this would happen, telling her that the Beauty Trials were a bad idea, telling her that Belles would never be safe.

I yank myself awake and sit up. My nightgown is soaked through. I scoop the leeches off my arms and into the small water dish on my nightstand. I inch out of bed. My feet feel wobbly at first, but I drag myself across the room to the doors leading onto the terrace. I stare out.

I watch the ships until my lips are blue and my entire body shivers. But I want to remember everything that's happened and let the cold wake me from this ever-present haze until it all comes back.

"Lady Edel, you must come inside." A servant wraps a coat over my shoulders. "You will get sick. You're still recovering."

Rain starts to fall and soak my nightgown. I let her coax me back inside the Belle apartments at the palace, and in front of the blazing hearth. She hands me a cup of hot chocolate. My arcana levels rise slowly as I sit watching the grains in the hourglass fall from one side to another.

"Bring me the papers," I ask.

"But you're supposed to rest. On orders of the—"

"I need them *now*," I bark with all my strength and feel like a punctured post-balloon losing air.

She skitters off and returns with a stack, setting them one by one in my lap. Their animated headlines whip and snap, each one begging to be read first.

OUT WITH THE NEW, IN WITH THE BETTER AS NEW
QUEEN TO BE CROWNED AFTER THE BEAUTY TRIALS

FORMER QUEEN CHARLOTTE IN EXILE

QUEEN BLAIS DENE WILL PASS AN EDICT SENDING ALL
BELLES BACK TO TEAHOUSES TO RESUME BEAUTY WORK

My mind is a tangle of images—Violetta pulled down and down into a whirlpool, Blais placing her hat on my head, my face rising out of the ground.

"I want to see Queen Charlotte!" I yell.

A servant rushes in.

I try to rise from my chair, but my legs are weak and wobbly and unable to sustain my weight. "Bring me a rolling chair."

"Charlotte is in exile. She hasn't been seen," the servant replies. "You must wait for your strength to gather."

The hot chocolate bubbles up in my stomach, and I have to sit back down.

"I'll bring you your post-balloons. There are many, Lady Edel. Open these, and I'll change your bandages in an hourglass." She disappears through a side door.

The exhaustion hits me in waves, and I lie back in the chair.

The first balloon is a brilliant crimson, blazing with the Belle-symbol.

Edel,

I've instructed all Belles in all teahouses to come to Maison Rouge to seek refuge until we know what the new laws will be. We've made every room available. Rémy has recruited a few ex-soldiers from the House of War to provide security for the island.

Your nurses send me daily reports on your condition. They say you are improving. I was with you while you slept. Hana, Rémy, and I would have waited. They removed us. For your benefit, they said.

Rémy will return for you as soon as you send word you are

well enough to travel. I am worried they will trap you there. I don't know what is going to happen, but I know I need you here and safe with us.

Love,
Camille

I open another.

Edel,
I'm writing to wish you a successful recovery and tell you good-bye. I wish I could stay and see how this whole thing will shake out, but I am afraid—as I know you can understand—and must leave with my husband. After what happened last time, I cannot bear to be locked away again.
I will write again when safe.
Leave when you can.
Love,
Gustave
Minister of Fashion

With every letter, the truth sinks in more deeply, like a knife in my heart. I open a third—it must be from an Iron Lady. The spiderwebs glisten over the body of the post-balloon.

Edel,
It is with my greatest sorrow to be writing you this letter to tell you the Iron Ladies plan to leave court for our own safety.

The new acting queen will take none of our initiatives and ideas into account as she builds her new cabinet. The Jolie Society has much favor.

When you are well, send word.

Best,

Lady Arane

The final one, a gold-and-white palace post-balloon, almost hisses, wanting my attention. I open the back to make it go silent. A mix of gold and black calligraphy announces new acting queen Blais Dene's presentation tea for tomorrow, held in her private salon. It's to celebrate her impending coronation. Glittery stars gleam on the parchment.

There is a note.

Your presence is requested at the queen-in-waiting's first official event. All accommodations for your condition have been arranged. We will provide a rolling chair, and an attending nurse shall be brought for your convenience.

Anger flushes through me.

"Up for some company?" a voice whispers.

I find Quentin staring down at me with a gentle frown. I can't imagine this visit was sanctioned.

"How did you get in here?" I ask.

"I have my ways," he replies. "But how—" The rest of his sentence breaks off as his eyes comb over me.

"It looks worse than it is," I lie.

"They said you were dead," he says softly.

"I have to know what happened in those woods. How *this* happened."

"Only Blais's testimony is recorded. She says a creature pushed you into a thorned bush."

I hold my head in my hands. It's wrong. I know it. But as I will my mind to remember, it feels like trying to grasp smoke.

He goes on. "Blais has built a new cabinet with Calandre as head."

My eyes fly open, and my hands drop.

"Did you say Calandre? That doesn't make any sense," I cry. "She refused to enter Beauty's Labyrinth. She belongs to the Goddess of Death. How is this possible?"

"Your memory isn't fully damaged, then," he says.

"Of course not," I snort. "She was taken by Encerclant. I saw it with my own eyes."

"I don't know. I have no answers." He pauses. "You should leave."

"What?"

"I fear it isn't safe here." He balls his fists. "The Jolie Society is being given too much influence," he says with a tone of warning.

"I need to meet with the Iron Ladies."

"They're starting to jail them," he replies. "They're being labeled traitors, rabble-rousers, and threats to the peaceful transfer of power."

Lady Arane's letter must have been written before that development. I swallow a lump in my throat—what if she's already in the Everlasting Rose? My hands start to shake with rage and sickness.

"I need you to help me figure out what to do," I whisper.

His hands grasping mine makes my body soften, the quivers lessen. Everything feels crooked, wrong. Like that forest. Like something crawling under the ground. But Quentin is warm like sun and sand. I sigh deeply, relaxing. I let my head fall forward against his chest.

A voice from the doorway breaks the silence.

"I came for nothing, I see."

It's Gaelle. She's taking in Quentin, his hands wrapped around mine. But he doesn't exist to her. Just me.

Her heart breaks in the center of her eyes. She turns sharply.

"Gaelle—" I start.

I try to stand and nearly fall down.

"You're not strong enough yet," Quentin says, pushing me gently back into the cushions. "You cannot walk!"

"I need to go after her," I say. It comes out like a sob, grating my throat.

"Whoever she is can wait," he says. "I need to tell you something, Edel. You must listen—"

I turn on him with my eyes full of fire.

"Listen to what? Why? You think you know what's best for me? You don't know me at all. Get out."

"Edel, I—"

"Out!"

His eyes close off, unreadable as stone again. He pauses, then reaches to his hip, where he pulls his knife from its sheath. He places it on the table by my chair. In a moment, he is sand. The next, he is gone.

THIRTY-SIX

The court opera singer croons as I'm wheeled inside the grand salon. Distinguished courtiers pour in behind me. It is a royal party and has been decorated accordingly. Flower-lanterns bathe every possible corner. The room is thick with men in tuxedos and women in jewel-tone gowns. Waiters hand out goblets and flutes of fizzy liquid, and present plates of beautiful food. A teacup monkey feasts on a tiered-dessert platter.

Blais sits on a throne-like chair on a raised platform. All her new ladies-of-honor hug the periphery, one covering her mouth with a jade-green fan as she whispers to Blais. Calandre perches nearby, busy brushing the brown coat of Queen Sophia's teacup monkey, Singe. I scowl at him. I never liked that monkey.

Calandre's wailing screams seem a distant memory. She doesn't seem like that same girl carried off by Encerclant before we entered Beauty's Labyrinth. One who might've faced the Goddess of Death herself and lived. Something's changed in her. Her sun-kissed skin is perfect and smooth. Her hairtower brims over with jewels and teacup sloths. Her grin is mischevious.

"You look beautiful, Your Majesty," one of the fawning courtiers says to Blais. She wears the crown over one of her usual garish hats, featuring her new royal emblem. The ruby sits in the center of her gold crown like a glittering red chicken egg.

Gossip-balloons swarm overhead as if they can hear and record the queen's words. Imperial guards use tall poles and nets to swat them away, but they dodge and soar higher up to the grand ceilings and seem to revel in a game of cat and mouse.

One of the ladies-in-waiting catches my eye. "Oh, our little Belle is here," she announces with a clap. The entire room breaks off to join her in applauding me.

As best I can from my chair, I acknowledge them with a bow. Blais motions grandly for me to be wheeled to her left. A servant fluffs a massive blue floor pillow for me.

"I will remain in my chair," I reply.

Blais smiles.

"A survivor, you are. And as long as you are loyal to me, a survivor you shall remain," she whispers.

I keep my mouth shut. Three years ago, I would have burst out with every curse I could conjure. *Charm*, I hear Camille's voice echoing. Or is this survival?

"Amazing that you're alive at all," she says. She speaks up so that those attempting to eavesdrop don't have to work very hard. "When I grasped the mirror and won the throne, I could have let you die. I chose to let you live."

I want to grumble back that she's not a queen yet. I want to ask her what really happened in the woods. I want my memories to clear like smoke being fanned away.

Smoke. I remember my breath like smoke before my mouth. A shape forming—a wolf eating a bird. It fades, and I shake my head.

A woman with flame-red hair approaches. I think she's the only woman in the entire room who isn't wearing a low bun. Everything about her is bright—her yellow dress shimmers around her like sunlight woven into silk. Tall and stately, she towers over both the queen and me.

I've seen her before, but my mind is a sluggish maze.

"Your Majesty," she says.

"Grand Duchess Georgiana Fabry," a court attendant says.

Georgiana—Auguste's mother. I remember sitting veiled in Lady Joseline's beauty party—Georgiana dropped off the blood-infused facials, they said. My skin prickles as her eyes wash over me.

My memory before the forest is just fine, as Quentin pointed out.

Blais introduces her to her ladies-of-honor. "This is the Grand Duchess Georgiana Fabry. She is an expert at new serums and products," Blais says. "Georgiana is also from the second-oldest family in the kingdom of Orléans after the House of Orléans."

"Historians still argue that point," Georgiana says. They laugh back and forth like old friends. I wish I could leap from this chair and choke the life out of her. She was once a criminal. Now she is at court, smiling and bowing as if she isn't as guilty as Sophia.

Blais introduces each one of her ladies-of-honor. When she gets to Calandre, she kisses her cheek and pets Singe affectionately, who lounges comfortably on Calandre's lap.

"Georgiana, this is, as you well know, Edelweiss Beauregard, a Belle we're fortunate to have at court. She is in recovery after our celebrated Beauty Trials."

I bow my head, and when I lift my face, Georgiana's eyes are cold and hard. I try to keep my face relaxed so my thoughts don't betray me, but I feel suddenly uneasy.

"May I speak frankly, Your Majesty?" Georgiana says.

"You always do, old friend." She gestures her approval.

"This is your opportunity to consider ending the Belle tradition as we know it," she says. "Outlaw beauty work. Close the teahouses." Gossip-balloons swirl and whisper their rumors into the room.

Outlaw?

"You never shy away from controversy," Blais says.

"And neither should you." Georgiana squeezes the queen's hand.

"It's time for a new era," another voice says, joining the conversation. I know that voice. Lady Angéle, of Gravier Palace. She appears at Georgiana's elbow, smiling primly. Blais greets her with a warm smile.

"Why allow the Belles to profit over something that we can take into our own hands? If it's in anyone's hands, it should be yours."

"I look forward to discussing the factory," Georgiana says before they lapse into whispers.

I excuse myself from the conversation. I feel Georgiana's gaze on my back as I wheel away to the long tables laid with food. I focus on a small plate of sweets, to stop my hands from shaking. I use one of the tiny forks to jab the fruit full of holes.

"Oh, what did that snowmelon ever do to deserve such torture?"

My eyes snap up and land on a handsome and familiar face. Sculpted cheekbones and piercing blue eyes, a shadow of a beard around his jaw. He smooths one eyebrow with a well-manicured hand, nails painted gold.

"You," I say. I recognize him now. The young man from outside the Everlasting Rose. He has no bronze butterflies with him today. "Who are you?"

He tips his hat.

"Barnabé Dene," he says dramatically. "At your service."

"Oh good. You've met my brother," Blais calls, and the

room's attention again hovers around me. "Careful with him, Edel, he has a funny sense of humor!"

"Still campaigning for the Jolie Society?" I say, not bothering to hide my scorn.

"Of course!" he says proudly.

"You do realize the object of your cause is dead," I say nastily.

"Death doesn't stop good business," he says cheerfully, then turns to join his sister. He leans against Calandre's chair, where Georgiana and Angéle also cluster around Blais.

I don't know how I expected this tournament to turn out. But it wasn't like this.

THIRTY-SEVEN

Servants help me prepare for bed as usual, supporting me as I hobble around. I take a long bath. The nurses check and record my levels, and remove the sangsues from the crooks of my arms. They pull down the covers and slide a bed warmer under the blankets. I let them close the bed curtains.

Then count to thirty.

Weeks have passed, and I have been waiting to heal enough to do what I have to do. But I have been sure not to show anyone I have healed.

I slip out and open the wardrobe closet to find the brown day dress I requested. A fury of chocolate ruffles cascade in all directions, scalloped skirts in caramels, and tiers of mahogany-cerise silk, plus beige tulle and pearl lace.

I finger the rich fabrics and imagine the dress stripped of its frippery. Then I get to work. I rip away the layers of lace to shrink the volume. I remove lux ornaments. What remains is a simple dress, brown and plain.

Identical to the ones worn by household servants.

I braid my hair. I fashion a tiny servant cap from a handkerchief. I look in the mirror. Aside from my amber eyes, I look no different from the gracious women who attend to our apartments.

I watch the hourglasses. I wait for the night star to rise. I drift in and out of angry dreams. Maman's face appears. *Be strong and clever, little one,* she says. Blais's laughter cuts through like a sharp knife, erasing her face and slicing at her words.

I sit up. I can't close my eyes anymore. I can't handle what awaits me even in dreams.

Finally, three tiny knocks whisper into the room.

I ease out of bed. I look at the hourglasses. The night star has risen. I creep to the hidden wall panel, the one I have been told about.

Adele stares back at me. She inspects me, her expression frank. It's a look I've come to respect.

"This is not what I thought you meant when you sent me that note," she says, frowning. "I thought you meant to meet a lover. Instead you look . . ."

"Like you," I say, climbing into the small space. The metal base wheezes under our weight. "And this is more important than any lover."

Still, my heart squeezes when I say it. I think of Gaelle,

who hasn't returned my post-balloons. I think of Quentin, whom I don't even know how to reach.

"Quickly," Adele says, adjusting to my plan with speed. She pulls the wall panel closed and turns the dumbwaiter's wheel. It inches down. I press against her back. I feel the excited thud of her heartbeat against my chest.

She takes us to the palace kitchens. She must have known they'd be dark and empty at this time. A monstrous potbellied stove lurks in the corner like a fire-breathing demon. Its low fire washes the floor in reds and oranges and yellows. Jars of bright spices and dried herbs clutter a wall of shelves. Dishes are stacked in towers.

"This way." She tugs me forward to a counter with two trays of tea and marzipan cookies and macaroons. "Grab one. The ladies-of-honor ordered these from the western palace kitchen." Adele looks left, then right before motioning me forward.

"Keep your eyes down."

I nod.

We step into one of the golden chariots that cart people from different palace wings along beautiful wires. She tells the chariot porter to take us to the western wing. We sail high above the various balconies. I try to keep my head down, but it's hard not to look. I've never seen the palace from this perspective. I spot a few courtiers stealing kisses in dark corners. I see newsies rushing from balcony to balcony looking for their last late-night story. I see servants rushing with linens and trays and carts from room to room. I thought the palace slept when I did, but I realize only a few of us have that luxury.

In the western wing, the guards watch us, their gazes fluttering over us, but Adele doesn't pause or hesitate; instead, she tromps right to the queen's door. The portal looks like a great eye. I don't want to go back inside there. But we're too late. Other servants are bustling up, also ready to enter. I feel flushed from head to toe. I almost drop the tray in fear.

"What are you doing here?" a servant asks Adele, a spot of angry red on each cheek.

"We got an order." She lifts the tray.

"It was for the western kitchen."

"Well, we got it, too," Adele snaps. She is a good actress. "Anyway, they won't say no to extra tea and cookies."

The woman concedes. As the doors open, Adele hangs back a little, letting the other trio of servants enter first.

"I'll follow them," she whispers. "Go to the left. I'll tap the servants' entrance with my foot so you know which door. Push and it will open."

I nod and squash a spasm of fear.

Adele saunters in and soundlessly taps a spot on the wall her foot as if she's adjusting her grip. I set the tray down and pretend to struggle. "I'll be right there," I say, trying to change the pitch of my voice.

"Hurry up, now. The ladies are waiting," says the other woman impatiently.

Adele scampers forward. "She's new. She'll catch up." She steals a glance back.

I mouth, *Thank you,* and she disappears. I pick up the tray again and push the hidden door open with my hip. The door swivels, and just like that, I'm inside.

The most massive canopy bed I've ever seen sits right the middle of the room. A gauzy white veil hangs from gilded posts, and the sleeping occupant drowns in pillows and blankets. Tiny clusters of beauty-lanterns drift over like stars.

Servants wheel in tiered trays bursting with skin color pastilles and rouge pots, brushes and combs and barrel irons, tonics and creams, bei powder bundles, waxes and perfumes, measuring rods and metal instruments, and sharpened kohl pencils. A beauty caisse sits on a side table, fanned open so the medley of instruments inside twinkle in the subtle light.

My old tools.

I set the tray on a tea table and approach the bed.

THIRTY-EIGHT

Calandre sleeps in the center of the bed, curled up with Singe and several of Sophia's other teacup pets that I always saw her at court with. What is she doing here?

Everything feels...off. I feel the ground stirring under my feet, like I'm in the forest again. Hands reaching up. Pink slime. I want to retch.

Suddenly, Georgiana bursts in. She whispers her orders viciously, so as not to wake Calandre. She pauses in front of the fireplace to inspect a beauty board. I smooth the front of my uniform and pretend to arrange sweets on a tray. I steal glances at Georgiana.

Her hair has a copper hue that looks as if it might burst into flames at any moment. She sparkles, from her lux dress in pewter and charcoal, to the matching lines of rouge paint around her brilliant brown eyes.

She pulls an attendant to the side.

"Yes, Grand Duchesse," the attendant replies.

She clicks her nails along the mantel. "Where are the rest of the beauty boards?" she hisses.

The attendant freezes in place. "My lady—"

"Grand Duchesse," she corrects.

"Grand Duchesse—"

"Do you want to be the one who tells the queen?"

"N-no, Grand Duchesse."

Servants scurry from the room. I pick up an empty tray, and I tuck myself into a shadowy corner, close to some loose items. I pretend to organize them while keeping an eye on the massive bed. Why would Calandre need so many beauty boards? Is Blais making her some special cabinet member? Why all the fuss over her?

Calandre stirs. Singe stretches and climbs to the headboard to watch. Calandre yawns like a cat. Her eyes find Georgiana.

"Well?" she says. Calandre's voice was so soft in the carriages. The type of person who was easily frightened or scared of their own shadow. Even when she was complaining at the Gravier Palace. Her voice now is so arrogant, so sharp. One word cuts through the air.

"Any moment," Georgiana assures her.

A door swings open, and she sags with relief.

It's Blais. I sink deeper into shadow, then quickly summon a glamour. A maid's uniform is not enough. She might recognize me.

"Bring it to me," Calandre says in the same imperious voice.

Blais crosses quickly to the bed, where Calandre sits perched on the edge like a little girl, idly kicking her feet.

Blais presents a bottle to Calandre. "Things should be much easier now."

"Oh, lovely packaging," she says, smiling broadly. Her teeth are bright red. My breath catches in my throat.

That ax-sharp voice cuts across the room: "You! Yes, you!"

She's addressing a servant in the corner, who has been standing awaiting instructions. I'm relieved I chose a glamour. I concentrate on keeping it up.

Calandre extends the bottle to the servant. "Drink."

The terrified woman looks wary, but Calandre pushes the bottle closer to her face. She purses her lips, take two sips, and then coughs violently. One time. Two times. The third, she turns away and a streak of blood appears across the plush white rug. There is a sound like a melon hitting the ground.

Dead.

I clap my hand over my mouth. What did Calandre make the servant drink? What just happened? What did Blais give her? Blais makes a groan like a rusty wheel.

"You thought that would work like a charm, didn't you?" Calandre crows, throwing back her head with laughter. I know that laugh. The way it echoed down the corridor of the Rose. My heart knocks against my chest as a wave of memory and recognition settles over me.

"Wait," Blais says, moving away. "Wait. I didn't—"

"Not so easy, though," says Calandre.

Every hair on my body stands on end. Like my breath in the dark forest, something is beginning to take shape. I know that voice. We all do. My heartbeat slows. The cup in my hand almost drops to the floor.

Sophia. It's Sophia. The realization sends a wave of nausea through me.

"When the time is right," Sophia says, "I will wear your face. But for now, you will stay here and do what you're told."

Georgiana holds a lamp. She strikes the back of Blais's head with a sickening thud. Blais crumples to the carpet.

"Tie her up," says Sophia.

I melt back into the wall panel before I even let myself breathe.

I don't wait for Adele. I follow our path back to my quarters, my mind churning like the maelstrom. All the pieces swimming together.

Georgiana. Lady Angéle. Blais.

Sophia.

The hands are bursting through the forest floor, covered in slime.

I sat and watched the blade come down. I saw the blood and allowed myself to feel relieved. I was a fool to think her execution meant anything.

But my fear is gone. There is nothing more to fear because everything is worse than I ever could have imagined.

And I can't run from what is to come.

I slip back into my quarters and immediately write two post-balloons.

Gaelle—

You must forgive me. Nothing is what you think. I need your help.

If there is any love in your heart, you will meet me at the salon one half mile from Lady Joseline's grounds. There is an Iron Ladies sign in the window.

I have a plan.

Edel

And then I write to Quentin.

Quentin,

It all makes sense now—you and your family used Calandre as a fake Sophia. Is this why you were late to the final trial? Flying her back in the palace? I will make this right without your help. I've figured it out, and I'm going to the center of all things.

Do not bother to reply.

Edel

I should write to Camille as well, but she'd only try to stop me. I will tell her, but not yet. Things have been put into motion that can't be stopped.

I watch the balloons sail out through the night air, and press my hand against my chest. My heartbeat, finally, is level.

THIRTY-NINE

The streets around Lady Joseline's house are just beginning to wake when my carriage pulls up, ringing with cheerful good mornings between shopkeepers. I am heading for a particular destination.

Adele found me a courtier's dress and fetched me a carriage, while I conjured a glamour, pretending to be a lady from the Spice Isles returning home. If Sophia could wear a different face to work her schemes, I could, too.

"Here," I call to the driver, using a high voice not my own. The sign is still there, propped in the window—hand-drawn. WE STAND WITH BELLES.

I'll see if that is the truth.

Determination vibrates through me. I had let my glamour lapse in the privacy of the carriage, but now I draw it up again. With weeks of my not using the arcana, my blood feels fresh and strong. Almost hungry.

The little bell tinkles when I step inside the salon with

the Belle poster in the window, and the smell of ink washes over me. I breathe it in, remembering how much Camille loves quills and ink. Perhaps I should have written her. *No,* I think. *Too early. When I call on her, it will be when I'm ready.*

"Early shopping, dearie?" the woman at the counter sing-songs. She's laying out packages of sparkling ink, unwrapping new sheafs of fancy paper. Her skin is graying, but she hasn't powdered it. She wears mascara, her hair piled high on top of her head. Despite the gray, she looks lovely: round cheeks and prominent cheekbones.

Perhaps it would be easier to appreciate people's natural templates if they didn't try to hide them so much, I think.

"I have business nearby and am passing some time," I say, circulating slowly. Will Gaelle find the shop? I wonder. Will she even come?

"Good business, I hope," she says, still focused on her tasks.

"I hear talk of vaults," I say, trying to keep my voice light. I need to know before Gaelle gets here if this is a safe place to talk.

"Vaults," she repeats.

"Blood vaults. Good business for Belle blood, I hear."

Something slams down on the counter—I snap my head to look at her. She glares.

"Begone with you," she snaps. "I don't need your money. You see the sign in the window." She marches around the counter, grasps my arm, and pulls me toward the door.

"Vaults," she cries. "I won't hear of any such merde. Here is the door—to the dirt with you."

Gaelle stands in the entryway, her eyes wide. They swing right over my disguised face.

"Benilde, whatever is the matter?" Gaelle says.

"This cretin is in my shop talking about blood vaults!" the woman cries. "I don't allow that kind of—"

Gaelle stares right into my face, unseeing. I let the glamour drop in a blink. "Edel!" she cries, and throws her arms around me.

The shopkeeper sputters, confused, and Gaelle draws back.

"Benilde, you are mistaken," Gaelle cries, and turns me so I face her. "Look."

Shock registers, then recognition.

"Edelweiss Beauregard," she says.

"I'm sorry for deceiving you," I say quickly. "I needed to know if this place was safe."

"It is safe for all Belles," she says thickly. "I thought you were one of Lady Joseline's people."

"I have come to speak with Gaelle," I say. "You know each other?"

Gaelle nods. "Benilde is a good friend. She's proven herself trustworthy many times."

"Good," I say. "Because what I have to say can only be said to the most trustworthy."

I tell them that Sophia is alive—in the body of Calandre.

First there is disbelief, then rage. "It's impossible," Gaelle cries, but Benilde only shakes her head.

"Impossible?" she says. "*Nothing* is for that evil woman. The tournament was the perfect distraction."

Gaelle is still studying me—her trust has waned. Her eyes narrow, like Quentin's.

"It's true, Gaelle," I say. "I was in the room. It's her."

"What about Blais Dene?" she says. "She won the crown."

"Sophia and Blais were working together," I say. "Blais is captive now after attempting to assassinate her. Lady Angéle was at the palace yesterday. She and Georgiana are involved." I take a deep breath. "The Arnoux family is also connected, I think." I don't confess Quentin is an Arnoux. It feels like I'm lying to her again. But right now, it will only muddy the waters.

"A bunch of power-hungry serpents," Benilde mutters.

"You said you had a plan, Edel," Gaelle prompts me.

"I need to get back inside Gravier Palace," I say quickly. "Sophia said something when I went to see her at the Rose—"

"You went to see her at the Rose?" she interrupts, looking incredulous. "How?!"

"Never mind that now. Sophia said the plan was at *the center of all things*. That's Gravier. Has to be. It's where we all were during the Trials. We know how Sophia gloats. But Angéle will never let me in—not now that the tournament is over. And a glamour won't last."

Gaelle frowns, her lips poked out the way I love. I want

to take her in my arms, tell her how much I missed her. But now is not the time. She goes on thinking, and I don't interrupt her.

"One of my suitors mentioned something," she says slowly. I ignore the squeeze my heart gives at the word *suitor*. "Gravier orders huge amounts of bellamy—a flower I'm not familiar with. But it smells very strong apparently."

"Yes," I cry. "That smell! Gravier was saturated with it, remember?"

She nods, remembering. "Shipments are delivered into their subterranean canal. Perhaps if we got to the docks..."

"I could smuggle myself in," I say, the pieces coming together.

"We would have to go now," she says. "It will take hours to get to the docks. I will need to work my magic to find the boat."

"It won't be hard," I say. "The smell."

"Good point."

"Take my carriage," Benilde says quickly. "My wife has it at the moment, but it can be here within the hour."

"Thank you," I say. I look straight into her reddening eyes.

"The sign in the window is not just a sign," she says.

 # FORTY

These docks are not like the ones where the courtiers catch ferries—here every kind of person is coming and going, merchants shouting and sailors carrying nets. Everything smells of sweat and salt. And drifting just between, the scent of the bellamy flowers for Gravier Palace.

"I doubt it's locked," Gaelle says when she returns from charming the dockyard manager. We're both wrapped in nondescript traveling cloaks. "But I can manage the lock if it is."

She taps her extravagant hairpins. I see now why they are there.

"Thank you, Gaelle."

"Don't," she says. I hear the undertone of hurt. Now is not the time or place to delve into what's between us. But I say one thing:

"I can't be everything you want me to be, or everything you deserve. But I do love you."

I catch the sparkle of a tear in her eye, but she sniffs it away. "Let me come with you," she says. The smell of the bellamy is strong—we must be close. "You can't do this alone."

"I'm already not doing it alone," I remind her. "But for the next part, I need you to rally my sisters."

"Write them a post-balloon."

"Gaelle," I say gently. "You will know what to say." We both know who is better at convincing.

We're approaching a green boat, bobbing low in the choppy water. The smell of bellamy is overwhelming.

"Unlocked," she says, sounding a little disappointed.

"You can pick other locks," I say, trying to joke.

"Let me come with you, Edel."

"No."

My feelings roil inside me. I can never talk about them. Instead, I grab her hand, turning it palm up. I point to the only line I know.

"There's your life line," I say. "With me on it."

She tries to read mine. I pull away.

"Not today," I say. And I kiss her good-bye.

I creep into the hold. I remember too late how much seasickness affects me, and the flowers make it even worse. Now my head thrums from the odor, somewhere between heady and headache. The petals are soft but the stems are stiff, and I have to burrow deeper into them every time I hear footsteps on the deck. Even though my hiding spot is dark, I squeeze my eyes shut tight to fend off the nausea.

At my hip is Quentin's knife. I resent it—but it's the kind of weapon I need on a mission like this.

The port is under the palace. If the competitors were allowed to wander more, perhaps I would have a better idea about where to begin. But pieces are coming together. Angéle and her empty rooms. Her ease with Joseline. Their allegiance to Sophia. Their talk of factories and vaults.

Gravier Palace is where they are keeping the missing Belles. It has to be. And I will get them out. Or die trying.

The boat is slowing, and rocks left and right as the waves slap its sides. We're gliding into a port under stone archways. I wonder if Gaelle's post-balloon has reached Camille yet, if she is already pacing. Doubt nags at me. Maybe I should've gone straight to Maison Rouge—surely Camille would have come up with a better plan than mine. Especially since I have none to speak of.

But it's too late—I can hear the shouts of the crew, and the grinding of the anchor chain. Any moment, they'll be coming down to unload the cargo.

I start to push my way through the bellamy, using my elbows to widen a pathway. The doorway to the hold is somewhere up to my right, and I tunnel that direction. The scent of the flowers is stirred by all my movement—pollen rises into the close, tight air. I feel faint.

And that's when I get the idea.

I position myself in the bellamy and wait. I don't have to wait long. I hear the wheel turn, grating as the door is unlatched and swings open.

"Make it quick, you two," a voice says. "I'm going up to meet the Lady."

"Your turn on the barrow," one says, high-voiced.

"Yes, yes," says the other.

I wait until I hear the rustling of their hands in the soft petals, and then I reach for my arcana. It thrums eagerly. The bellamy was picked recently enough that it responds right away. I hold my breath and let it surge.

"It's heavy," one of the boatmen says, his voice suddenly tired.

I hear one collapse—I don't wait for the other. I claw out of my hiding spot and see two unconscious bodies. I rush past them, out into the clean air. "Sweet dreams," I whisper before I close the staircase door.

I silently thank the darkness under the palace. No one is in sight. I glance around. Behind me is a wide dark tunnel encasing a curving path—littered with dead bellamy blossoms. That must be the way the cargo is transported. But I see which way the captain must have gone: a stone staircase, a torch aligned with every step.

"I'm coming, girls," I whisper, and up I go.

The palace is shrouded in darkness—so different from during the tournament. I skulk around the corridors, looking for anything familiar. All I ever saw inside was the Game Salon and my quarters. Even my meals had been in my room. I try a few doors, but they're all locked and silent.

I wonder if Angéle thought Charlotte would stop by any moment. Maybe she should have. Maybe Charlotte should have been paying closer attention, rather than trying to keep everyone happy.

I remember the smell of blood in St. Nanterre, but I don't smell it now. What if I am wrong?

I hear voices and dodge down another hallway to escape them. Small glass doors sit on each side. I rush toward them, hoping I can get my bearings. The garden. I walked those paths with Quentin that night. My cheeks burn at the thought of him. I wonder if this is how Camille felt after Auguste. But I don't have time to feel foolish.

If that's the garden, I realize, I'm on the wrong side of the palace. I suck in my breath with frustration. Far off, I hear more voices. They might be coming closer; they might not. The cool weather has created a cover of fog. It would be easier to make my way unseen outdoors than indoors, but there's the matter of getting back in.

Then I remember.

I slip out the door and into the cool air. The gardens are empty, and I smell ocean air. Staying close to the building's edge, I make my way along its perimeter, fast and silent. The balcony I shared with the other competitors is empty.

I creep up over the stone barrier and onto the deserted

balcony. It's been weeks since I've been here, but it feels like years—like a different lifetime. I stalk over to the doorway that was mine during my time here, and I find the window to its left, my heart leaping. If it's been repaired...

It hasn't. The glass is still loose in its panel, and it wiggles under my fingertips. I slip my fingers inside and under, then give it one quick wrench. It comes loose in my palms. Rather than letting it fall, I ease it down inside the room. Then reach through and unlock the door.

It opens quietly and I slip through.

I expected it to be empty.

But when I turn to face the room, I'm staring at one of the missing Belles, Delphine.

FORTY-ONE

"Edel," she gasps.

I don't know if I'm relieved or angry. She's alive—but she's here.

"Why have you not sent a balloon?" I snap, forgetting to keep my voice down. "I thought you were dead!"

She closes the space between us in three strides, grabbing my arm.

"Edel—"

"Delphine, where have you been? I have been so worried!"

"Edel, you—"

"The others, Delphine? Where are they? Are you—"

She shakes me, hard enough for my teeth to rattle.

"Shut your mouth!" she hisses, then drags me to the closet. She shoves me into a deep row of luxurious dresses and closes me into darkness. "Hide and be quiet. Don't breathe!"

The door to the bedroom opens, and chatter floods into the room.

"Oh, good, you're ready" comes a voice I know. It's Lady Angéle, and through the crack I can just make out that she escorts someone in with her—they both twitter happily. "Delphine, I don't think you've met Lady Renoir. She's a good friend of my dear Duchesse Georgiana Fabry. You'll take good care of her, won't you? Of course you will."

If I shut one eye, I can see Delphine's arms through the crack by the hinges. There are the tools of a beauty session.

Lady Angéle turns to Lady Renoir while Delphine stands silently.

"Delphine is one of the good ones," she says. "She's been a godsend, doing beauty work while we work out the kinks in the system."

"Of course," Lady Renoir purrs. "I must admit I was shocked to see the little army you have around the front gates. I thought I was entering a battleground!"

"Just precautionary measures," Lady Angéle says airily. "You've heard of the Arnoux family, of course. Of the Grottos."

"No wonder they looked so mysterious and strange. Coming out of their caves now—so odd!" Renoir says with a tone of surprise.

"Not as odd as you might think." Lady Angéle chuckles.

"As it turns out, those who cheat Death make fabulous business partners. I see no reason to think they will cheat us, however."

I will my heartbeat to stop hammering. The thought of Quentin pretending to want to help me survive, while he helped imprison the Belles...I try to remember what Delphine said before she pushed me in the closet, and hold my breath.

But why are they outside Gravier Palace? Safeguarding their investment? What do they gain by helping to reinstall Sophia on the throne?

Riches, like everyone else, I suppose. Is this kingdom so banal, from top to bottom, that it can't simply come up with someone new?

I can just see Lady Renoir sit down at the beauty table. She hasn't even gotten undressed. Delphine uncorks a bottle just like Blais gave to Sophia. The pungent smell of the bellamy floods the room.

"Such an odd smell," Lady Renoir says. "Pleasant but... strong."

"We have the flowers shipped by the boatload," says Lady Angéle. "It take pounds and pounds to make a bottle. But it stabilizes the formula—and masks the taste of blood, of course." She laughs.

I stiffen, and maybe I imagine it, but Delphine does, too. *One of the good ones.* It makes me clench my teeth so hard my jaw aches. I watch as Delphine uses a delicate brush to spread the burnt-red concoction all over Lady Renoir's face, from her hairline down to her throat.

"The mirror," Lady Angéle commands, and Delphine presents it. I have the perfect view of her reflection. Smeared with blood, she looks wild, like something from the dark forest.

But I have enough bad memories.

"Now drink," Lady Angéle commands.

Obediently, Lady Renoir takes several sips. She slurps a little, and a red bubble bursts, the elixir making her lips even redder. Nausea rocks me as if I'm still on the boat.

"Now try," Lady Angéle says. I can hear the grin in her voice.

Lady Renoir raises her hands to her face and, pressing with her fingers and thumbs, begins to mold her features. Her face is disturbingly malleable, like wet clay. She sculpts her nose like it's no more than stiff mud. She shapes her cheekbones, smooths her forehead. There are moments she looks hideous, inhuman. I can see the combination of horror and fascination in her own eyes.

Delphine looks on silently, still holding the mirror. Her eyes look out of focus.

I stifle a whimper.

"We're still working on what to do with the hair," Lady Angéle says. "But for now, wigs."

"What do you think, Delphine?" Lady Angéle says to get her attention. "Amazing, isn't it?"

"Yes, my lady," Delphine answers softly.

"Just think," Angéle boasts. "Soon we won't need you Belles at all." She pauses. "At least, not for this."

 # FORTY-TWO

When Lady Renoir is wiped clear of blood, her new face at least symmetrical—and free of gray—she and Lady Angéle stroll out, leaving Delphine to clean up. She flings open the door.

"You heard everything?" she demands. "They are trafficking Belles. All the missing girls? They're here. They're here in Gravier!"

I feel like slumping to the floor and staying there. "She lured them here?"

"They promise Belles protection and safe working conditions." Delphine nods, tears in her eyes. "And then once they're here, they lock them in blood vaults."

"What about you?" I say, my suspicion rising. "She called you one of the good ones."

"I look after them," she says. "Some have died. There was

nothing I could do. But without me, there would have been more deaths. "

My tears sting. I was right. But I didn't want to be. I wanted every room in this hideous palace to be empty.

But my sisters are here.

"You need to leave, Edel," Delphine says, sounding choked. "If they find you, you will die in a vault. The hoses like never-ending leeches. Worse than the Rose. I've seen the way it happens, and I—"

"So have I," I interrupt. "And not a single other Belle will die that way. Not while I'm breathing air."

"That's the thing, Edel," she cries. "Lady Angéle is just as bad as Sophia; she merely hides it better."

"Every door that hides a Belle must be open. I'll break them down if I have to."

"They're all locked," she says shakily. "These doors are good thick wood. It would take hours to beat them all down."

"Then where is Lady Angéle's study? I will find her."

Delphine's face is drained of color. Her eyes flicker over my face. "Did you really want to be queen, Edel?"

I'm so surprised by the question that the truth pops out. "Yes," I say. "I wanted to rule so that I could put a stop to all this. But I know better now. A queen cannot stop these things. Only people like us. With whatever gifts we have." I squeeze her hand. "Be brave," I tell her. "And be ready. I'm going to get the keys, and when I return, we are freeing our sisters."

"What are you going to do?"

Before I can answer, we both jump at a rumbling crash—the floor trembles. Shouts and screams fill the air.

"What in the gods...?"

We rush out on the balcony.

"Vultures?" Delphine says. "Is that what I see?"

They number in the hundreds, and they descend from the sky, wings outstretched, thick like clouds. Again and again, they slam the guards on the wall, sending them tumbling down. I look for movement. It does not look like there are any survivors.

Another shadow passes over the ground. The sun seems to flicker. And all the shouting and chaos momentarily goes silent.

I look up.

The bird is the size of a blimp. And when it opens its massive curving beak, a sound like grating gears shakes the palace walls.

Encerclant. And sitting astride her now-massive back is Quentin.

Quentin and Encerclant swoop toward the ground, lower and lower, and when they come near, they swoop through the ranks of the soldiers from the Grottos. Bodies scatter, flying like pebbles. The massive vulture swoops back into the sky, wheeling around and passing over the balcony.

"What are you doing here, Quentin?" I whisper.

"You didn't come alone," Delphine says, staring up in shock.

"I did," I reply, still watching as Quentin and Encerclant swoop down for another strike. "And so did he. That's his family he's fighting."

"Why does he fight his own?" she gasps.

"The same reason we fought Amber. She turned on us," I say grimly, and spin to dash inside.

FORTY-THREE

I can hear feet rushing everywhere: heavy boots of guards and the lighter feet of servants and attendants. They will die. Most of them didn't ask for this. But then I remember that these exact attendants must be cleaning up the blood, removing the bodies. At what point does fear become compliance?

Outside, more bodies fall like hail. My stomach turns. My pulse races. It doesn't matter if I am in the caves or the forest. There is blood and death everywhere I go.

I step into the hallway, a glamour already settled on my face. It will only provide the barest cover—after all, I'm wearing pants coated in bellamy pollen. Luckily, Quentin's assault is keeping the palace too busy to notice me. "Stay long enough for me to find her," I whisper, holding the wish inside my chest as I move as fast as I can.

All I remember from my time in the palace is once hearing Lady Angéle tell her attendant, *"I'll be upstairs waiting."* It's almost nothing to go on, but it's all I have.

The curving staircase is just by the Game Salon, and I take the stairs two at a time until I reach the top. Thankfully, the rooms up here all have open archways rather than doors: music rooms arranged with flocks of pianos, art rooms populated with graceful sculptures. I want to destroy everything I see. But Quentin is already doing so. I have to focus. If Blais hears of the assault on Gravier and sends reinforcements from the imperial army, the tide could turn quickly.

The smell of bellamy is stronger upstairs. I begin to race through rooms, trying to find the source. It's not difficult. There is only one room with a door on the second floor, and I know before I open it that it's Lady Angéle's. The even more pungent smell of bellamy makes my nose throb.

This is the right place. All that remains to be seen is if I'm the right person to stop this.

I let the glamour drop, and swing open the door.

Lady Angéle is behind her desk, shoulders hunched, writing feverishly. She only looks shocked for a heartbeat as I enter, then slowly leans back in the chair, placing the quill on the desk.

"You," she says, almost sneering. "Why couldn't you just die?"

"Are *you* ready to die?" I ask her. The words come easily, naturally. I realize it's all I have come to say, to do.

I close the door behind me and slowly cross the room. "Where are my sisters?" I say. "Where are you keeping the Belles?"

"She never should have let you compete," she says. Her hands are beginning to shake. "Your kind can never leave well enough alone, can you?"

I walk around behind the desk until I'm standing right beside her. I don't remember taking the knife from my hip, but it's in my hand.

"Where are the keys?" I say. "Where are you keeping the Belles?"

She snarls up at me, and I stare down at her red gums, her red teeth. She laughs in my face and turns around, continuing her hurried correspondence as if I'm a horsefly let in the room and unworthy of her attention. I cannot hold my anger inside anymore.

"There will be no more Belle blood," I say calmly, and then thrust the knife into her back, through to her heart.

Her flesh begins to curdle, like bad milk. It peels away, dissolving down to the bone. Soon, only a splash of blood is left, like the rest of her was taken by wolves.

In the center of what's left of her, there is a key. She kept it on her person.

I glance down at her desk, where her quill was so busy scratching.

For the one and only Queen Sophia,

We are under attack. I think it is wise to relocate those in the vaults until

Even at the very end, she was thinking about profit. Over the lives of Belles. Over the lives of the people in her palace. Even, perhaps, over her own.

A sickness worse than Gris, I think.

I pick up the key. It's time to free my sisters.

FORTY-FOUR

When I pass the room where I left Delphine, all I hear is the sound of her weeping. I open the door quickly, knowing we need every second if we're going to release every Belle being held prisoner here.

"Where?" I ask.

She points. "There are twelve," she replies.

I barrel down the hall, to the parts of Gravier where Lady Angéle forbade us from wandering. Almost immediately, I see the row of heavy oak doors Delphine told me about, all locked tight. My sympathy for the bodies on the balcony wanes. Every guard, every attendant knew what was happening here. I fit the master key into the first lock and find the first Belle.

She sits upright in a bed facing away from the windows, her wrists strapped to the headrest. Her arms are full of tubes. The room smells like blood and bellamy, the floral scent so thick it coats my tongue. I wonder if I'll taste it for the rest of my days.

"Who are you?" she asks, fear tucked between her words. Her fists clench. The sight of her so helpless and afraid makes me want to burn Gravier to the ground.

"There are many of us," I say, pulling her free of the tubes and needles, snatching bandages from the table and wrapping the wounds that bleed freely. "I will explain everything, but first we must get you out of here."

"Where?" she cries, trying to rise.

I grit my teeth. "I don't know yet. But Lady Angéle is dead, and the guards are occupied with giant vultures, so we have some time to figure it out."

"Rosette," says a voice at the door. I whirl, but it's only Delphine. "Are you all right?"

"I might live," Rosette says. Though she smiles, she's not joking. I've felt the arcana of other Belles when we are near one another—but I cannot feel hers.

"Did they damage you?" I say. "Do you still have your gifts?"

"They are waning," she says, her eyes filling with tears. "How did you know?"

Delphine does not move from the door. "Did you kill Lady Angéle?" she asks me, her eyes wary.

"Yes," I say without hesitation.

She springs into action.

"You keep getting them loose. I will get them out onto

the balcony. All the guards have taken shelter in the front of the palace. It should be safe."

"What about the vultures?" I ask.

"They're dropping bodies into the ocean now," she says, helping Rosette stand.

As I free them, some of the Belles can walk and some of them can't. Opening the doors and removing their tubes is quicker work than supporting the weak, wounded women as they make their way from the cells. Some of them weep; some of them don't speak, shocked that someone came for them. "We never forgot you," I keep telling them as I work, rubbing feeling back into their arms and legs before I let them attempt to walk. "We've been searching and searching."

Some of them nod. Some of them blink. In many, I see the same kind of rage I carry. I wonder if we'll ever be rid of it.

These women are better cared for than the woman who died surrounded by blood bags in St. Nanterre. I know it has nothing to do with care or empathy. Lady Angéle and her evil allies were protecting their investments—feeding them sufficiently, measuring their blood levels. But my sisters have been nothing more than animals bred for slaughter, if that.

I think about if this would've happened if I'd won the Beauty Trials. If I could've prevented it all. I think about all I've done. Those I've killed. It's true: I never could have been a queen. A queen wouldn't do what I plan to do. What I have to do.

Better cared for or not, the Belles are weak and getting

them out onto the balcony takes time. No matter what speed I move, they cannot keep up with my pace. Outside the palace, it is now silent. As I slip the key into the lock of the final room, my stomach briefly knots at the idea of Quentin and Encerclant lying dead on the grounds somewhere.

I put it out of my head and swing the door open.

This Belle is neither asleep, nor awake. She is dead. And she's not alone.

A young man stands beside her bed, his hands busy. A silver tray is filled with vials of blood.

"You," I gasp, and he jerks away from the tray. It's Blais's brother. Barnabé Dene. The man with the butterflies.

FORTY-FIVE

"You killed her," I say, staring at the dead Belle, her eyes dull and open. I advance on him; all the rage inside me turns into a storm I can't control. The knife from the Grottos is in my fist. I am ready to end him.

"I assure you I did not," he says, his hands up in placation, and backs away. "She was already dead."

"I hear that a lot," I say. "You are part of the Jolie Society. I know what you advocate for. Even if you didn't kill her, your little club would. By law."

He leaps to the other side of the bed, using it as a shield. I see his eyes flick down to my dress, where the first splash of Angéle's blood landed.

He holds up one finger, his eyes wide and serious.

"What if I told you I was not part of the Jolie Society?" he asks. "That you and I are actually working to accomplish the same goal?"

"Start making sense," I snap, pointing at him with the knife. "This blade is from the Grottos and all it takes is one slice and you'll be forever sand. Test me if you don't believe me."

"I believe anyone who breaks into the Everlasting Rose and then survives the Beauty Trials. But please believe me: I did not kill this woman."

"Elaborate," I say.

"Certain secrets have yet to play out," he says, and dares to offer a sly smile. "But I can assure you: we both will do much to help those we love."

"Those we love," I snap. "Are you referring to your homicidal sister?"

A huge boom sounds outside. I hear shouting from inside the palace now—the pounding of many pairs of boots. I wonder if the boots I hear belong to imperial guards. I wonder again if Quentin is dead. Either way, we're running out of time.

"Blais's methods aren't always genteel," he says, shrugging. He has the nerve to be cavalier. "I'm a scientist, nothing more."

I raise my knife. "A scientist?" I snap. "Using the blood of tortured subjects?"

"Ah, but you see, I did not draw this blood," he says. "I can assure you, I have never drawn a Belle's blood in my life."

"Then what are you doing with it?"

"It's pertinent to my studies."

"You talk in riddles," I say. "And I don't have time for it."

As if to illustrate my point, the sound of boots draws nearer.

Barnabé reaches into his jacket pocket and I start to lunge, but he shouts, "Wait!" He withdraws a slim vial, colored a deep crimson.

"As a gesture of good faith," he says, grinning. "Calandre would enjoy it," he says, drawling her name.

Then he's gone, slipping backward out the open window before I have a chance to stop him. I throw my head out the window. He's gone, like smoke. How did he do that? What is in this vial? I lift it up to the light, unable to decipher whatever he's left behind.

Someone shouts my name, yanking me out the room and back to the balcony.

Delphine has all the Belles on the balcony safe and sound, except for the dead sister I had to leave behind, the one I was too late to save. I try to remember her face, memorizing it so she will never be forgotten.

The air is filled with the sound of humming, and a shadow falls over the balcony. I look up, expecting more vultures.

It's a hulking crimson zeppellin. It's Camille. My heart soars. I haven't felt this surge of relief in days. I cheer her name.

I spot her and Rémy working quickly to send a basket

down over the balcony. I watch Delphine help the weakened Belles climb in.

I rush the others forward, helping the last of them lift their frail and energy-less bodies over the railing and into safety.

"Edel!" Camille shouts. "Watch out!"

Guards burst onto the balcony. I slip the tiny vial into my hair and let them take me prisoner so that the others may get away.

FORTY-SIX

The carriage ride to the palace should be the hardest of my life, but I have seen worse. I have done worse. My sisters are free and flying above the rotten ground of this rotten kingdom. There is still nowhere in Orléans where they will be safe. Eventually, they will have to land. If only that zeppelin could take my sisters across a rainbow to another world.

"You are being taken to the Rose," the guard tells me. They dragged me out, narrowly missed by a crowd of descending vultures the imperial guards were attempting to fell with catapults.

My only regret is, I don't know whether I will die hating or loving Quentin. I don't know why he attacked Gravier Palace. And maybe I never will.

"Did you hear me?" the guard says, nudging me.

"Yes, yes, the Rose, blah, blah, blah," I say.

"After your audience with Queen Blais," he adds. "Pay attention."

"No," I reply easily. He growls in response, and I growl back. Pay attention to what? Queen Blais? There's no such thing. Only Queen Calandre, which is to say, Queen Sophia.

I could shout it from the windows of the carriage—but what good would it do? Will she return, miraculously, from the dead? But she saw how the Beauty Trials sated the kingdom. Perhaps she will wear Blais's face forever.

"Rouse yourself," the guard says, nudging me unnecessarily. "We'll be getting out in a moment."

"I'm well aware," I say. "I've been to the palace a time or two."

He merely grunts in reply. He nudges me out of the carriage, and follows me too closely on the long walk through the palace, now furnished in the gaudy, shimmering styles Queen Charlotte removed. But as we wait to be admitted to the queen's quarters, I find him studying me.

"What?" I snap.

"Some say you would have been queen, had you not stopped to help her."

I cannot say yes or no. It is still a blur. I shrug in answer.

"Why?" he asks.

"Perhaps I thought it was the only way out," I say. "For any of us."

Before he speaks, the door swings open. I only glance back quickly. His face is heavy with sorrow.

Blais sits on the throne, attempting to seem queenly. I can see the bruises along her wrists from bonds only recently untied. Sophia, wearing Calandre's face, lounges beside her. They regard me with disdain.

"Edel," Blais says. "You might recall that I said you would be kept alive for as long as you remained loyal to the throne. Releasing the Belles we carefully collected is the opposite of loyalty."

She speaks evenly, with a characteristic sly tone. But Calandre—which is to say, Sophia—is furious. She scratches Singe's back vigorously, her eyes bouncing from surface to surface.

"Out with the old and in with the new," I say breezily, knowing it'll irritate them. Maybe enough to get one of them to lose focus and drop their glamours. They don't have the true powers of the Belles. "Or should I say, out with the new and in with the old?"

Sophia slowly raises her eyes to mine. They dance with joyous evil.

Blais jumps when she sharply claps her hands.

"You have only delayed the inevitable, Edel," Sophia says. She stands abruptly, sending Singe scampering. She knows I know and has cast aside the charade. "I'm not pleased, it's true. But we'll get our blood back. And in the meantime, I have you.

"Sometimes there's the perfect time and place, and I think this is it," she says. "Blais, come sit at the beauty table, my sweet."

She turns to me.

"Edel, you know how this goes. Or do you? No. Out with the old, in with the new as you said!"

The beauty table is laid out just the way that Delphine's was at Gravier Palace. No more tools. I remember what I told Gaelle—there is no need for them; only our gifts. I wish I could take it back. Here are only a mirror, and vials of deep red blood.

"Prepare the elixir, Edel," Sophia says, and leans back in her chair. "You need the practice."

I cross to the table, feeling numb. "It feels good to be in my chair again," Sophia says. "They brought me one to my room at the Rose, but it's not quite the same."

She closes her eyes, her head tilted back, ready to be served.

And I remember the vial.

Calandre would like this, Barnabé had said.

I drop my head as if examining the tray, and the vial in my hair drops neatly into my palm. I turn back to the queens.

Sophia opens her eyes and winks at me. "Take a little sippy, dear Blais," she says. "You first."

Blais reaches wordlessly for the vial, and I hand it to her, my face expressionless. It's possible that Barnabé tricked me—perhaps what I am about to give Sophia will make her even more powerful. Maybe it will do nothing. I have nothing and everything to lose.

Blais takes a sip, and then another.

The three of us sit in silence, waiting. Sophia, despite her jokes, is intent, studying Blais's face for a reaction.

Nothing.

Blais shrugs, eyes downcast.

"Give it to me," Sophia says, and I take it from Blais. Sophia drinks the whole thing down.

"I like everything but your eyebrows, Blais," she says. The heady floral scent wafts off her breath. "I'll be doing a little molding there. Edel, have you seen self-work? Your blood is all we ever..."

Then she stops speaking.

It's as if there is something inside her body that is trying to get out. It ricochets against her cheekbones, her skin bulging like a bullfrog's throat, contracting and snapping closed. A ragged wail tears from her throat with each stretch, each bulge. Her teeth move like piano keys, her mouth wide open.

It reaches her eyes, and they bubble, one after the other.

I leap back just as it bursts, blood splashing the floor like water against rock. Bloody at first, as if scraped, layer after layer of skin peels away. She is gray, exposed, even her tongue a lump of ash. She comes apart, becoming nothing but a pile of rubble, stinking of bellamy, drifting in and out of the folds of her once-fine dress.

 # FORTY-SEVEN

What was once Sophia is ashes drifting to the floor. She's dead. Truly dead.

Calandre's face, Calandre's hair, even her clothes and her hands. None of it masked Sophia, not truly. How many people at court knew? How many will find out now? I only wish she was wearing her true face when she died.

Blais grabs me, looking elated. "It actually works!" she says. "Clever girl, where did you get my brother's elixir?"

"I...I saw him at Gravier Palace," I say, stunned.

"Yes. You caused quite a ruckus today," she says. "Sophia was furious. You know how she is...was! Doesn't do well when things don't go according to plan. But that's life, isn't it?"

"He wouldn't tell me what the blood was for," I say, still processing.

"It was your idea, actually," Blais says. "A personalized poison."

"Me?" I choke.

"That idea you brought to Charlotte. She didn't take you seriously when she should've. Your individualized beauty boxes were extraordinary. An elixir tailored to a user makes for a perfect assassination, don't you see? We used your work to make an incredibe weapon."

It washes over me, truth and lies and all the things I assumed wrong.

"How . . . how?" I stutter.

Blais laughs. "Initially all my brother's experiment could do was return the subject back to Gris. It took a little longer for him to make it target someone's blood. And he had his little bronze beauties for that."

"The butterflies," I whisper. "At the Rose."

"They're really more like little mechanical mosquitoes," Blais says. "A bite you don't even notice. A few attempts and he had Sophia's blood." She claps. "Oh, Maman will be so pleased."

"You've been planning this for months," I say.

"Sophia and I have been working together for some time to get her back on the throne. But poor Sophia, she always thought she was the only one who could possibly want what she wanted as badly as she did."

"Why even play her game?" I say, feeling a familiar

desperation. "Why not just win the tournament and take the crown?"

"Sophia has influence." Blais shrugs. "The Jolie Society loved her. Call it cult of personality. Whatever it is, aligning with her was smart when it was smart. But you have to know when to change strategies."

"And now?" I say, feeling dizzy.

"Well, if you hadn't freed all the Belles that Georgiana and Angéle and I have spent months gathering, I might've gifted you a position in my cabinet. So sad. So it's back to the vaults, mon chéri!"

She reaches for the bell to call the guards at the same moment the door bursts open.

 # FORTY-EIGHT

Gaelle stands in the doorway. Her face is smudged with dirt, her dress is torn, and her eyes are as fiery as the candle she holds in her right hand.

"What in the gods..." Blais says, as if amused.

"Gravier Palace has fallen," Gaelle reports.

Blais straightens her spine. "Impossible."

"The Iron Ladies have rallied," Gaelle says. "Because everyone you know supports you, you think everyone in Orléans does as well. But you will find St. Nanterre is not the only place looking for a fight."

"Sophia was alive, Gaelle," I say quickly. "Blais's elixir—"

Blais's speed is like a viper's—she slaps me, digging her nails into my skin. The pain is immediate.

"Don't touch her!" Gaelle screams. She flings the candle, and Blais's side of the room is immediately concealed in a purple-black fog. I can hear her coughing and the alarm bell. I'm aware of Gaelle grabbing my arm and dragging me through the door, out into the hall.

"It's time to go, my love!" she shouts, and we take off down the stairs.

"Where is everyone?" I pant. We haven't seen a single servant or attendant.

"Fighting or gone," she cries over her shoulder.

We reach the bottom of the stairs just as the words leave her mouth, and like a curtain being lifted, the sound of sword on sword, of screams that only come from violence, reaches my ears. The walls that Blais and Sophia and even Charlotte took such care to wallpaper with gilded adornments is streaked with blood and smoke.

"Who are they fighting for?" I holler over the noise. She's pulling me back away from the fighting, toward the salons. "Are they loyal to Charlotte?"

"I don't think they're loyal to anyone!" she yells. "The newsies spread a rumor that Blais was going to pass the throne to Calandre and violate the tournament results. Everything exploded."

An earsplitting crash rends the air. The massive stained-glass window is shards. All we see are talons.

It has to be Encerclant.

I start to move toward the window, but Gaelle drags me back.

"The Iron Ladies will take it from here," she says.

But Blais is blocking our way. She clutches a vial of blood elixir, her eyes lit with frenzy.

"They will take nothing!" she says, chest heaving. Her face is streaked with soot. "Not while I am queen."

"I hardly recognize you without a hat, Blais," Gaelle mocks. I love her, I realize in that moment. I truly love her.

Poison. Hat. It makes sense now.

"You poisoned me," I cry. "In the forest. There was something in the hat. . . ."

"Of course I did!" she screams, almost laughing. "And I won the crown."

"Not quite," calls a voice. I can't place it yet. But the look on Blais's face tells me she knows exactly who it is.

We turn around to find Violetta.

"Impossible," Blais says. "I saw you in the waters. You were dead. You're supposed to have died."

"No, *you* are," Violetta says. "You just don't know it yet."

"You were killed in the caves," Blais says.

"I met Death in the caves; it's true," Violetta says. Her gray skin is sheathed in sweat and glows like silver. She easily hefts a sword over her shoulder that I couldn't even lift. "We had much to discuss."

I marvel at her. "You met . . . the Goddess? She's . . . alive?"

I realize how foolish a question it is.

"Dead, actually." Violetta laughs. "But she is always with us."

Blais's face blanches. "I won the tournament!" she screams.

"The tournament is overseen by Death, and you violated the rules," Violetta says calmly. "And so did the family Arnoux."

"I am queen!"

"A deal is only a deal as long as the terms are upheld," Violetta says. "It seems the youngest child renegotiated the terms last night."

Quentin.

"Death and I agreed that she would let me go if I helped eliminate those who had cheated her. Terms that suited both of us." She pauses to grin. "And Quentin Arnoux agreed to void his family's immortality in exchange for your life."

"My life?" Blais says. "*My* life?"

"It's a shame that he must die at dusk to do so," Violetta says.

"Dusk," I whisper. No one hears me over Blais's howls.

Behind Blais, a burst of fire explodes through a stone wall. All but Violetta cower.

"The queen's chambers are burning!"

Gaelle scoffs. "Blais, how can you run a kingdom if you can't even put out a little fire?"

Blais gapes at her, turning her face from the stairs to us and back again.

"The vials," she says. "The serum. It's all there."

Smoke drifts down the staircase, but she plunges toward the inferno anyway. I shudder, reminded again of the forest behind Maison Rouge. The smoke and the screaming. The face like my own. The face like Blais. Did we leave them behind in the trees, or are they with us now, inside us? Will they always be?

"Good," says Gaelle. "Let it all burn. Her included."

I love her.

"Leave, ladies," Violetta says. "My deal is not complete until the palace is flattened, eviscerated."

"The whole palace?" I gasp, even as the walls shake.

"Every stone." Then she's striding away, swinging the sword down off her shoulder.

"Benilde is waiting," Gaelle says. "It's time to go."

"I will," I say. "But there's one more thing I have to do."

FORTY-NINE

We find Quentin by following Encerclant through the dusty back streets outside the city. Her massive shape circles in the dying light of the day like a beacon as we weave through the wreckage. She's so big that we can feel a breeze every time she flaps her wings, even from here. I will never doubt the storybooks again.

Benilde urges her horses forward slowly. "Are you sure this is a good idea?" she says. All Gaelle and Benilde know of the vultures is death and rot. By now, I know better.

"This is the boy I saw you with," Gaelle says.

"It's not what you think," I answer, but I can barely look at her.

"Care to elaborate?"

I sigh. Is there an easy way to explain how love can be stored in different parts of the heart? That what I feel toward Quentin isn't the kind of love that grips my heart for

Gaelle, but cradles something frail inside me? The strange, scared child, growing up in a world full of death, lies, and money?

"We both were born with blessings and curses," I say quietly. "We understand each other. Sometimes it felt like more. But mostly, he is my good, decent friend."

She nods. And suddenly, in the shadow of Encerclant's wing, I see Quentin's body in the grass, his arms placed behind his head.

He might already be dead.

I leap out of the carriage and sprint down the road. "Quentin!" I scream as I close the space between us. "Not yet!"

He sits up. My heart tumbles, then catches itself.

"What are you doing here?" he says, shocked. "You should be at Maison Rouge!"

I throw myself down on the ground beside him. "I saw Violetta. She told me what you did," I say. "What if I had come looking for you? What if I had never known?"

"You wouldn't have looked for me," he says.

"I would," I insist. "After what happened at Gravier Palace..."

"You've heard."

"Quentin, I was there."

"You were *there*?" he demands. He claps a hand over his eyes. "Gods, even when I try to protect you I put you in danger."

"You did no such thing," I snap. "You made it possible for me to free the Belles."

"Then they are free? I did the best I could."

"They are okay now."

"You should be gone, Edel. Go to your home while Violetta sweeps the city. You shouldn't be here."

"What did you *do*?" I ask. "Why do you have to go?"

"On the day of the third trial, I learned that my family had broken their agreement with Death," Quentin says. "They made a lucrative deal with Sophia. But Death did not agree to give Calandre's death for Sophia's life. Death does not take kindly to anyone doing her business for her. The family Arnoux deserves ashes."

Trying not to cry, I reach for his hand.

"Has Violetta told you of her plans?" he says.

"No," I say. "All I saw was her and her sword, and everything burning down."

"Violetta has already captured Barnabé Dene to prevent his experimentation from going any farther. The elixir will be altered. The Gris affliction will become a natural condition. Beauty work will be outlawed."

"I know a lot of Belles who won't know what to do with themselves without beauty work." I laugh.

"They will follow your example," he says.

"I am just a person."

"You are the bravest person I have ever known," he says softly. "And I have lived quite a long time."

"I could have killed Blais myself and you could still be here."

Only a sliver of the sun is visible above the horizon.

"I'm dying." He smiles. "Something new after so many years. Except the sun. That always feels new."

"What happens now?" I ask.

"When I'm gone, Encerclant will take my body to the Grottos. I'll be there forever, if you want to stop by."

He closes his eyes, smiling. I hold his hand until the sky is black and his grip loosens with the life leaving him, and only when Encerclant lands nearby do I let go. I hear a rhythmic growling in her throat, like a purr.

"Take good care of him," I say, and gently as a mother kitten, she gathers Quentin's body in her massive talons and takes to the sky.

EPILOGUE

The only thing left standing in the imperial city of Trianon is the Everlasting Rose, where the remaining members of the Dene family are imprisoned. Violetta heads a small council to govern Orléans, and she lives in the same house near the Grottos that she's lived in for twenty years.

And so do I—Maison Rouge.

This is one house of dozens, now, with gardens that extend as far as the eye can see and my Belle sisters tending to their tiny crops. From where I stand on the back porch, I can see Gaelle making her way up from ours. My arcana breathe a sigh of contentment as the sun pours down. Soon visitors from the Spice Isles will be stopping by to trade. Gaelle loves company. She has gone to gather the best strawberries for them. She will charm them into giving extra cinnamon. This is the way of things now. We grow things; some of it we sell, much of it we eat. We trade for what else we need.

All across Orléans, people are discovering and rediscovering what to do with their time, what to do with their talents. There are so many Irons now, as we call them. Most of the kingdom embraces this new reality.

The back door opens—I don't have to look to know it's Camille. She smells like bread and milk now.

"He's asleep," she says. She means the baby. "Both of them, actually."

The baby and Rémy.

I reach for a blueberry in the jar on the rail. I roll it around in my palm before eating it. Gaelle waves from the gardens when she looks up and sees us waiting. We both wave back. I feel my heart swell at the sight of her.

"You have a talent for making things grow," my sister says. "Who would've thought."

"I did," I say. "Me."

ACKNOWLEDGMENTS

Returning to the world of the Belles while *our* world struggled with the Covid pandemic was the hardest thing I've had to do. This book is about a chaotic, crumbling environment, and a competition where death awaits. During the writing process, I was losing people, just as Edel does in the text, which made it hard to stay tethered to the page. I thought I wasn't going to be able to dive back into this fantasy world, but so many of my friends, family, editors—my champions— helped get me through.

I have so many people to thank.

My amazing literary agent, Molly Ker Hawn. Thank you for the wisdom and being ready to strategize at every turn.

My fantastic editor, Lizzie Skurnick. You are a genius.

The Hyperion team: Elanna Heda, Jocelyn Davies, Cassidy Leyendecker, Ann Day, Crystal McCoy, Holly Nagel,

Dina Sherman, Shane Rebenschied, Matt Schweitzer, Andrew Sansone.

Thank you to my friends, my love nests, my group chats, my Slack channels, my covens. All those who keep me human. You know who you are.

Thank you, Mom and Dad, for all the things.

And thank you to the readers. Thanks for coming back into this strange world with me.